THE LONG FALL:

BOOK 1 THE INCEPTION OF HORROR

Kathleen McCluskey

The Long Fall *Book 1 The Inception of Horror*/Kathleen McCluskey
ISBN: 978-1-947605-03-9
Ebook: 978-1-947605-04-6

C<small>HAPTER</small> 1

The Beginning

Jehovah studied the debate before him, mesmerized by the fierce war of words clashing between these great orators. Brothers turned adversaries, they spit obscenities, each one condemning the other. He sat above them on his bench, a mighty gavel laced in gold tucked tightly in his hand.

Growing impatient with their bickering, God slammed the gavel down.

"Enough!" The audience shuddered under the thunderous boom of his voice. "This is a courtroom, not a playground. Now, get on with your case."

Lucifer began to speak, his large feathery wings raised from tension. "Your Almighty, my Father, and members of the jury, I come here today to see if mankind can repent. Although doubtful, I do believe they shall reap what they sow." Lucifer paused and looked at his mighty brother Michael, forever at the Father's side.

Arms crossed, with the hilt of his sword glinting in the sunlight, Michael glared at his cunning younger brother Lucifer. Michael and Lucifer were Jehovah's firstborn and second-born. They took sibling rivalry to a new level. They loved yet despised each other. Michael, being the strongest and the eldest, loathed Lucifer's cunning and intelligence.

Lucifer smirked at Michael and continued his case. "Humanity, Father, is but a curse upon the planet. They destroy everything they come in contact with. You annihilated this awful species once and were gracious enough to give them a second chance."

Lucifer looked at the jury, full of subangels, and gave a confident smile. "Do not be swayed by his presence, or mine, or of my brothers and sisters. We are angels, like all of you, created by Father, and in his own image. The only exception being we are stronger and more respectful of what the Father has created than the pathetic humans. We all know only the righteous have these beautiful white wings. Except you are all seraphim. You are one of my kind. I am a seraph as well. We all started out as seraphim, except, my brothers and sisters, I was the first created, so we are archangels. I am the angel of the light. I am the one to shine a judging eye on all that I see. He has given me the gift to shine a light onto these pathetic excuses. I am here to persuade you to persecute the human race. My victory will be complete. However, if I am to lose, Father will never judge me. I am one of the archangels."

Lucifer scanned the jury and said, "Where is Saraqael? Your leader?" Lucifer turned sharply at God and said, "Really, Saraqael isn't here. Curious, Father, very curious." Again, Lucifer casually turned back to the jury, smiling coyly at the terrified angels. His smile was filled with deceit. The jury listened, unable to see his malice. Arrogantly he leaned against the railing, looking his Father in the eye.

"Father, you covered this planet with water once yet spared a few measly humans to continue. Are you that arrogant to keep your greatest creation? Made in your image? Are we not all that reside in heaven created in your image? Why then, Father, you let a few made in your image to live? An ungodly act, even for you, Father. They are awful, spiteful creatures that will do anything to feed their greed and lust. They maim, murder, and steal from one another."

Gabriel bellowed out, "Objection, Father!"

Jehovah responded with "Overruled. Continue, my son."

Lucifer spoke again, grinning at Gabriel. "Father, and members of the jury, my beloved brotherhood, I will present to you all the atrocities this species has rained upon this planet, and in the following days, you will come to despise them as much as I do."

Lucifer went over to his large stone desk, put his legs up, and crossed his feet, hovering with his wings. He had a look of complete victory on his face not geared toward the Father but at Michael as he sat down, staring at Michael the entire time as he began to hover and then sit. Their eyes locked in an unseen battle with thoughts.

Michael stepped down and stood in front of his Father's bench. He stared at Lucifer, his big green eyes sparkling as thoughts of killing his brother ran through his head. He had always had a deep hatred for his younger brother. Even when they were just children, Lucifer's mind games had made Michael so angry that he wanted to tear the boy's wings off.

Michael, being much older than his mischievous younger brother, had a long-standing resentment toward him. He could remember the games he would play, ones that left Michael confused and angry. They would often go to the planet and watch the humans in their daily routines. Michael, his chest puffed out, like a proud father, and Lucifer laughing as the drought and famine would wreak havoc on them.

Michael knew that with his strength and size, he could easily kill his brother. He also knew he could never get close enough to his intelligent younger brother. The wrath of the Father would be fierce and extreme. Rule number one in heaven was to never kill one's brother. The Father would say, "You are your brother's keeper."

Michael thought of Cain and Abel, and a twinge of revenge filled his heart. Father had let Cain live; maybe Michael would be granted the same courtesy. *Doubtful*, Michael thought. *I am not a human.* He stretched out his massive, thick feathery wings and sighed. He tightly gripped the hilt of his mighty sword and thought of Lucifer's head dangling on the tip. He could only imagine the victory he would feel. He turned and, with feathers floating behind him, returned to his Father's side.

Jehovah, knowing what he was thinking, shook his head at his mighty son. This winged soldier, his warrior-angel, would never defy any of his laws. He smiled.

Lucifer said, "One more thing, they are unworthy to be granted life."

Gabriel bellowed out, "Objection, Father!" startling the audience.

Jehovah responded with "Sustained. Please strike that from the record. Finished, son?"

Lucifer smirked and nodded yes.

Gabriel arose. His sheer presence would kill a human in an instant. His massive white wings dragged behind him. No tension within himself, he approached the jury.

He began to speak. "Humanity? Hmm . . . a strong word. Father created them in his own image. They are flesh of your flesh and bone of your bone, Father. How can we not love them? They have given the land love and strength. They have tended the fields and raised animals to sacrifice to you, Father."

Lucifer jumped from his seat, feathers flying around his feet as he sprang. "Objection! Fucking objection!"

Jehovah, in his calm tone, said, "Sustained. Please strike from the record. Any talk of sacrificial lambs will be forbidden. And, Lucifer, my son, watch your language. This is a courtroom, not a brothel."

Lucifer nodded and grinned at his younger brother Gabriel.

"My Father," Gabriel continued, "the humans have given everything in your name, have spread the word of one true god throughout the land. The days of many gods have disappeared, and Jehovah is the only god they pray to. Your name, Father, has reigned for centuries." Gabriel looked over his shoulder at his older brother and smiled back, a middle finger poking through his feathers as he walked past him. Resting on the railing in front of the jurors, he studied the jury. He continued, "I will show you in the coming days the repentance of the humans and how they have bowed to Father for the rising and setting of the sun daily. Their complete devotion to him is grand and absolute." Gabriel looked at the jury, his ever-loving, stark blue eyes glistening as he spoke. "As angels, it is our duty to protect and love all of mankind, the great and the small, the poor and the wealthy, the righteous and the sinner." Gabriel sighed and looked down at his feet for a brief moment. As he lifted his head, he spoke again. "As my brother so eloquently spoke, yes, indeed, you are all seraphim, but I, too, was once one of you. Father saw fit to make me the angel of life and death. I am here to give the humans life and not destroy this planet again. Do not be swayed by our presence, or of our Father's. We are angels like yourselves." He smiled again, a soft sweet smile; unlike Lucifer's, it was void of malice.

Jehovah, tired from the day's events and seeing his children at odds with one another, broke court until the next day. As he stepped from the courtroom, Michael at his side, he strode down the marble-floored corridors of heaven. God abruptly stopped, and with one mighty sweep of his hand, earth was visible. Heaven was continually filled with clouds, and he had to make a space in them to see the planet.

Jehovah said, "Look how beautiful my creation is, heaven and earth, water and creatures in the sea, the land and the animals, and of course, my beloved humans." He asked Michael, his confidant, his warrior, "What do you make of this entire mess?"

Michael, every loyal and ever present beside God, bowed his head, went to one knee, the hilt of his sword in his palms, and answered, "Father, Lucifer does have a point. Why would you spare a few humans when you unleashed the great flood?"

Jehovah, stunned at Michael's admission, said, "My son, I spared a few as they are made in my image and I couldn't bear to lose them all. Noah is a righteous and God-fearing man, and I made the right decision."

Michael looked up at his Father, his long dark hair blowing in the constant breeze in heaven, and spoke. "Father, Noah might have been a righteous and God-fearing man, but the stench that rises from that planet daily because of the sin and destruction is not worthy of your love."

Jehovah became annoyed and pursed his lips.

Michael, seeing the irritation in God's face, said, "As you wish, Father, I will never go against you, ever. You know that, and I know that. I love you, Father."

Jehovah, tired of his yes-man, was angered and kicked Michael's sword out from under him, the razor-sharp point flying in the air as Michael tumbled to his side. God bellowed, "This is my fucking planet, and I will do as I please! They are mine! Do you understand? Mine and mine alone." God, looking down at his loyal son, extended his hand for Michael to grab.

Michael, in a defiant move, pushed God's hand away and arose. "Father, this is the arrogance I must deal with daily on earth. The worshipping of the other gods still persists. And I, Michael, your beloved firstborn, protects thee and your name. I ensure that you are the only deity that they pray to, I ensure that you are the only one that they ask forgiveness from, and this is how you repay me?" Then understanding his outburst, Michael began to sob, "I am sorry, Father, I will always protect thee." He grabbed God's hands and bowed and kissed them lovingly.

Jehovah and Michael heard the rustling of large wings, those only granted to the archangels, and looked down the clouded corridor. Emerging out of the mist was Raphael. His wings constantly and playfully fluttered in heaven's breezes. He loved to feel the wind between his feathers and flaunted their size and beauty daily. Being the youngest of the brothers, and with his head cocked in confusion, he took his eldest brother by the hand and said, "Father, forgive me for interrupting. May I please have an audience with my brother?"

God, knowing Raphael as a spoiled and frightened child, always gave this angel a second glance. He also knew that Raphael wielded a great power, the power to heal the sick and resurrect the dead. Jehovah smiled at his son and let him lead Michael away.

Michael pleadingly looked at his Father and reluctantly went with Raphael.

"Go, my sons. Maybe you, Raphael, can talk some sense into your strong yet weak-willed brother."

Halfway down the corridor, Michael threw his arm away from Raphael. "What do you want? You make me ill with your deceit and your arrogance because of your abilities to heal the wounded and bring back anyone you deem worthy. Remember, dear brother, I am older than you by centuries."

Raphael threw his head back and laughed sarcastically. "Yes, brother, you are older than me, but none the wiser." Raphael took Michael's hand in his and said, "Dear brother, I love you more than you know, and you are right. Lucifer has a valid point." They entered Raphael's bedchamber.

Michael, confused by this, said, "How did you know, you sneaking, eavesdropping snake?"

Raphael smiled and said, "Dear, dear brother, we are all linked together, in our hearts and our minds. My ability is strong as the last born. My mind is more linked to all of my older brothers and sisters as I am the strongest telepath in all of heaven. My bond with all of you, with the exception of Gabriel, as he is the bringer of life and death—he loathes my ability to strip away his control over death—is strong. Yet he is still very psychic. Gabriel has the ability to give life or to strip it away. With that great responsibility comes the uncanny and unusual ability to block telepathic influences on him. I, however, can penetrate his mind and his thoughts, especially when he's tired or weak. After the great battle of the Tower of Babel, I had access to his mind for weeks." Raphael, with his loving green eyes and blond hair, said to his brother, "I can read you, brother, and I am confused by your thoughts. You would take sides with him over us? Your beloved brothers and sisters? You would rather have humanity's stench rise up here into heaven for eternity? You would betray our race and our kind to satisfy him?"

Michael was very annoyed at his younger sibling and said, "His name is Father, not *him*."

Raphael chuckled. "He may be Father to you, but to me he is an arrogant tyrant and not my father."

Michael, still confused, answered, "How can Father not know your thoughts if you are a great telepath?"

"I am the greatest telepath. I block his thoughts from mine and mine from his. He has no idea that I block him, he just thinks I'm stupid. Michael, Lucifer and I need you and need your mighty sword and your incredible size to help us rid this gorgeous blue planet from the human interlopers."

Michael, confused as always, had to leave the chamber and rid himself of Raphael.

As he was walking away, Michael turned over his shoulder and said, "Raphael, such blasphemy will get you into trouble with Father and the rest of us. You should be careful what you say and whom you say it to. I will never betray you, just be careful."

Michael, his head still reeling from his confrontation with Raphael and with the Father, entered the clouded corridor. He spotted a blurred figure standing in the hallway. Noticing wings raised high and armor shining in the sunlight, he knew in an instant who it was. Her broad shoulders and mighty size rivaled Michael's. His younger sister Uriel was almost as big as he was and twice as cunning as Lucifer was. Michael instinctively reached for his sword. Her subangels upheld God's laws.

"What do you want?" Michael's command to the leader of the dominations made the angel turn and smile at him. Her gentle brown eyes hid a mind as sharp as the Father's. Her long dark hair flowed in the breeze.

Looking at Michael's hand on his sword, she spoke. "Why do you always try and fight me, brother?" She shook her head. Her heavy large arms and massive breasts bounced as she did. "I am your sister and would never go against Father or you, my brother. My brethren and I will follow you into the bleakest of battle for Father and for the preservation of heaven. You, dear brother, are the mightiest of all of us. I do not wish to battle with thee. Your fantastic devotion to being the right hand of Father is known throughout heaven. We love Father and uphold his laws and defend him as you do. We are your ever-loyal army. All the laws that we stand for will not be usurped. You may summon us at your will, my dear brother. We will be there when you need us."

Michael turned and said, "You expect a battle in heaven? Over humanity? Are you insane? Father would never let us battle. You of all angels should remember Father's first rule!"

Uriel spoke. "Of course I do. We are our brothers' keepers, but if something does go awry, I want you to know that we are with thee." With that being said, Uriel bowed to her older brother, turned from Michael, and retreated down the corridor.

Shaking his head, Michael thought, *A battle in heaven or on earth for the humans?* He pushed the thought from his mind. Getting confused more and more by the intelligence spewed in his direction, he just wanted to go to bed and rest his weary yet divine head.

Lying on his bed, Raphael smiled, knowing exactly what had just transpired in the hallway. The grin was that of utter victory as he knew that Saraqael would unleash the seraphim. They would destroy the dominations in one epic battle. He wondered where the virtues were. They were hard to read for Raphael; they were just too pure. They had nothing to hide. This annoyed Raphael, he wanted to know everything that went on in heaven and on earth. He also knew with Lucifer, Michael, and himself, he would finally be rid of that annoying Gabriel. Gabriel, with his ability to grant life or to take it away, gave Raphael a sick feeling in his gut. Raphael, being the angel of healing, knew that his Father would call upon him to heal Gabriel. However, he would be the first that Raphael killed. He would dangle his precious gift in front of Gabriel as he killed him.

The thought of ramming his sword into Gabriel's heart and looking into his brother's eyes as the life force drained from him made him smile. He would beg Raphael to spare him and heal him, yet Raphael would not grant such luxury, even if his mighty Father persuaded him to do so. Oh, what delight he thought at having Raqael release the four horsemen upon the earth, and with Gabriel finally dead, Raphael would be feared by all. He thought of the four horsemen and the sheer agony they would bring with them. These thoughts were just too delightful that he began to giggle and laugh hysterically at the thought of God's precious planet in ruins.

Raqael, standing in the stables, looked at her beloved four horses. She knew one day Lucifer would call upon her to wake the horsemen. With bags of grain, she went to each of the mighty steeds.

She went to Pestilence and gave the horse a scratch. The horse smelled of death and disease. She filled his grain bowl and refilled his water. Pestilence gave her a nudge with his head and said, "Thanks."

Raqael then went to Famine. This steed was asleep and grunted as she refilled his hay supply. She was thankful that Famine was asleep; this steed always pulled on her heartstrings, with his ribs sticking out and him being continually hungry. It was all she could do to not cry every time she saw this steed. Although mighty and large, Famine was thin and wiry. She would return to his pen and lay his bony head upon her lap and brush his long mane. Most mornings she awoke lying down with Famine.

Next, she spotted War. This stud always gave Raqael a twinge of fear. This steed was aggressive and would bite any chance he got. War spoke. "What do you want, filthy angel? I can smell your fear. Get out! I don't need anything from you. All I want is Lucifer to allow my rider and me to battle." The horse constantly asked about Lucifer and his rider. It annoyed Raqael, but she would never dare say so.

The last of the pens housed Death. This pale horse scared her. She shivered as she got closer. Her breath visible as she went into the pen, the air around her became frigid. Death had his back to her. His giant haunches flicked and twitched as his massive tail swayed back and forth. Raqael refilled the hay and grain. Death spoke. "Don't forget my water, fool. Lucifer would not be amused if anything would happen to me. I am his greatest stud, and only he and my rider may sit upon my back. Now get out! Your stench fills my nostrils, and I fear I may be sick."

Raqael nodded and did as she was told. She was thankful that Death had his back to her. The eyes that were held in the horse's skull were fire red and burned straight into her soul.

Michael, finally at his bedchamber door, felt a moment of relief wash over him. He turned the knob, and his relief soon turned into fear. Michael feared nobody but the Father and one other archangel, Ramiel, the leader of the virtues. Ramiel had a large army at his disposal, and at any time, he could destroy Michael and the Father and overthrow heaven itself.

Michael cleared his thoughts, and in a strong and stern voice, he said, "Why are you in here? Get out."

Ramiel said, "You know exactly why I am here. My army of virtues and I are none too amused by Lucifer's and Gabriel's antics in court today. You, above all other of our brothers and sisters, should realize that this is all wrong. Humans, although flawed, do uphold Father's laws and are virtuous. I will not allow the destruction of earth nor that of our beloved home. Heaven is a sacred place, and I will not let you or anybody else destroy it, Michael. You may wield a sword and be Father's right hand, but I have the mighty judgment of Father himself. In his hand are all the rules that bind not only angels but humans as well." Ramiel turned and walked toward the door. "Remember, I am on nobody's side in this but Father's.

I would not enjoy a battle with the seraphim. That army is as mighty as the virtues and dominations together. The battle would be massive and bloody, and many angels would die. That saddens my heart, and I will not let it happen. Good night, brother. I love you." He closed the door behind him, his large white yet bloodstained wings fluttering behind him.

Michael knew that, being the leader of the virtues, Ramiel often had to do tortuous and bloody work on angels and humans alike. Michael, standing in the middle of his room, could only stand with a slack-jawed gaze and be even more confused.

CHAPTER 2

The First Witness

awn ascended. The morning sun broke into heaven and illuminated Jehovah sitting in his chambers. He looked down and studied everything dealing with his beautiful blue planet. He thought of all his children, angelic and human alike. His thoughts immediately went to his angelic children and their conflict. Why couldn't the boys just get along? They were always at one another, in one way or another. Michael and Gabriel together, most of the time, made God smile. The thought of Lucifer and Raphael together constantly brought a frown to the Almighty's face. The four boys were always trying to be more superior than the other. The constant barrage of insults flung from each side made the inhabitants of heaven nervous and leery. Being archangels, they needed to set an example. The examples that they set now were abysmal, to say the least. The two girls were never in competition, never at each other, and always supported each other. The girls were loners, one with the horses and the other continually training her army. The other angels were always tied up with their own tasks. Jehovah knew that Ramiel was always looking for lawbreakers and Saraqael was constantly pushing and training new tactics to his seraphim army.

He looked down upon his amazing creation, and a smile began to show on his timeworn face. He was overcome by the wave of scent of sin and human greed. His nose wrinkled as the foul stench entered his nostrils. He could see the two cities, sisters in their abundant debauchery. His ears were assaulted by the hatred and loathing of one true god. He saw lewd dancing and orgies encircling graven images. He could not sense any righteousness in these twin cities.

His first thought was to wipe the planet clean of these cities. He raised his hand and was about to rain fire upon the earth when a thought came to him. He knew that righteous men and women were being held captive in these cities. He scanned and scanned, yet none were sensed. His instinct told him that there had to be, had to be good in these awful metropolises. He wanted desperately to rid the planet of such irreverent behavior.

Jehovah raised his mighty hand, lightning and brimstone about to be released. Yet God relented, a large tear running down his face. He lowered his head, and he tried to forgive. He knew this was perfect and grinned. He could use this to his advantage in today's court proceedings. He would suggest to the boys that each send an angel down to the planet disguised as humans. The twin cities were a perfect place to find sin and sinner and the righteous and God-fearing. Jehovah also thought he would contact two humans. The two humans. One would help the angels sent to the planet; the other would help him prove that mankind was worthy. He would visit Abraham and have him gather fifty God-fearing men of the great city of Sodom. He would also contact Lot to give shelter to the angels chosen. The Lord thought, *Oh, this plan is brilliant. Lucifer will see that mankind is righteous. He wouldn't have to destroy Sodom and Gomorrah.* He knew, as judge and executioner, he couldn't take sides. He did want Gabriel to reign supreme in the battle over his beloved humans. He could not bear to lose them again.

Jehovah readied himself for the day. As he entered the courtroom, he heard Michael say, "All rise!" He could see all the angels standing and their heads bowed in respect to him, all except Lucifer, who stared at his Father as he entered. Taken aback by such utter disrespect, Jehovah paused and stared back at his son. For a second they were locked in a battle with their minds. Jehovah had a glimpse into the cunning and often-spiteful mind of his second-born. He could feel the sheer hatred aimed at Michael. Jehovah knew, if the boys were left to do as they pleased, they would certainly kill each other. He knew Lucifer was extremely intelligent, and a twinge of fear entered his heart. An unfamiliar shiver ran down his back as he sat. Jehovah knew that a battle was coming, and he hated the thought of his home in ruins. He leaned back in his large chair and looked out at the court. He saw all the angels beginning to sit. He noticed Gabriel, busy with his papers, and then he looked again at Lucifer. He pondered the question in his mind: *Is he truly divine, or is he evil in its purest form?*

Lucifer inwardly smiled as he knew exactly what his Father was thinking.

The prosecution went first, as always. Lucifer began to speak. "Good morning, brothers and sisters, and to you, Father. I will call my first witness this morning." Lucifer grinned as the large oak doors at the back of the courtroom opened.

The only sound that could be heard was the creaking of ancient hinges as the doors slid shut. A hush filled the courtroom as all the angels couldn't believe who had come in. The stench of centuries filled the air. The smell of deceit and of pure hatred filled every molecule of air in the room. He wriggled across the room, hissing and showing his gleaming white fangs as he did. His black scales shimmered like diamonds in the morning sun. His forked tongue flicked in and out of his mouth. The bright-yellow color of his eyes was matched only by the ferocity of the sun. His massive body was still at the end of the hallway and near the audience as he passed by Lucifer. They recoiled as he passed them, gasping and whispering among themselves. He smiled as the hatred spewed toward him filled the room. A sense of superiority filled the snake's face. The mighty serpent slinked across the floor and onto the witness stand. His massive tail began to curl around the legs of the chair. He was coiled like a viper ready to strike.

Lucifer spoke to the serpent, who glared at Jehovah. "Welcome, serpent."

Not hearing Lucifer, the snake stared at Jehovah.

He hissed, "You have made me eat dusssst and crawl along my stomach for eternity. How I have waited to confront you. You unforgiving assssssshole. Oh, how I loathe you."

Lucifer, shocked at the snake's remarks to the Father, said, "Hush now. This is not why I called you testify today."

"I will not hush! This basssssstard has dissssssciplined me with missssssssery. Yet hisssss beloved Adam and Eve got minimum punishment."

Lucifer, wanting the snake's eyes on him, began to weave in front of it. He walked back and forth in front of the serpent to keep his attention and began his questions.

"You are the serpent from the Garden of Eden, are you not?"

The snake nodded and said, "Yessssss."

"Please tell the court of the forbidden fruit tree and what transpired that day."

The serpent, with its yellow eyes, stared at Lucifer. He didn't trust this angel and was afraid to say the wrong thing. He knew, if he didn't say exactly as Lucifer had told him to, his punishment would be torture from Ramiel.

Lucifer scolded the great serpent and said, "Enough with the s sounds! You are beginning to irritate me."

The great snake leaned forward, his long upper body tense with rage, and said, "I will speak asssss you wish." His long fangs, dripping with venom, came very close to Lucifer's cheek as he began to lean back into the witness chair.

Lucifer, indignant to the serpent's venom, did not flinch. He was quite cavalier about the potential for death.

The serpent began his story. "On the day in question, I was walking." When he said *walking*, he glared at Jehovah. "And I came upon this human being standing in the middle of the garden, under the apple tree. Being the inquiring animal that I am, I wanted to know why she only stood under the beautiful fruit tree but did not eat. I told her to eat."

Lucifer grinned and interrupted. "What did she say?"

"'I cannot eat of this tree. It is forbidden by God. We are permitted to eat of all the trees except this one. The Lord said that it was poisonous.' I told her, 'The fruit of this tree is not poison, it is delicious, with its white insides and the delicious red skin. Besides, who is to know? There is only you and me here.' Without hesitation, she pulled an apple off the tree and bit into its red skin. Her husband came running over and scorned her for eating of the tree. She said, 'It is delicious. God lied to us and said we would die. I am not dead, Adam.'"

Lucifer asked, "And what did you do?"

"I chuckled as they finally realized they were naked and became embarrassed. They scrambled around and fumbled. They grabbed figs and leaves to cover themselves—quite comical to watch. I knew there were to be repercussions, but I never expected the punishment I was handed. *He*"—he shot a look to the Almighty—"took my legs away. Only punished his humans with childbirth and tending the fields. How bad can that be? I am to go on my belly for all eternity, eating dust, yet they defied him as blatantly as I did, and he didn't take their legs and arms."

"That is all," Lucifer said as he went over to Gabriel's desk, palms on the stone edge, and leaned in. He asked, "Cross-examination?"

Gabriel looked down at the floor and shook his head.

"I didn't think so," Lucifer said triumphantly. "See, Father? Even Gabriel knows the humans, even when only two inhabited the planet, were untrustworthy." He looked at the great serpent and said, "You may step down."

When Lucifer said *step*, the serpent fixed on him with a bold stare and hissed defiantly. Lucifer then watched and chuckled to himself as the great serpent clumsily fell onto its side and slid off the chair. Their eyes locked in an absolute hatred.

The serpent whispered so only Lucifer could hear, "Lucifer, you think you're so smart. You wait until *he* punishes you for interfering with his beloved humanssss. Allow to unleash Ramiel onto you. We will see who gets the last laugh, then, won't we?"

Lucifer just grinned as the serpent slithered off the witness stand and out of the courtroom.

Lucifer walked in front of the bench and said, "Father, I can feel that you have something to say or do. Care to enlighten my brother and me?"

Jehovah studied Lucifer with great intent. He couldn't figure out how he knew that he was planning something. He didn't think he had any details, just an inkling of what he was planning. He knew Lucifer could see part of his design, as he was a strong psychic, but Jehovah also knew that he could not fully penetrate his mind. All the archangels were psychics, Raphael being the strongest. Even Raphael couldn't penetrate his mind, or so he thought.

Jehovah spoke. "I have been watching the planet this morning and noticed twin cities that are in need of some divine intervention."

Lucifer, his eyes glinting, said, "Objection, Father."

Jehovah answered with an "Overruled. You will like this plan, my son. Lucifer, I am going to send two angels down to the planet. You can choose one, and, Gabriel, you can choose one. I have spoken to Abraham via dreams and told him to find fifty righteous men of Sodom and Gomorrah. He has yet to tell me his results. I want your angels to seek out and find a man named Lot. He will give them shelter and welcome them into his home, as I have spoken to him as well via dreams. Bring back your angels disguised as humans." God raised his gavel and banged it. "Court dismissed for lunch. Be back here in one hour."

Court was back in session after lunch, and Jehovah began to speak to the court. "I have sent my two sons to find two angels, one apiece. Have you brought your angels, my sons?"

Gabriel and Lucifer looked at each other then to their Father and nodded.

The Lord spoke. "Let the record show that the defense and the prosecution both have confirmed they have brought their angels." Nodding at his sons, he continued, "Angels, step forward."

Two subangels came in front of the bench, disguised as humans, and bowed their heads before the Almighty.

He spoke to them. "You will go to the city of Sodom and seek out a man named Lot. He will give you shelter and welcome you into his home. You are to find righteousness is this offensive city. I know mankind will prove to my son Lucifer that they are worthy of my love and the love of the angels. Now go. Blessed are they among the travelers, and blessings to you, my angels. Lucifer, Gabriel, and members of the jury will stay as we all watch what transpires on the planet. The rest of you may leave, if so desired."

Jehovah banged his mighty gavel, and with a wave of his large hand, the city of Sodom was visible to the remaining angels that were in the courtroom. They all watched as the events of the twin cities began to unfold. Lucifer sat with his arms crossed over his chest and a smirk on his face. He was very interested in what was about to happen, but he could feel that this was going to be a decisive victory for the prosecution. He couldn't help but chuckle to himself.

CHAPTER 3

Sodom and Gomorrah

The angels descended from heaven to earth and found themselves outside the gates of Sodom. They nervously looked at each other as the smell of sins, great and small, was inflicted upon them. They opened the gates of the great city and were immediately assaulted by a woman. She smelled of sex and was filthy. The angels cringed as she writhed around them, singing and dancing. They pushed her away and tried to brush off her filth.

They continued to survey and walk. All types of people filled the common area of the city. People lay behind some of the vendors, covered in their own vomit. Some were having sex in the open. It was hard for the angels to look upon such irreverence.

A moment of happiness filled their hearts as they saw people praying.

But their happiness was short-lived when the angels saw there were only a few.

They kept walking through the decrepit and dirty city until they came out of the common area. They strode into the housing district. These streets were cleaner yet still unrefined. The men and women of the community glared at the angels and whispered among themselves, pointing accusing fingers and untrusting the strangers. Some of the men began to follow the two interlopers. Walking faster, the angels could feel the presence of the man they came to seek out, Lot. They could feel him in the small and humble home at the end of the street. The angels proceeded to the modest abode and knocked upon the door.

Lot welcomed his visitors with delight and baked unfermented cakes, and they feasted. Lot washed the angel's feet and made beds for them to rest.

Before they could lie down, the men of the city surrounded the house. A giant mob, men and boys alike. They demanded Lot bring the angels out so they could rape them.

Lot went outside and begged the men not to hurt the strangers. "They are my guests, and I will protect them!" Lot shouted. Lot even offered the men of the city his virgin daughters instead of the angels.

But they didn't want the daughters; they wanted to know the angels. The mob of the angry men of Sodom burst through the door of Lot's home. They searched and searched. Nobody was in there. The men ransacked Lot's home and, finally satisfied, left Lot in the mess that their destruction had created.

Jehovah, Gabriel, and Lucifer were watching the entire scene on the planet. They all were mortified by the story unfolding in Sodom. The Almighty, angry at how this transpired, said, "I am going to destroy these fucking cities. But I want my angels and Lot and his wife and daughters to be safe. These cities have no right to even exist on my precious earth!" He closed his eyes and sent a message to the angels. Then he said, "I am going down to these cities and find Abraham to see if he has found the fifty righteous men I've asked for. You may watch as I destroy these terrible cities."

Lucifer went to say something to his Father when Michael grabbed him by the arm. Concern in his eyes, he shook his head no. Gabriel was crying, yet Lucifer was grinning from sacred ear to sacred ear.

The Lord disappeared in a puff of smoke and departed for the planet.

The angels, who were keeping Lot's family safe with invisibility, heard the voice of God in their heads and immediately told Lot and his family they had to leave. "Jehovah is about to bring this city and the city of Gomorrah to ruin. Do not hesitate. Seek out Abraham outside the city gates and the other righteous men of Sodom and flee."

Lot, knowing these men were of divine flesh, heeded their warning and left his home. He took only his family with him and fled.

Jehovah stood outside the gates of Sodom. He saw Abraham and eighteen righteous men come through the city gate. He asked Abraham, "This is all you could find? I said at least fifty."

Abraham lowered his head, looked at his feet, and said, "Yes, my Lord, this is all I could find. I am sorry, but it was extremely difficult to find honest men in this horrific city. Most of the men here thought I was insane."

Jehovah stared at Abraham, debating on whether or not to kill him. His thoughts, however, were more occupied with destroying the cities, and he let Abraham and the eighteen men leave. The Almighty could feel the angels were back safely in the bosom of heaven. He knew that Lot and his wife and daughters were on their way as well. He thought about Lot and how he offered up his virgin daughters. This irritated Jehovah. He closed his eyes and spoke to Lot with his mind. He told him to not look back at the cities as they were being destroyed or he would be turned into a pillar of salt. Jehovah knew that the temptation of looking back would be so great that his entire family would soon be salt. He opened his eyes and stared at the city gates.

The twin cities were being destroyed together, as their fates would be exactly the same. A great cyclone of sand and wind surrounded Jehovah. Lightning cracked within the cyclone. He held hail, wind, fire, and brimstone in his divine hands. He raised his hands up to the heavens and unleashed his fury. It had been a very long time since such rage filled his heart. Not since the great flood had he felt such a desire to destroy his creation. He loathed what these cities represented and wanted them gone from his beautiful blue planet. His long white beard and long gray hair flew around in the wind. His once-pale blue eyes rolled over white, and he began.

Jehovah sealed the cities by melting the gates together. The skies began to darken, and the wind blew ferociously, lightning cracked, and thunder boomed. Hail the size of oranges fell to the earth and crashed in a cascade of shattering ice. Shards flew everywhere and pierced the flesh of the closest sinners. The residents of the doomed cities began to cry and scream.

The Almighty could hear the repentance and prayers coming from the sinners, yet he gave no forgiveness. Fists clenched and teeth gritting, he unleashed his might onto the cities and its inhabitants. The prayers were so loud in his head that he thought his head was going to explode.

How dare they! he thought. *Even those blasphemous assholes who were willing to rape my beloved angels asked for mercy. Never, never, never.*

Balls of fire flew forth from the blackened clouds. God's fury was incredible. The streets began to fill with a river of molten rock and ignite fires as it flowed. Fires erupted in almost every home and business. Brimstone fell in great blasts and exploded on impact. Giant unequivocal globs splattered with every collision either with ground or building or even a sinner. God would not relent. He opened the clouds and allowed rain that burned the skin on humans and animals alike. The smell of burning flesh could be smelled for miles.

To the Almighty, it smelled like victory. God could hear the begging and pleading coming from the mouths of the wicked, yet still no forgiveness was to be found in his heart. He wanted these cities to be examples of his wrath. His vengeance would be complete.

Lightning lashed at the ground, bringing great electric shocks to the remaining few that had survived the fire and brimstone. The Almighty was done. The cities lay in ruin, and with a smile on his face, he returned to heaven.

He reappeared in the courtroom a few minutes after he had left. The angels looked at him with anxious faces, and a soft murmur filled the room. He sat down on his great chair and sighed. He pushed his damp hair back, moistened by the sweat of his brow, and looked around the room. He saw his ever-loyal Michael, concern and tears in his eyes. He saw Gabriel with his head hung low. And then he looked at Lucifer. He was grinning at his Father, a triumphant smirk upon his face.

Jehovah spoke. "Tell me, son, what did you think about that?"

Lucifer, trying to hold back his feeling of superiority, said, "Father, you just destroyed the wicked and the sinners of two great cities. I feel vindicated. You have shown the court that mankind is truly unworthy of your love and understanding. Did any of them repent as you were killing them, Father?"

The Lord spoke to his sons and the court. "Indeed, I have destroyed two cities on the planet. However, I did save twenty or so from the destruction. There are still righteousness and good among the humans. I have just proven that. To answer your question, my son, yes, several did pray to me and ask for forgiveness. I declined to accompany their requests on the grounds that they should have left when given the chance. I did not grant salvation on the simple fact that they all have free will and chose not to use it."

Gabriel spoke. "Father, you look exhausted. You need to rest after such events. I remember your sleep after the great flood. We were shocked at the centuries that passed on the planet while you slumbered. I'm worried about you."

Jehovah looked at his dutiful son and said, "Yes, you're right. Your concern is only matched by your love, Gabriel." When he said this, Jehovah did not look at Gabriel but at Lucifer, who only stood there and grinned.

"Court adjourned. We will reconvene in three days, centuries on the planet."

With a mighty bang of his gavel, all the angels stood and bowed their heads as Jehovah exited the courtroom. All except for Lucifer, of course.

Michael bolted to Lucifer and grabbed his brother by the throat. He lifted him off the marble floor. Michael's other hand was on his sword. Michael spoke through gritted teeth. "What the fuck is wrong with you? I should kill you where you stand. I despise you and would rid myself, Father, and the rest of heaven of your presence if given the chance. I would take every second of punishment our brother would deal out to me just to see you die. Even your beloved Raphael would not be able to save you, as I would remove your heart. Bastard."

Lucifer beat Michael on the shoulders with his wings, feathers flying every which way, but to no avail. He clutched Michael's hand, and his legs kicked wildly. Surprisingly, Gabriel came to his aid. Pulling Michael off their gasping brother, Gabriel pushed Michael back and held him. Lucifer hit the floor with a loud thud and looked up at Michael.

Lucifer spoke, his words filled with hate. "How dare you touch me, brother!" Rubbing at his throat, he continued, "Do you realize the consequences for such actions? Ramiel's torture would be nothing compared to what I would do. I could banish you to the stables and convince Father to remove your wings. A fate worse than death for any angel, even you, Michael. Do you understand me, moron?"

Michael, still being held by Gabriel, responded, "You have to taunt Father, don't you? Why? He loves you as he loves all of us, yet you provoke him. You make me sick, and I cannot wait until this nonsense is behind us. You better sleep with one eye open, brother."

Lucifer was stunned at his brother's brashness. "You couldn't sneak up on a deaf-mute, you ignoramus! Fuck you! You think, because you have that sword, you could kill me? You call me arrogant? Look in the mirror, dear, dear brother, and I guarantee you'll hate what you'll fucking see. Your threats mean nothing to me, do you understand? Nothing!"

Michael turned and left the courtroom with rage and revenge filling his heart.

Gabriel, watching the scene unfold before him, noticed something in Lucifer's eyes, something he had never seen in his older brother. What he saw was fear.

Gabriel went to the aid of Lucifer. He knelt beside his brother and said, "Michael knows not what he does. His brains reside in his muscles and his sword. You above all of us should know Michael's limits. You two have been at odds with each other for all time."

He pushed Gabriel's hand off him, stood, and said, "Why did you help me? We are locked in this confrontation for humanity. Never thought that my adversary would become my ally."

He smiled at his older brother and said, "I am not an ally. I just don't like to see my two brothers fighting with each other."

Lucifer began to walk out of the courtroom and uttered over his shoulder, "Gabriel, do you think that Michael would show you the same courtesy?

Jehovah slept.

CHAPTER 4

Jehovah Awoke

Jehovah awoke in the darkness. He could hear his beloved humans screaming in agony. He closed his eyes and scanned the planet. There in Egypt he could feel the children of Israel crying out for guidance. The time of many gods still reigned in Egypt, and it was time to rid himself once and for all of them. He could see elaborate temples erected to other gods. This angered him, and he chose to destroy all of Egypt.

Jehovah chose two brothers to lead the righteous. Aaron and Moses were chosen to bring them out of bondage and into a life of freedom. He knew that the pharaoh was not going to bow down easily. He sent Moses to Ramses. The pharaoh would not relent. Jehovah smote the land with plagues, and still the pharaoh wouldn't budge. He sent Gabriel to the planet, not as the angel of life, but as the angel of death.

Finally, his people were free to preach his Word and uphold his Ten Commandments. They gave praise to him and his glory.

Gabriel appeared at his Father's bedside. Fresh from the planet, he was spoken to by the Almighty. "You must never let Lucifer find out about this. He would use it in court against the humans. The ones that I just destroyed were not worthy. They need not trouble you with another thought. I must ask you to wash this from your mind and your memory.

Lucifer will be able to sense it in you if you don't. Gabriel, this is crucial. You must do as I ask."

Gabriel said, "Yes, Father," and rid himself of all memory of the passing over of the Jewish homes. He washed away all the death of the Egyptian firstborns.

Jehovah could feel Gabriel rinsing his memory and smiled. Gabriel left his bedchamber in a daze. Jehovah rested his head and smiled. Now that the planet was quiet again and the Egyptian crisis had been averted, he could go back to sleep.

Raphael knew exactly what had happened on the planet.

Gabriel was exhausted as he lay his head down and began to sleep. He couldn't remember the last time he had been this drained. He tried to shield his mind from his younger brother Raphael, as he knew he would try to scan his memories.

Raphael knew that Gabriel was trying to block him and waited patiently for the right moment to enter his brother's memories. Gabriel's guard was finally let down, and Raphael didn't waste a minute and dived into his mind. He couldn't believe the sights he saw. He read his older brother's mind and couldn't wait to inform Lucifer. Raphael thought, *What delicious deception! So even the boorish Gabriel is capable of such deceit? Oh, this is just too fantastic!* He could see into Gabriel's mind and rummaged through his memories. *He tried to rinse his mind. How clever, trying to keep his memories hidden from me,* Raphael thought. He saw frogs, lice, flies, darkness, hail, bloody water, dying cattle, boils, and finally the death of the firstborn of Egypt. Raphael thought, *Oh, Lucifer is going to love hearing about all this!* He spoke aloud. "This is the ammunition we need to finally rid the planet. Gabriel won't even see my strike against him coming. The fool!" Raphael laughed and was content. He thought of Gabriel and his loving and disgustingly pure heart, and Raphael cringed. He smiled again at the thought of dangling his healing power in front of Gabriel's face as he lay dying.

The dawn rose and found Jehovah in heaven's kitchen. The exact place that he created earth and all the beings that lived upon it. His first try with beings had been a disaster. The mighty lizards proved to be a burden on the planet. They ate everything and anything and had not one prayer of thanks to their Creator. He couldn't control the beasts, as he forgot to bless them with the capacity of rational thought. Jehovah had no recourse but to destroy the inhabitants and almost the entire planet with a meteor. He didn't want to destroy the planet again.

His thoughts went to his beloved humans. He stood in the kitchen for a moment and was the proud Creator. He shook his head and could feel the hunger rise in his stomach. Right now all he wanted was a sandwich. He had only slept for three days in heaven, but centuries had passed on the planet. He felt refreshed and energized as he finished his meal. He entered the hallway, and waiting by the door was Michael.

Jehovah spoke to his son. "Good morning, Michael."

Michael bowed his head and said, "Good morning, Father." Side by side they strode, and Michael spoke. "Father, Lucifer and Raphael were together the entire time you slept. I have not seen Gabriel or any of my other brothers and sisters. Heaven has been quite quiet since you had rested. Mercifully, Ramiel hasn't even had to unleash punishments."

Jehovah looked over at his son as they walked and said, "Yes, indeed. Mercifully." A pang of restlessness filled Jehovah's heart at the thought of Raphael and Lucifer together for days. "We will be reconvening court this afternoon. I have another idea."

Michael said, "As you wish, Father."

Court settled in for the afternoon session, and Jehovah spoke. "While I slumbered, I had another idea about humanity and the extent they will go through to prove their love for me. I am to let you, Lucifer, have a human of your choice to torture as you wish. You may not kill him. Gabriel will not interfere. You will see the repentance of the species in this one man. The destruction of the twin cities did not produce the outcome I wished. There were sinners and saints, survivors and victims of my wrath. We need to try again. The floor is yours, Lucifer, to let us know what you thought of the devastation."

Lucifer walked over to the jury and spoke, his back to Jehovah. "The twin cities were full of sin. They were full of sinners, they were full of such debauchery, yet Father seems to think they were righteous. I am here today to tell you that he is wrong."

When Lucifer said *wrong*, the courtroom erupted in gasping and calls of "Never."

Lucifer turned and looked at the audience. He peered at them through half-closed lids and squinted. The audience quieted down without Lucifer saying a word. He continued, "Indeed, Father found twenty-plus men to come out of the city and turn their back on sin. However, there were thousands of souls in those cities. It's laughable. Most of them, not all, repented when the end came near. Yet Father did not grant forgiveness. Hmmm, I wonder why. Members of the jury, this is a wonderful conquest for the prosecution." He turned and looked at his Father. "Thank you for this decisive win, Father. I can feel the jury members swaying toward ridding the planet of the scourge of humans." Lucifer turned and leaned his hands on the railing. "Father decided that the events of the twin cities would neither benefit me or Gabriel. I do think that most of you agree with me, that there should have been more souls leaving the doomed metropolises. As for Lot and his family, his wife was turned into a pillar of salt. She could not resist the temptation to not look back upon the destruction. I believe that the events of the past day in court were to my benefit. It showed just how untrustworthy and deceitful humans can be. Now Father gives me a new challenge to choose a human to torture to see if he will renounce the Word of God. I will bring in my brother Ramiel to subsequently hand down the punishment."

When he said the name of his younger brother Ramiel, the jury cringed. All the angels looked at the floor and were terrified.

Jehovah spoke. "Lucifer, I said you could torture the human, not Ramiel. I said nothing about him."

Lucifer said, "Exactly, Father. You spoke of Gabriel but failed to mention Ramiel. If you are to speak of one of my brothers, you should speak of them all." A slight victory filled Lucifer's eyes, and Jehovah knew that his second-born was right.

The Almighty spoke. "Have you decided on whom you will curse with the afflictions of Ramiel?"

Lucifer thought for a moment, and he said, "Indeed, I have, Father. The man I choose is Job. Your ever-faithful and ever-subservient Job. He is a blameless and upright man, and I will assure you that Ramiel will not kill him."

Jehovah was stunned that Lucifer even knew about Job.

"Thank you, Father," Lucifer said and sat back down at his marble desk.

Gabriel got up out of his seat and spoke to the jury. "My brother would like to think that the twin cities were a victory for him. He could not be more wrong. Although Abraham only found eighteen men to accompany him out of the city, they were the most righteous of mankind. This destruction is a victory for the defense. Some, nay, I say most of the men, women, and children of the doomed cities repented and asked Father for forgiveness. The only deity that they prayed to in the end of their lives was Jehovah. I did not hear any prayers to other gods. Did any of you hear it?"

The seraphim in the jury all shook their heads no.

Gabriel did not rest as Lucifer did against the railing but walked in front of the jury as he spoke. He continued, "Father did not grant forgiveness, not to punish them even more, but to teach a lesson. They all have free will, as do we, but they chose not to use it and leave. Although repentance while dying is enough for any human soul to enter the kingdom of heaven, Father saw fit to deny it. Their souls will not rest until they have paid their penance in purgatory. Then and only then will they be granted access to our beautiful home. That is Father's decision to make when he feels ready to make it. We cannot and will not judge Father for the things he does. Now my brother wishes to bring Ramiel into this discussion. A bold move, I must admit. You will see Job suffer greatly as many of you have from Ramiel in the past. I will leave you with this thought: would any of you want the wrath of Ramiel? I can feel your empathy for Job already. Thank you. That is all."

Gabriel walked past his Father and nodded in his direction and said, "Thank you, Father."

Lucifer stood and said, "May the court please welcome our brother Ramiel?"

The tension skyrocketed as Ramiel crossed the threshold and into the courtroom. They could hear a pin drop as the audience all looked at the floor. Ramiel tried to look into their eyes, but none would dare look at him. Any eye contact with Ramiel was taken as a challenge and he would spring into action. All the angels were scared, all except Lucifer, who smiled and looked at his younger sibling. He knew that Ramiel was the perfect choice to torture this pathetic human.

Ramiel passed Lucifer with a sneer and went straight to the front of the bench. He went to one knee and bowed his head to the Father. He spoke in his soft voice. "Hello, Father. I promise to not kill this human. I take no pleasure in this. I would rather not be involved. Do I have to be used as Lucifer's pawn?"

Jehovah spoke. "Yes, my son, you do. If I had not misspoken, you would be able to decline Lucifer's proposal. I am sorry."

Ramiel stood and looked lovingly at his Father, his bloodstained wings dragging the floor behind him as he turned to Lucifer. "Let's get this done, brother."

Lucifer smiled.

CHAPTER 5

Job

Job, a man blameless and upright, was a servant of Jehovah. He dutifully prayed in the morning, at noon, and at night and thanked God for his bountiful life. He praised Jehovah at meals. He tended his flock, which numbered seven thousand and more. He sacrificed beautiful lambs in Jehovah's name and gave thanks for every healthy birth, either human or animal. He prayed to the Almighty daily and honorably. Jehovah allowed Gabriel to bless him with seven sons and three daughters. He prospered and was happy. Lucifer wanted nothing more than to have this man blaspheme his Father and fall from grace. It would be a great victory for the prosecution, and Lucifer allowed Ramiel to do as he wished. The only rule was, he could not kill him.

A day came to pass when a stranger came calling for Job. The man was in shambles, his hair strewn about his face. The smell of fire surrounded the stranger. His robes were tattered and worn. Job inquired why he was in such disarray. The man told Job that he was in the field and a ball of fire came from the sky. He spoke of a bloodred sky that unleashed the mayhem, the likes of which he had never seen. The flock was instantly turned to ash, and all the camels were stolen.

Job went to his knees and prayed to Jehovah, thanking him for sparing himself, his wife, his children, and his grandchildren. The stranger and Job prayed for hours. Lucifer watched in disbelief as Job was turned into a pauper yet still prayed. Not one harsh word was sent in the Almighty's direction. Only praise and love. Lucifer told Ramiel to destroy the house that had his family in it and kill them all. Ramiel obeyed and folded the four corners of the home onto the floor, crushing everyone inside. The cries of his beloved children screamed out for Job to help. But Ramiel made sure that the walls held tight to the floor. He tried with all his might to free his family yet never once asked God for help. Instead, he prayed the entire time he fruitlessly tried to save their lives.

When the agonizing screams finally subsided, Job was crazy with grief. He stripped off his clothing, went to his knees, and prayed aloud, "Naked I came out of my mother's belly, and naked shall I return there. Jehovah has given and Jehovah has taken away. Let the name of Jehovah continue to be praised."

After calling out to his Lord, Job collapsed in the sand and slept.

Lucifer was becoming more and more irritated. He had Ramiel kill Job's wife. She suffered greatly with a sickness. She fought with and swore at Job; she writhed in pain and cursed Jehovah. Job continued to pray for her immortal soul as she lay dying. The home they created lay in ruin beside the fire that kept them warm. Job held his wife's hand as the life finally drained from her body and said, "Jehovah, please welcome this servant into heaven. She is a loving and humble woman. She always did as instructed. I hope to see her again in the kingdom of heaven. Thank you, mighty Jehovah, for the years we spent together. I praise thee. Let the name of Jehovah continue to be praised."

Job collapsed in the sand next to his dead wife and slept.

Lucifer's next plan for Ramiel was brutal and unforgiving. He had Ramiel inflict Job with a boil that went from the soles of his feet to the top of his head. Job was in agony yet did not renounce Jehovah. He limped over to the ruins of his home and found a shard of a broken pot. He began to rub his skin with the piece to remove the boil. Although in extreme pain, Job still prayed to Jehovah. He cried out, "Jehovah, great and powerful, has blessed me with the ability to feel pain. What does not kill me only makes me stronger. Let Jehovah's name continue to be praised."

Job continued to clean the boil off him. The pain was so great that he fainted a few times, yet each time he awoke, he would pray to Jehovah. He would bow his head and thank the Almighty over and over.

In the courtroom, Jehovah smiled as he could feel Job's unwavering devotion to him. He thought, *My plan is working perfectly.*

Lucifer became angry and wanted Ramiel to unleash more pain and agony. Ramiel obeyed. Job stumbled off his knees, his skin oozing, and buried his wife. Once finished, Job turned, and only darkness came to his eyes. He had been struck blind. Job said, "Let the day I was born be consumed in darkness. I need not to see. I can see the kingdom of heaven that awaits me. Jehovah has seen fit to strike me down with blindness. So let it be. He must have a reason. Let the name of Jehovah continue to be praised."

Lucifer screamed in the courtroom, startling everyone there. Gabriel let out a hearty giggle. Lucifer, enraged, looked at his younger sibling.

Lucifer spoke to Gabriel. "Laugh it up! You will see. *All* of you will see!"

He wanted nothing more than to kill his brother on the spot. Thoughts of murder and destruction ran through his head. This seemed to calm him, and he regained control of his divine emotions. He leaned back in his chair and thought of an even more appropriate punishment for this irritating Job.

Lucifer sent Ramiel back to do more damage. Ramiel stood by the fire as he watched the pathetic blind and wounded Job stumble about. He knew of several torturing scenarios he could inflict upon him, but Lucifer wanted a specific torture, and he obeyed. He hated being Lucifer's message boy, but he was bound by his devotion to the Father and did as he was told. Ramiel watched as Job stumbled around the fire. He came close to Ramiel without touching the man. With a soft puff from his mouth, he sent Job flying into the flames. Job screamed as the fire licked at his already-raw feet. Ramiel puffed again, and Job lay in the sand, his skin smoking and bubbling.

Job began to pray. "By a fire I was born, and by a fire I shall die. The kingdom of heaven awaits me. I shall bask in Jehovah's light and glory. Let the name of Jehovah continue to be praised."

Death would not come to Job.

Lucifer called Ramiel back to heaven and to his side. Ramiel spoke to Lucifer. "Do not call on me again. The smug look on your face will earn you a personal visit from me."

Lucifer just smiled at his brother and said, "You think you can get close enough to me? Doubtful. I am the second-born, and Father would have your wings if you dealt any punishment my way."

Ramiel spoke. "Your arrogance makes me sick, brother. May I go now?"

Lucifer gave a crooked smirk and sarcastically said, "Of course you can. Your services are no longer needed. You may go."

Looking up at his Father, Ramiel said, "If you need me again, Father, I will be with thee."

Lucifer arose. "I concede. Ramiel cannot inflict any more damage without killing this human. You and Gabriel have played this game very well, Father. One victory for me with the twin cities and one for him with Job."

Jehovah spoke. "Now my sons have witnessed the evil and the righteous on the planet. They have seen how the humans have the capacity for repentance and the desire to give in to temptation."

Lucifer interrupted. "They are a scourge on the planet. All mankind is not worthy."

Gabriel shouted, "Objection, Father!"

Before Jehovah could answer, Lucifer hissed, "Shut up, brother. Just shut up!"

Jehovah said, "Sustained. The court will strike from the record Lucifer's outburst."

The doors at the back of the courtroom opened slightly, and Raphael emerged. He took a seat at the back of the room, and angels around him slid away. They knew of Raphael and did not want anything to do with this archangel. All of them knew Raphael as a spoiled and arrogant child. His unsettled restraint with his temper was well-known in heaven.

Lucifer looked over his shoulder and smiled at Raphael. He could feel the love and support of his younger brother from across the room. He also knew that Raphael had something to tell him; he could sense it was very important. Jehovah, knowing that Raphael was hiding something, studied his last-born with great intent.

Jehovah spoke. "The events witnessed today have been brutal. We will reconvene tomorrow morning and discuss what transpired on the planet. This will give the defense and the prosecution a chance to reevaluate their positions and work on their statements about today." Jehovah banged his gavel and said, "Court dismissed."

All the angels rose as Jehovah left the courtroom.

Lucifer went straight to Raphael. He knew he had some news and anxiously wanted to know what it was.

CHAPTER 6

Raphael Talks

Lucifer and Raphael walked down the marbled corridors of heaven, and Lucifer spoke. "What did you want to tell me, brother?"

"We cannot talk here. With all the marble columns, I cannot block everyone. There is too much interference."

Lucifer curiously looked at his younger brother, and Raphael spoke. "Brother, they will think we are invisible once inside of my room." With a broad grin, Raphael clapped his arm around Lucifer's shoulder and walked him to his bedchamber.

As they entered Raphael's bedchamber, he motioned for Lucifer to sit. He said, "You're going to need a drink for what I am about to tell you, brother. You and I are closer than any brother or sister could be in heaven or on earth. He thinks he can make us all close, but he is so wrong. As you already know, Michael has a deep hatred for you and I for Gabriel. The story I am about to tell you will sound even too fantastic for you to believe. Remember that I am your closest ally and I will never lie to you." Raphael gave Lucifer a tall glass filled with ice and scotch. He had one as well. Raphael sat across his beloved brother, sipped his scotch, and began his tale.

Lucifer sat across Raphael and listened as he spoke. He began, "Do you remember when he slept? After the destruction of Sodom and Gomorrah? A definite victory for you, my dear brother. A decisive win, for sure. Now, what I have to tell you, I stole from that wretched Gabriel's mind. He doesn't know I was in there, fiddling around with his memories. I had such fun in there. I even erased a few. It was delightful for me to erase the memory of his first kiss from him, his first steps, and the first time he developed white feathers instead of the prepubescent brown ones."

Lucifer downed his scotch and handed his glass to Raphael and said, "On with it. I could care less about your measly conquests over our brother. I don't give a shit."

Raphael giggled and refilled his brother's glass and sat back down. He smiled at his brother, leaned back in his chair, and sighed.

Lucifer spoke. "Get the fuck out of my head! Do *not* try to read me, Raphael! I will destroy you. I love you as my brother and my best friend, but everyone has limits. No more games! You called me in here for a reason, now get to the fucking point. Right now, on with it, or I swear I will leave. I've had enough of this childish behavior from Gabriel. I do not need or want it from you."

When Lucifer said Gabriel, Raphael jumped out of his seat and hissed at his older brother. "Fine, I will tell you all that I know. Read my thoughts, brother, and know I speak the truth."

Lucifer looked at his sibling and studied him intently and finally said, "Go on. I know you speak the truth, but no more fucking games. Do you understand?"

"Brother, as angels, you do know we cannot feel the effects of alcohol."

Lucifer, enraged by this, began to get up and leave. He spoke. "Do not tell me of rules, brother. You haven't played by them since you were a child. That is why I and only I trust you. Either spill what you fucking know or I am going to leave. I am sick of this bullshit."

Raphael smiled and said, "Sorry, brother. Just pointing out the obvious, and I know nobody likes me here. They fear me, and quite frankly, I don't give a fuck."

Raphael and Lucifer sat back down, and the former began his tale of the Egyptians and the exodus from Egypt.

"Dear brother, do you remember a small yet insignificant spot on the beautiful planet that goes by the name Egypt?"

Lucifer nodded and said, "Yeah, what about it?"

Raphael continued, "They worshipped many gods, and they had massive temples and pyramids erected in their honor. He was annoyed by this worship, as he wanted to be the only god that reigned supreme on this pathetic excuse for a planet. Are you feeling my wrath, brother? I can surely feel yours. I loathe the humans as much as thee, yet wait till you hear the rest, dear brother. Do you need another drink?"

Lucifer nodded and said, "Please, my confidant, continue as you pour me another. I do loathe the humans yet envy them in a way."

When Lucifer said *envy*, Raphael spun around so quickly he dropped the glass and it shattered on the floor. "What in *the* fuck? Brother, you are prosecuting them. You mustn't ever let that feeling be present in your mind, or that wretched Gabriel will sense it as well as he will. I know you all call him Father, yet that name makes me sick. Why do you envy such flawed and defective excuse for life? Enlighten me, brother." Raphael spoke with a condescending tone.

Lucifer leaped from the table and grabbed his beloved brother by the top of his wings. Raphael had his wings in a relaxed position, dragging on the floor and low near his shoulders. He was shocked at his brother's aggression, their noses touching.

Lucifer spoke. "Do not *ever* take that tone with me. Do you understand? I only envy them because they can feel the effects of this delicious drink. Don't you ever judge me again. Listen to me, my beloved best friend, my sibling, you are the last-born. Michael and I are the firstborn of everything created. Father made us before he created the earth, before the inhabitants of that fucking planet and all the other angels. I am the second created, *ever*. It will do you well to remember your spot in the pecking order before we continue. As I said, you are my brother and my closest and dearest friend. I watched your birth. I watched as Father created you from the dust of the heavens and breathed life into you. I was the first to hold you and cuddle you. I love you as flesh of my flesh and bone of my bone, but more importantly, I love you for being the soul of my soul."

Raphael smiled widely as he knew Lucifer was right. He loved his brother and knew that he loved him. "Okay, my beloved brother, I know you are most powerful. I will continue as you have asked." As he spoke, he motioned for Lucifer to once again sit and release his cherished wings from his grasp.

Lucifer looked at his younger brother and gave his wings one last squeeze, relented, and then sat. He sipped his scotch and was ready for the tale to be told.

Raphael rubbed his sore and almost-broken wings, sighed, and sat down across his brother. He sat back in his chair and smiled at Lucifer. Lucifer said, "Enough of the smiling and the bullshit. If I really wanted to know what the fuck was going on, trust me, I could find out. You are my trusted confidant, my brother. Although the last-born, I trust you completely. Please tell me more about this land called Egypt."

Raphael gave a triumphant smile and began to spew his tale.

Raphael spoke. "Remember how he slept after the debacle for the defense? Do you, brother?" Lucifer nodded. "Well, he was very, very naughty. I scanned and fiddled about in Gabriel's memory, and oh, the sights I saw! I will start at the start. There was a pharaoh, his name was—although it does not matter—Ramses. He had his beloved humans in bondage and slavery. Brother, you may need another drink."

Lucifer was grasping the crystal glass so tightly that it shattered in his hand. "Fuck that drink! What happened next?"

Raphael continued, "Let me tell you, brother, that Gabriel was indeed involved. He was the hand of death. The Lord—the word makes me want to vomit—he punished Egypt and the pharaoh with plagues. And in his divine audacity, he chose two men to try to confront the pharaoh. The two men, Aaron and Moses, tried and tried. You would've loved Ramses. He defied him as you and I do."

Lucifer leaped across the table and grabbed his younger brother by the throat and said, "How dare you! I did not defy Father, and never will I defy the humans! I loathe them. They're corrupt, and their greed make me sick. I, being the second-born of everyone and of everything on earth and in heaven. It has been home to us and to our kind for centuries. Now Father is all consumed with these pathetic humans that defy his laws, yet he still stands by them on the planet. He is trying to save them, and I am trying to destroy the species. Chance after chance they get, and Father allows them to repent. The humans are nothing more than a blemish on this planet. Now continue and allow me to hear what happened."

Raphael continued, "He smote the land with flies, lice, darkness, bloody water, boils, cattle dying . . . yet the pharaoh would not relent. I will speak of this in more detail as I tell more of my story. He sent—brother, are you sincerely ready to hear this? He sent your brother, not mine, Gabriel to the planet to act on his behalf and kill every firstborn of the nonbelievers of one true god. Again, I will get into greater detail of Gabriel and his nighttime visits to the homes of Egypt. He sent that fucking Gabriel to kill the Egyptian firstborn! Yet Gabriel, your adversary, chose to keep this from you and from all of us. He tried to rinse his memories, but in his weakened state, I was able to infiltrate his mind and extract what I wanted. Now, my brother, my love, my confidant, I shall begin. But when I am finished, I want to know what you think of all that transpired."

Lucifer nodded.

And Raphael began his story. "After the destruction of Sodom and Gomorrah, Jehovah slept. I refuse to call him Father, or our Lord, or the Almighty. He slept for centuries on the planet and was awoken by pain and anguish coming from the planet. He scanned and scanned until finally seeing the bondage of his people in Egypt. The only ones that believed in one true god. Oh, the arrogance of such a tyrant makes me want to kill him myself! He chose two slaves to be his messengers and preach the Word of God. The pharaoh was not amused by any talk of one true god. He brought Moses to his chambers. Moses brought his brother Aaron and a faithful servant to the Lord named Joshua. Moses spoke to Ramses and demanded from the great pharaoh to release his people from bondage. Moses threw down his staff and said, 'Watch the power of the one true god.' Moses's stick immediately changed into a serpent. The wizards that were ever present near the pharaoh threw down their staffs, and they, too, turned to serpents. Moses's staff consumed the other three snakes, went back to Moses, and was his staff again."

Lucifer raised an eyebrow and said, "You mean to tell me that Father gave divine powers to a pathetic human? What type of blasphemy is that? Why would he do that? Just to prove a point? It's his own fucking rule that we may never interfere with their lives unless instructed." Lucifer smashed his hand, fists clenched, onto the table. He took a deep breath and said, "Continue, brother."

Raphael spoke again. "The first plague was that he turned the water of the Nile to blood. Quite clever, if I do say so myself. Even for him to come up with this was brilliant. The horrified Egyptian elite could do nothing but pray to their god Rah. The Egyptians could not drink, cook, tend their flocks—nothing. The plan was sheer brilliance. Still, Ramses would not relent. Ramses had such arrogance for a human. The arrogance of an archangel. The second plague was even better. He sent frogs to leap everywhere in the city. The city streets were filled with frogs. No person could walk the streets or step out of their homes without stepping on and squishing them. All ribbiting and making noise day and night. My, what a sight to behold! The next plague, which happens to be my personal favorite, was flies and lice. Watching his chosen children run around, scratching at every part of their body that had hair, was hysterical. The gnats flew in every orifice a human could have. The eyes, nose, mouth, privates . . . oh, what sheer delight I took in their agony!

"Just when I thought it couldn't get any worse, he sent in swarms of flies, their constant buzzing driving his beloved children to the brink of madness. How I wish I could have been there. I only have these memories from that loathsome Gabriel. He and his crying with sympathy made me want to vomit. The next plague was pedestrian, to say the least, the death of the livestock. Big fucking deal. That was unimpressive. Oh, the next one was sheer brilliance. He inflicted every Egyptian with boils. Like the ones Ramiel unleashed on Job. It was such wonderful sorrow to watch. They cried and screamed to their gods yet found no comfort. Every time a new plague would hit the Egyptians, your Father would send Moses back to Ramses, and yet he did not relent. I kinda like this Ramses fella. He has my capacity to watch suffering and not give a fuck. The next plague again was a bit pedestrian to me. Wind and rain? Really? That falls from the sky daily on the planet, even in the desert. It was a big fucking deal that they finally got rain on the parched soil. It then began to hail, a nice touch to the rain, but I was still unmoved. Just seems beneath your Father to perform such a mundane curse.

"Now the next plague was locust. Great swarms of them blackened out the sun and hit Egypt with such force. Their hunger was insatiable—it was amazing! They ate all the crops that weren't destroyed by the hail. Now the Egyptians had no livestock and no vegetation. Oh, what a wonderful affliction he dealt to them! I really enjoyed watching these plagues. I especially loved watching Ramses defy your Father with sheer hatred. Ramses even laughed in the face of Moses, who brought the news to the pharaoh of the upcoming plaques to hit Egypt. The darkness that followed was a nice touch, yet not really worthy of a curse. It gets dark every night. Big deal if the darkness stayed for an entire day. It was not his greatest torture."

Raphael stood and got two more glasses of scotch, handed one to Lucifer, and continued.

"Now, dear brother, this is the last curse. This is the one that is going to enrage you. I beg you, do not kill the messenger. I am but a storyteller and letting you know exactly what happened while he slumbered. Your Father was very busy, and a very naughty boy, indeed.

"Your Father sent messages to his true believers and instructed them to paint the tops and sides of their entryway doors with sacrificial lambs' blood. It was a sign to Gabriel, sent as the angel of death, to bypass that home. He told them that any firstborn caught outside or unprotected by the blood would be killed. He made them stay inside and protected them. He also gave them bread and pheasant while they stayed inside. He fed them, do you believe it? I can't understand why he loves these pathetic creatures as he does. He told them to stay inside their homes. The cries and screams that came from the Egyptian homes were wonderful. They begged and pleaded to their gods, but it was fruitless. Even Ramses's own son fell victim to his rage. Yet Ramses refused to pray to Jehovah. Some, in the end, and terrified, renounced their gods and prayed to Jehovah. He granted them forgiveness, and they reside here in heaven with us."

Lucifer raised an eyebrow.

"He is keeping them away from the rest of us for their protection and the protection of Gabriel."

Raphael seemed to be relieved from the burden of such a great secret.

Lucifer sat there for a moment, his arms crossed over his chest. An eerie quietness filled the room. Raphael became a bit frightened as he had never seen his brother so calm in the face of such a betrayal. Lucifer was usually quick to react on his fiery temper, but now he sat quietly, contemplating the next move. The rage that filled the heart of this mighty archangel was foreign to him, as he was always in control of his hatred and anger. Raphael motioned to his brother, his palms raised up, saying, "Now what, brother?"

Lucifer just stared at his brother and said nothing. Raphael could feel the seething rage building in his brother's heart, yet Lucifer remained calm. Raphael did not know what to do. He tried to read his brother, and Lucifer burst from his chair and screamed, "I told you once to not get in my fucking head, and I will tell you only once more! Get out, for your safety. I have such a loathing for the deceit of Father and Gabriel I want to kill them both."

Lucifer sighed and threw his glass against the wall in a great shatter. Shards of glass flew about the room. Raphael cringed in fear, bowed his head to his very angry and very powerful brother, and said, "I will never try to read you again, brother, unless you need me to block something from any angel or him."

Lucifer sat for a moment and said, "Raphael, block this Egyptian thing from my mind so Father and that loathsome and traitorous Gabriel won't sense it. I will need you in my head only to block these thoughts, but I warn you." Lucifer rose from his seat and grabbed his younger brother by his already-wounded wings and hissed in his ear, "If you try to access anything else of mine in my memories, I will kill you on the spot. Do you understand?" Lucifer spoke calmly, scaring Raphael even more. "Now, brother, I am going to my bedchamber again. Block this nonsense from my head. I need to think. My revenge on our kingdom and on earth is going to be fantastic. I am about to overthrow Father himself. Just need to figure out how."

Lucifer went out the door, and Raphael, although terrified of his cunning and intelligent brother, knew heaven would be a better place with him in charge, and surely, he would be his second-in-command. He grinned with delight at the thought of Lucifer's tyranny on the planet and smiled widely.

C<small>HAPTER</small> 7

Gabriel's Righteous Witness

T he next day in court found the two attorneys at their desks. Michael bellowed out, "All rise." To Michael's surprise and confusion, even Lucifer stood and bowed his head. Michael knew his intelligent brother had something brewing in his cunning mind.

Jehovah entered the courtroom and saw Lucifer standing with his head bowed and was shocked. Pausing for a moment to look at his second-born, he gave a loving smile to his son. Michael looked at his Father and said, "Lucifer has risen for you, something he has not done from the beginning. There is something amiss. Please do not trust him. I have a bad feeling."

Instinctively, Michael grabbed the hilt of his razor-sharp sword and stared at his younger brother. Lucifer, looking over his eyebrows at his older sibling, just grinned and stared into Michael's eyes. Michael started to step down from Jehovah's bench and was abruptly stopped by the Father's hand on his shoulder.

Jehovah spoke. "My son, your brother has finally seen the light and knows he needs to show me respect." Then Jehovah turned to the court. "Welcome, brothers, sisters, sons, and daughters. I have been told by the prosecution that they would like to let the defense have a witness." The Almighty looked at Lucifer and said, "Lucifer, care to enlighten the court as to your decision this morning?"

Lucifer rose from his massive marble desk and spoke. "Father, my first witness, the serpent, was a decisive win for the prosecution. Job was a decisive witness for the defense. The twin cities, although you and Gabriel think it was a win for the righteous humans, was not, Father. I won that battle with the destruction and death on the planet of the sinners. I would like to give my beloved"—when he said *beloved*, a smirk ran across his face—"brother a chance, and he needs to call a witness. As I am pathetically crushing my brother in the case. The jury is swayed in my direction. I can feel it, as can you and Gabriel. I would like to give my brother a chance."

Jehovah studied his second-born with great intent and could not sense any deception. He spoke. "Gabriel, would you like to call your witness?"

Gabriel stood triumphantly and glared at his older brother and said, "Of course, Father. Lucifer is not as smart as he thinks."

Michael nervously looked at both of his brothers. He knew that the deception of Lucifer could not be matched in heaven or on the planet. He did not trust him, and an uneasy feeling filled his heart. He obeyed Jehovah and stood beside him on the bench and tensely watched what was about to happen.

Gabriel rose and said, "Father, I call your beloved Noah to the stand."

When he said *beloved*, Lucifer bellowed out, "Objection. What the fuck! I give you a chance, and you already have to piss me off by calling him beloved?"

Jehovah spoke. "Overruled. Watch your tongue, Lucifer. This is uncalled for."

Lucifer sat back down, victorious with his acting ability at being outraged. He knew what was coming, and all of heaven would have a front-row seat to the deception of Gabriel and the Father. He just had to bide his time.

Noah entered the courtroom from the large oak doors at the back of the room, a falcon resting peacefully on his shoulder, sparrows flying about him. He had a rabbit in his hands as the deer followed behind. Noah was blessed with the ability to have animals with him at all times, and this time was no different. The tension in the courtroom seemed to dissipate as such a gentle man entered the room.

Lucifer sneered at Noah and thought, *Righteous my ass! Nice touch with the critters.*

Gabriel motioned for him to sit at the witness stand and, in a subservient manner, grabbed Jehovah's hand and kissed it. Michael pulled his sword and said, "I will skewer you where you stand. Get away from Father." His sword was at Noah's throat.

Jehovah said, "Forgive my overprotective son. Nice to see you again, Noah."

Michael, feeling the Father's ease at seeing his old friend again, sheathed his sword and stood back into his protective role at his side. Lucifer was smug in his thoughts of how pathetic his older brother was protecting the Father and mankind. Leaning back in his chair, he awaited the Noah debate.

Gabriel said to Noah, "Please tell the court of the events of the ark."

Noah began, "Jehovah came to me and said for me to build an ark of resinous tree and make compartments in the ark. God gave me instructions, three hundred cubits in length, fifty cubits in width, and thirty cubits in height. I was to make the entrance to the ark on the side as a ramp."

Gabriel smiled and spoke. "What did you bring into the ark?"

"The Almighty gave me seven days to gather male and female of all the living animals, birds, and insect on the planet to save them."

"How many men and women were on your ark, Noah?"

"We had eighteen souls with us. All righteous and God-fearing men and women."

"Really? Righteous? Ha!" Lucifer spat out.

Jehovah stared at his son for a moment, not wanting to believe his audacity and disrespect. "The jury will disregard my second-born and his remarks."

Lucifer sat at his desk, ever the sneering critic, and could not wait to unleash the great secret he and Raphael held.

Gabriel asked Noah, "Then what happened?"

Noah began his tale of the great flood. "The rains came from the heavens in great sheets, the rivers rose, the oceans broke from their tides. For forty days and forty nights, the storms raged. There were many that begged and pleaded to be let into the ark when the ground beneath them was turned to liquid. But to the Lord's instructions, once the ark was sealed, the seal could not be broken until the disaster was over. I, being the ever-loyal servant to the Lord, obeyed. Even when the men and women all called me crazy for building an ark. I mean, who builds an ark in the middle of the desert? But once the rains began, I didn't seem so crazy."

Jehovah noticed a distinct change in Noah's demeanor. He went from gentle and kind to mean and spiteful as he spoke of the days before the great flood.

"The Lord brought the earth and all the inhabitants to ruin. He destroyed everything, except what was in the ark. A hundred and fifty days passed, and I sent out a raven to see if it had a resting place. The bird came back with nothing. I waited another seven days and sent the raven out again, and again, it returned with nothing. After another seven days, I sent out the dove to see if it could find a place to rest its weary wings. It returned to me with a freshly plucked branch of an olive tree. I knew then that the waters have finally begun to recede. I waited again for seven days, and when the dove did not return, I knew it had found its permanent resting place. The Lord made great winds form, and we landed on a spot of dry land. We named this mountain Ararat. Jehovah spoke to me and said, 'Go forth and prosper, you and all the beasts of the land.' He told me that he did not want to destroy the planet but had no choice. The evil and sinners were everywhere. He said that a covenant between himself and the remaining righteous was a beautiful symbol in the sky. A sight that I had never seen. Such beauty in the colors. The Lord told me that it was called a rainbow. This was his emblem of solidarity to the planet. Therefore, I have no idea why we are even discussing the destruction of mankind. Jehovah promised me that he would never do it again. Yet here we are."

Gabriel spoke to the court. "Do you see, my brothers and sisters? Our Father has destroyed the planet once and gave his promise to never do it again. I am sickened by my brother Lucifer and his standards on who is to live and who is to die." Gabriel leaned over his brother's desk and said, "Cross-examination?"

Lucifer sat back in his chair and thought for a moment.

A pregnant silence filled the room, and Lucifer spoke. "As a matter of fact, I do."

Gabriel was drawn back to an upright position and nervously went back to his desk.

Lucifer arose, his large white wings flowing behind him, a smug look on his face. He went to Noah and stood beside him. He said, "I have only one question for you. How could you sit and watch as all of humanity perished before your eyes and did nothing to save them? The cries and screams of the mothers and their children, the agonizing terror that you were witness to. How can you live with yourself?"

Noah bowed his head, his shoulders rising and falling as the sobs became evident to the court. Noah finally spoke through tears, not looking at Lucifer, and said, "It was not my place to save them."

Lucifer looked at his brother Gabriel and said, "That is all, Noah. You may step down."

He walked over to the jury and leaned onto the railing. He spoke. "See? Was not his place to save them. However, we all know whose place it was, do we not? He chose to consume the planet in water, and yet here we are again. You would think that they would have learned their lesson the first time. These creatures are not only stupid, they are arrogant as well to think such atrocities cannot happen again. Maybe next time the earth should be consumed in fire."

Lucifer turned and sat back down at his desk, put his feet up, and gave a hearty sigh.

Jehovah had had enough; he was exhausted. Seeing his old friend and reliving such awful memories was almost too much for the old man. Court was adjourned until the next day.

After the Father had left, Lucifer and Gabriel each went out their respective doors, and waiting behind Lucifer's was Michael. Shocked at the sight of his older brother, Lucifer chuckled and said, "Brother, I've told you a thousand times, if I've told you once, you will never get close enough to me to kill me or do any real damage. What the fuck do you want?"

Michael, in a calm and soft tone, said, "I want your soul, brother."

Michael grabbed for his sword, Lucifer for his. They stood facing each other, ready for combat. Uriel appeared from the mist and stepped between her two brothers.

She spoke. "What in thee fuck is going on here? You two make me sick. Brothers yet mortal enemies." She snatched both swords and stepped back. "Now it's fair. I will not allow you two to kill each other, and any angel that interferes will deal with me. Let the boys fight. I am tired of this bullshit and ready to go back to the way it was, before all this human garbage. I will not stand idly by and let heaven come to ruin!" Her massive size and deep voice shook the very core of every angel present. She spoke again. "Beat each other senseless! I really do not care. Maybe when this is all said and done, you will be able to break bread with each other at Father's table."

The two brothers, locked in an eternal battle with each other, finally had the chance to inflict pain. Michael struck first. He grabbed Lucifer by the wings and threw him to the marble floor. Lucifer hissed and kicked up, catching the unaware Michael in the chest. Staggering back, fists raised, rage in his heart, Michael came at Lucifer again. They punched and kicked each other. Rolling upon the ground, wrestling, screaming obscenities at each other. Lucifer hissed at his brother the entire time. Michael struck at Lucifer's knee, and his brother dropped to the floor. Lucifer, at the perfect angle, struck up and hit his older brother right in the testicles. A moment of sanity filled the hallway as they caught their breath.

Lucifer spoke. "How dare you touch me! You are a fucking moron, and I loathe you. You defend what should not be defended. You love what has no right being loved."

Michael, out of breath, said, "I will defend Father till the bitter end, you heinous excuse for an angel!"

Lucifer giggled as he leaped for Michael and said, "Idiot! I was talking about the fucking humans."

Lucifer grabbed for Michael's throat, hands squeezing, and Michael, wheezing, was taken aback. He could feel his life force draining from his body, and in a desperate yet quick and precise strike, Michael landed a close-fisted punch to Lucifer's face. Lucifer hit the floor and cracked the marble as he slid away. Blood spewed everywhere. Lucifer, shocked, grabbed at his broken nose and busted lip.

Uriel stepped between the brothers and said, "Michael, I think he's learned his lesson." She turned to Lucifer, towering over him, and said, "Haven't you, brother? He will kill you."

Lucifer, mortified and embarrassed at the power of his older brother and the brashness of his younger sister, limped away, blood trailing behind him. Never answering his sister.

He found his way to his bedchamber and lay on his bed. Although beaten and wounded, he smiled through broken teeth and a busted lip. He spoke to the empty room. "Oh, tomorrow. Oh, tomorrow. I will have my day, and it will rain angel blood onto those fucking humans."

CHAPTER 8

Lucifer's Mighty Last Witness

The next day was a sunny, bright, beautiful day in heaven. The court was in session, and Jehovah spoke. "Well, I see today will be the day. There are no more witnesses being called, and this will be the final judgment of mankind."

Lucifer interrupted and said, "Oh, excuse me, Father, I do have one more witness."

Jehovah shuffled his papers and looked at the docket. "There are no more witnesses on the list, son."

"But, Father, I am calling one more today. I am calling you to the stand."

When he said this, every wing in the courtroom was raised in anxiety.

"What? You cannot and will not judge me. There is nothing for me to say."

Lucifer arose and walked in front of the bench and said, "Father, my dear Father, you are the great deceiver. You have a huge secret involving the humans, and I have a right as the prosecuting attorney to let all of heaven hear it."

Jehovah cocked his head to the side and said, "All right, boy. I have nothing to hide. I have no fear. Ask me anything you want."

Jehovah sat in the witness chair and awaited Lucifer's questions. Lucifer spoke. "Father, I have been told that there was a little thing on the planet that he"—he pointed an accusing finger at Gabriel—"and you know about."

Gabriel sprang from his chair. "I have done nothing, brother. I am innocent."

Lucifer turned with a sneer and said, "Brother, I do not blame you, as he had you rinse your memory, but with my ever-faithful and ever-loving younger brother, we saw. Oh, the sights we saw! Thank you, Gabriel, for being the weak-minded angel that you are." Lucifer turned to Jehovah and said, "Care to tell the court about Egypt, Father?"

Jehovah stood and called the name Raphael. Raphael appeared before Lucifer and the court and said, "Oh, I see my loving brother has spilled our little secret."

A wounded look crept onto the Almighty's face, and he said, "You have betrayed me, my son, my last-born. I cannot believe it."

Lucifer screamed, "Let us speak of betrayal, Father! You betrayed us all! Do not blame Raphael. He knows not what he does." Lucifer spun back around and looked at his Father. "Back to the question at hand. Care to enlighten us about Egypt? Do you want your version or mine?"

Now Jehovah spoke. "Really, it was no big deal. A few of my following children were enslaved, not brutally, by some of the Egyptian homes. They ate well, they lived well, and they were never beaten. It was really no big deal."

Lucifer laughed a hearty laugh. He spoke. "Father, are you kidding? A few of your followers?" He turned to the courtroom. "Let me tell you the story of the chosen few." *Few* was a word he almost choked on. "There were thousands of humans known as Hebrews. They were enslaved by the Egyptians. They had to build massive temples and statues to their many gods. This enraged Father to the point of no return. He lost his control and lashed out at a man named Ramses and his followers. He says, 'No big deal.' I'm here to tell you it was a very big deal." Lucifer turned to the jury and asked, "Turning the entire river Nile into blood was no big deal, Father? What about all the other punishments you dealt out? Plague after plague you inflicted upon the Egyptians." Lucifer then turned from the jury and leaned his massive wings on the railing, staring at his Father, arms crossed in a defiant manner. "The ultimate in punishment, as he calls 'no big deal,' was the death of the firstborn. He spared his beloved followers." He ran over and slammed his fists onto Gabriel's desk. "Courtesy of our beloved angel of life and death. The archangel I refer to was sent as the angel of death, and this angel is *him*."

Gabriel recoiled and said, "I never!"

Lucifer, with his smug and arrogant tone, said to his Father, "See? Even Gabriel doesn't remember. But I found out. You talk of salvation for the humans. All I witnessed was brutality. You call yourself benevolent and pure, but what I saw was malevolent and downright evil. So want to add anything else? The flies, lice, frogs, darkness, hail, wind, rain, death of the livestock, inflicting boils? The pharaoh finally relented after the death of his son and let Father's chosen flee. They found themselves at the base of a mountain that the humans named Sinai. God sent Moses to the top and spoke to Moses as a burning bush. Really, Father, a burning bush? You couldn't have come up with anything more dramatic! Father proceeded to hand down to Moses Ten Commandments. Laws that every human is to follow. One, thou shall not steal. Two, thou shall not kill. Three, thou shall not commit adultery. Four, thou shall not bear false witness. Five, thou shall not covet thy neighbor's wife. Six, thou shall not bow down to graven images of any god. Seven, honor thy mother and father. Eight, never use my name in vain. Nine, keep the Sabbath holy. And ten, and this is my personal favorite, you shall not worship any other god than Jehovah. Yet they break these laws daily. I assume you didn't make them laws, just polite suggestions? Have I missed anything, dear, dear Father?"

Jehovah, still strong-willed and defiant, said, "No, boy, you didn't miss anything. But let me tell you something. The humans needed laws and guidance from me and my divine intervention."

"Then why, Father, if Moses was so beloved by you, why was he never allowed into the land of milk and honey?"

Jehovah stood. "I need not explain anything to you, Lucifer, my son, and I am getting quite irritated with your own twist on how it happened. I will answer no more of your petulant questions. You are but a spoiled yet very intelligent creation of mine, and I am beginning to regret the day I made you the angel of light." Jehovah leaped down from the witness stand, and a mighty wind filled the courtroom. "I will show you true power, boy."

His hands raised palms up, he summoned lightning and thunder. Great bolts hit the floor of the courtroom, sending shards of marble flying in every direction. Thunder boomed, and shock filled the room. All the fury of nature was around him. He bellowed. Every angel in the courtroom began to cower and beg for mercy.

"I will show you my power as I am God, the Almighty! I am Jehovah. I am all powerful, boy. I could crush you with a single blow. I created you, all of you. I created the creatures and the angels that inhabit all heaven and earth. I answer to no one. Not you, not Michael, not Gabriel—none of you! I need not justify my actions. I made you, and I can break you."

He began to float over the audience, his eyes rolled in his head. His gray beard pushed back over his shoulder. His long white hair swirling about his face. He screamed at the court, "I have made every single one of you, and I can destroy every single one of you!" He looked in Lucifer's direction and screamed louder, "I have made up my mind, and you, Lucifer, are wrong. Dead wrong. I am right and always will be. I have no need for a jury or a courtroom. I did this to try and keep the peace between you and Michael. You lose. I find the humans to be innocent. Gabriel wins, and you, son, lose. You will pay dearly for your disrespect to me. You fucking ungrateful child! Get out of my sight before I lose my last bit of sanity and kill you."

Lucifer and Raphael ran from the courtroom, burst through the massive oak doors, and smiled at each other. Lucifer went toward the stables to see Raqael, and Raphael went to find their old friend and ally Saraqael. He needed to let them know that it had begun. He needed his army so he could hide them in the clouds, so God would not find them.

Lucifer burst through the barn doors, and Raqael bowed and covered her head with her wings. He said, "Where is he, bitch?"

She pointed in the direction of the last stable. Lucifer marched toward the final and darkness-ridden stall, his breath becoming visible as he walked closer.

The steed in the stall said with its back turned, "What the fuck do you want, you filth—oh, master, hello."

Death turned and saw Lucifer standing at the entryway of his stall. The horse's eyes began to glaze over and get even more ferocious flame to them. Death spoke, head bowed. "Master, no saddle, please. I want you to feel what I feel, become what I am, and be with me in our minds and spirits."

Lucifer looked at death and said, "Listen, you stinking, fucking animal. You remember who I am and what I stand for. Do not ever buck me or bite me. I will dismember you on the spot. Understood?"

Bending one front leg, the mighty steed bowed down to Lucifer and his might. The horse knew the rage and anger that was building inside Lucifer and wanted to eat it.

"We are going to ride, bareback, and where I say. We are going to start with fucking Father and everything he has created on this plane we call heaven. When we are through with this pathetic excuse for a home, we will make a visit to the unclean and despicable planet. We will have such fun burning their cities to the ground. He, it, the fucking great deceiver tried once with water. Now, my trusted companion, we will show them the true meaning of pain with fire."

Unbolting the door to the stall, Lucifer entered, his armor shining in the minimal light of the stables, his massive white wings teasing the hay that lay on the floor. He threw the bit in the horse's mouth, and the horse winced.

"Do not wince with me. You are Death. I need the bridle to control you. Without it, you have no master. No rider. I will ride you bareback, as you asked, only because I want to become death. I want to become nightmare. I want to become everything they fear."

Death exposed his back to Lucifer, bit in mouth, and said, "Let's roll, master. I have been waiting centuries for you or my rider."

When Death said "or my rider," Lucifer became enraged and smacked the horse in the face. "Do not ever compare me with another. Do you understand? I am Lucifer, the second of all created, and if I wanna ride you, I will. Your rider is beneath me and will never—and I mean *never*—match me. Understood?"

Lucifer stood beside Death and threw one leg over the horse's pale back. Lucifer almost blacked out and convulsed as he grabbed the horse's mane and bridle. Taken aback by this, Lucifer tried to dismount. Death would not allow him.

"Become me, see what I see, feel what I feel, inflict pain as I do . . . welcome to beautiful pain, my master Lucifer. How I love thee."

Lucifer grabbed death's mane and began to feel a transformation, a reckoning with his inner being, if you will. Convulsing and turning his hands palms up, he could see his once-gentle archangel hands change into black skin. Long talons began to emerge from his fingertips. Lucifer was shocked at this, and Death reassured his master, "Do not be afraid, my sir. This is your true being coming out."

Lucifer kicked Death and said, "I fear nothing. Transform me at your will."

Death spoke. "Oh, my sweet master, I am not the one transforming you. It is your true nature, your arrogance and hatred, making you this way. I am just the conduit that it comes from."

Mounting Death felt like the best orgasm Lucifer ever had. He was completely absorbed into the horse, and the horse completely absorbed into him. They were one. Another convulsion hit Lucifer, and his eyes began to water and burn. The smell of sulfur filled the stable, and Raqael was paralyzed with fear, sending a feeling of dread through her heart. She sensed her brother's true nature evolve.

Lucifer finally regained control, and when he opened his eyes, he could only see fire and brimstone everywhere he looked. Everything had a red twinge to it, and he knew he had become Death and Death had become him.

"I adore this feeling, my beautiful, pale friend. I finally feel whole and alive."

In all the centuries he had lived, he finally felt at home.

He gave the great steed a kick to the sides, and together they left the stall. As they passed the other stalls, the other horses bowed their heads in respect for both rider and horse. War knew, if Death had been released before him, he was soon to be ridden next. Maybe Famine and Pestilence had already occurred on the planet. War was a bit confused that Lucifer himself rode Death and not his rider. His anxiety and excitement filled the stalls with electricity. All the horses had an anxious awareness that filled the barn as the thought that their riders would soon come for them. They all bucked and whinnied as Death proudly rode past them.

Lucifer mounted on the massive pale horse and stopped beside his sister. She was still on her knees, and her wings covered her face. Lucifer spoke. "Do not wake the other riders. This is the only apocalyptic steed that is needed right now. If I find out you spoke to any other archangels about this, I will burst you into flames. Bitch, if you disobey me, it will be a painful and lengthy death. Understand?"

She nodded.

Lucifer said, "You look at me, bitch, when I talk to you, do you understand?"

Raqael raised her eyes and met Lucifer's fiery eyes. A moment of complete terror filled her heart. A tingle of fear ran up her spine, and she stumbled backward, trying to shield herself from his rage. She spoke with a tremble to her voice. "Yes, Lucifer, I will obey." Relieved at seeing him exit the barn, she began to cry.

When Jehovah's tantrum had calmed, he looked around the room, and Lucifer and Raphael were gone. He gritted his teeth and said to Gabriel, "Go seek out Ramiel and his virtues." To Michael he said, "Go seek out Uriel and her army of dominations. I have a feeling your brother Lucifer is about to bring mass destruction to heaven. He must be stopped. You, Michael, have my permission to kill him. I will allow you to break our first rule. Right now, you are not your brother's keeper, you are his assailant and his executioner."

Gabriel looked terrified, yet Michael smiled, bowed his head, and said, "Thank you, Father, finally. I will bring my sister to your bedchambers posthaste."

Gabriel said, "Father, Ramiel scares me, but I will do as I'm told and bring him to your bedchamber."

Jehovah spoke. "Tell them to ready their armies for battle. Tell them to leave their armies at the camps. Have them tell their blacksmiths that we will need every sword of both armies sharpened. Tell your brother and sister to come alone. I have only the need for my archangel generals. There is going to be a great massacre here in our beloved home." Jehovah slammed his fists down onto Gabriel's desk and screamed, "Everything righteous and merciful in my heart has been changed to rage at such betrayal by my own flesh and blood! Lucifer will pay dearly for beckoning Death and riding on him. He thinks he is going to let that pale steed ride through my creation? He better reconsider his ideas. I am the Almighty and will never lose in a battle."

Lucifer triumphantly emerged from the barn and into the moonlight. Standing before him was Raphael and Saraqael, neither bowing their head to their leader. Lucifer dismounted Death and grabbed his two brothers by the tips of their wings and threw them into a kneeling position. "You will show me the respect that I am due. You will bow before me as you do him. I am going to rule heaven, and it will be wise to be on the side of victory and the new-crowned king of heaven. Father—ugh, that name. From now on, anyone the says Father in my presence will be burst into flames. His new name is It. Saraqael, are your seraphim ready for battle?"

Saraqael, ever respectful and looking at the cloud tops, said, "Of course, all loyal and ready to die for you, sir."

Raphael spoke. "I have cloaked the armies between cloud layers to shield them from h—I mean Its prying mind. It thinks I am stupid, yet I found out about Egypt for you, dear brother. He will never pinpoint the location of the army."

Lucifer mounted the pale steed again, and his beautiful white feathers began to molt and fly in the breeze as he galloped away.

Raphael cried out to his brother, "Where are you going?"

Lucifer turned and said with no fear in his speech, "I am going to find that awful creature It calls Ramiel. Any virtue soldier-angels that come at you, don't kill them. I want Ramiel to witness their inevitable fate."

Raphael, scared and confused, said to his older brother, "Did you see his teeth? What kind of hideous creature is he becoming? His fangs were bigger than the serpent's of the Garden of Eden. To be honest, I am a bit scared of him and his power."

Saraqael answered and said, "Dear brother, you better not let those thoughts be ever forward in your mind, as Lucifer will sense them, as you are a great physic and your power can be a reward and a curse."

Raphael and Saraqael could only look at each other and began their journey to the hidden massive seraphim army.

Lucifer sat upon his very euphoric and ever-loyal steed. They rode through the hallways of heaven, shouting the entire time, "Ramiel, where are you? You are a pathetic excuse for a torturer! I know that you sense I ride on the mighty pale horse Death. Confront me, pussy! I have no intention of killing you. I want to eat your soul on the battlefield as I slaughter your so precious virtues in front of you. Come out, come out, wherever you are. All the angels fear you. I, however, never have and never will. Show yourself! If you are the mighty archangel you claim to be, then face me."

Lucifer's seething rage and uncontrollable arrogance made his words hold meaning.

Ramiel stood on the other side of the Father's bedchamber door, angered.

He said, "Father, fuck him! I will kill him and that fucking horse. I am tired of his fucking arrogance and games. He needs to be stopped, and I am just the protecting angel you need."

Before Jehovah could protest, Ramiel appeared in the hallway with some of his fiercer virtues in front of Lucifer and Death. The virtues, with their swords raised, were no match for the mighty pale horse; he brushed past most of them, and they fell dead. The more loyal soldiers stood close to their master and protected him.

Lucifer, with his great sword and with one sweep, slit the throats of the remaining virtues.

Ramiel now stood alone. "Step down from your furry protector, and let's converse."

Lucifer threw his head back and said, "Do you really think I am that stupid?"

Ramiel said, "No, but I do think you are that arrogant."

Death began to slowly walk toward Ramiel, eyes glaring at him. Ramiel retreated from this pale horse in terror. All his virtues lay dead and dying around him. Their protection of Ramiel was one of utter devotion. They had laid down their lives for him. Death just walked over the dead virtues, crushing some of their skulls with his mighty hooves. One touch from this apocalyptic steed could kill angel, human, and God.

Finally, in the corner, Lucifer dismounted and grabbed his brother by the wrists, chains in his hands, and said, "Put out those torturous hands palms together, dear brother. I will not fall victim to your touch. You have dished out such awful yet delightful pains in the centuries that I've admired your work. Such a shame that you are on the wrong side."

"I could and would never ever side with you. Your complete disregard for life here and on the planet makes me sick. Father loves you, yet you are too stupid to see."

Lucifer backhanded his brother and said, "Fuck you! Now you are my bait for the rest of your precious virtues to come to me and the seraphim. I want you to watch as I slaughter them one by one."

Lucifer shackled his brother's wrists tightly together, palms touching. He wrapped the chain around his brother's back and between his legs. His feet were then bound by irons of such strength that no angel or God could ever break. In one final insult, Lucifer slammed a two-inch-thick wrought iron collar onto his brother's throat and attached a leash. He could feel his brother's fear as he led him to his pale ride. Ramiel tried to resist, but the collar was suffocating.

Lucifer mounted Death then smiled at Ramiel. He said, "Don't let even one feather touch my beautiful horse. One touch from him, and you will die instantly. I don't want you to die, yet, brother. I want you to see the suffering and crying as I slaughter them one by one. It will bring me such pleasure to accomplish ridding myself of each of your precious soldiers and then of you, dear brother."

Death smiled at Ramiel and snorted in his direction. Ramiel recoiled and stumbled back. Lucifer gave a hearty laugh, and they started down the hallway, back to between the clouds to await the virtues' arrival. Ramiel knew his special-forces type angels would not go quietly or be captured. He couldn't wait to see Lucifer destroyed.

Lucifer spoke. "Be careful of your thoughts, brother. My psychic ability has grown stronger through this transformation. It would be wise of you to keep your thoughts to yourself. Such hatred you have for me, I may inflict torture on you just for laughs."

Walking back to the secret seraphim army, Ramiel noticed Lucifer's change. He could see his once-beautiful and very large feathery white wings gone now, just bones and substructure. Ramiel grew a bit more uneasy as he looked at his brother. His teeth, his eyes, his hands—what was happening to his brother?

Lucifer spoke. "I am becoming my true self. The centuries of hatred for mankind and for its laws have rotten me from my very core. My intelligence and my arrogance also played a huge part. I am smarter than all of you, even the piece of shit you call Father.

Lucifer entered the camp of the seraphim, and all were taken aback at the sight of Ramiel in chains. He placed his brother in a tent, bound to a support beam in the middle of his prison cell.

Lucifer closed his eyes and said, "Raphael."

Instantly Raphael appeared before his master. Raphael said, "Dear brother, you have summoned me, but may I ask what has happened to your wings? I have never seen such massive air dominance. Your wingspan has to be twenty feet. The feathers are gone, and is that leather, like a bat's?"

Lucifer proudly said, "Indeed it is. I am transforming into my destiny. I feel what always eluded me for centuries. I finally feel at home in my own skin. I want you to send a telepathic message to the virtue army, a visual picture of this once-powerful yet quite pathetic Ramiel."

"Master, I cannot read the virtues."

Lucifer, irritated, said, "I know, fool. I want you to send them a message, not to read them. We have their beloved leader, and I want them to come to try and make a rescue."

Raphael did as he was told. It was not easy to penetrate the virtue mind, but he did and sent the message. A wave of revenge came rushing at him, and he smiled. "Master, the virtues are on their way, and quite calm."

Lucifer grinned. "They won't be so calm when they see what I have in store for them. Again, none are to be killed unless absolutely necessary. I want them captured. I have something special for Ramiel to witness."

Lucifer shouted, "Saraqael," and the leader of the seraphim appeared before him. "I have a special task for you and twenty of your best warriors. I need our sister Uriel captured. Do not kill her, or my wrath will be merciless. I want her brought to me in chains. Do you understand?"

Saraqael responded, "Of course, master. Kill as many as the dominations as possible, but bring our sister alive."

The creature, once divine, said, "Remember, fool, if our sister even dies from a cold during this expedition, I will blame you and you will pay dearly. I need to convince her to join us and lead her dominations along with your seraphim to rid our home and the planet of the human stench. The smell makes me want to vomit each and every day. Now go, and be victorious."

CHAPTER 9

The War Begins

Lucifer was comfortably mounted on his friend and battle companion Death, awaiting his captives. He could see out in the mist Saraqael and two of his seraphim. Saraqael, bloodied, bruised, missing half a wing, limped over to Lucifer, bowed his head in defeat, and said, "I am sorry, master, we have failed. Your sister is too large and powerful. We could not take her alive."

Lucifer, enraged at the thought of his beloved sister dead, leaped down from his pale horse and slammed his boot onto Saraqael's throat. "You killed my fucking sister? Even after I gave you specific instructions?"

"No, master," he said as he began to sob, "we just couldn't get close enough to her. We were no match for your powerful sister. She has a heart and love of battle. Her size and her razor-sharp sword slaughtered us like sacrificial lambs. She lives." Gasping for air, she added, "Please, master, I speak the truth. Search your heart."

Lucifer pushed down even harder and said, "Heart? What? What the fuck is a heart? You're pathetic. I will search my very soul for her."

Lucifer closed his eyes and could see Uriel binding a deep gash on her forearm. He saw with envy her blood-splashed armor. He could not wait to have his armor look that grand. "I guess if I want something done right, I must do it myself."

Lucifer, irritated, mounted Death and called for Raphael. They made straight for the stables, his trusted compatriot at his side. They entered the barn, and Raqael cowered again.

Lucifer kicked her in the face and said, "Is War ready to ride?"

She pointed in the direction of the stall, and Lucifer approached. He bent and gabbed his sister under the chin and ran his long talons along the milky white skin of her face. He grinned and slashed open her cheek. "That was for fun. Now you know what I will do to you if you speak of this." He leaned down and licked her cheek. His once-almost-human tongue had become forked and dry. "What the fuck is this? I am not a serpent. This is Its doing! The bastard!"

Enraged, he patted Raqael on the head and said, "That's my girl."

They walked past the other stalls, and Pestilence and Famine knew that they were to be next. They made grunting and excited sounds. They approached the stall, and War said, "What the fuck do you want, Lucifer? You may not and will not ride me."

Lucifer spoke as he entered the stall, grabbing the horse by the nostrils, their eyes meeting. He said, "I am the only one besides your rider that is allowed to ride you. Remember your place with me, servant, or I will lash your back so hard no one will be able to ride you, ever! Understand?"

War was silent yet nodded.

"But I have no intention to ride you." He motioned with a large taloned hand. "Raphael is. If you give me one ounce of trouble about this, I will have you thrown to that hateful planet and used as a plow horse. Do you understand?"

Again, War was silent, all the time looking at Raphael, and nodded.

"I am the keeper of all of you and of your riders. I and only your riders may ride you. However, War, in your case, I sit upon Death, and we are in need of your special ability to inflict pain on the battlefield, so I give permission for my second-in-command to ride you. Any problems with this?"

The horse bowed his head to Raphael and said, "Ride me as you wish. I have been waiting centuries to be let out of the stench of my stall and to be rid of that pathetic sister of yours. She has no guts, no grit, no balls . . . let's ride."

Lucifer grabbed War by the throat, his long nails digging into the horse's flesh. "Remember, you will never give Raphael trouble, or I will send you to that fucking planet in one swift move. I hope we are clear. As for my sister, if you touch one feather on her, I will burst you into flames where you stand. No female archangel, even a pathetic one, will be killed. Do you understand?"

War, afraid of Lucifer, responded, "Yes, master, no trepidation will come to her by my hand. I also know that only you and my rider may mount me, but in this case, I will treat Raphael as I would treat you. That I vow to you." War turned his head and looked at Raphael. "Welcome, my new rider. I will obey you as if you were Lucifer himself. Let's ride."

Meanwhile, Jehovah, enraged that War had been released as well, said to Gabriel, "I need you to lead the virtue armies against Lucifer. Ramiel has been captured, and you are the perfect replacement. What better choice to fight the forces of darkness within the apocalyptic steed than the angel of death?"

Gabriel, being a gentle and soft-spoken archangel, bowed reluctantly and left the Father's bedchamber and found himself on the battlefield with the virtues.

Jehovah said to Michael, "You have one job, my son, and you know exactly what I want to happen to your disgustingly deceitful brother. I am giving you protection from the apocalyptic steed known as Death. He cannot hurt you. Touch him at your will. This will be the only way to get close enough to Lucifer to kill him. I want him dead. Bring me his head."

Michael went to one knee, the hilt of his sword resting upon his palms. "Father, what you ask will be almost impossible. I can personally feel Lucifer's psychic ability growing. He will feel me coming. You know as well as I that even as child, I could never ambush him. But I will do my best, dearest Father." He stood, kissed his Father on the cheek, and vanished.

Raphael, using all his psychic ability, located Uriel with ease. He could see her in her bedchamber, sword drawn and waiting by the door. Three dominations nervously paced the room. Raphael looked at Lucifer and telepathically sent the message. Lucifer smiled. *This is going to be easy.* They rode down the marbled corridor toward Uriel's door. Having apocalyptic steeds at their command, they absorbed through the door and caught Uriel by surprise.

"You cheating bastard! Had to bring two of the four horses of the apocalypse to help you capture me. How typical, how pathetic."

Lucifer smiled and said, "I need not the help of the steeds. You are my sister, and our powerful telepathic brother found you. Now, bow before me and allow me to capture you."

"NEVER!" she cried.

Her dominations made a move toward Lucifer and Raphael. War sprang into action and killed them all in one quick and bloodily dismembering blow. War looked at Lucifer and said, "That felt fantastic, thank you."

Uriel dropped her sword and spoke. "You will never defeat Father, and what the fuck is happening to you? Have you seen yourself?"

Lucifer could feel the transformation but hadn't seen it. His newly acquired tail swiped back and forth above his head. Noticing it for the first time, he said, "This is new. I kinda like it. Now bow before me, bitch, and let me bind you. Kneel before the new ruler of heaven and watch as I destroy all of heaven. Better yet, Raphael, come here." Lucifer turned to his brother. "I want you to bind and shackle this female angel."

As Raphael grew closer upon War, the steed just crushed and walked over the dead and dying dominations and seraphim alike.

Lucifer said, "Nice touch. That was an amazing sound. I do love the sound of crushing skulls. As for the planet, they will all know the meaning of agony and pain. Father, It, will be dead, and there will be no one to grant forgiveness." After she was shackled and chained, Lucifer said, "Now lick my boots, bitch."

Uriel hesitated, and Lucifer kicked her in the face. "You have no thoughts on the ideas of torture I have planned for those fucking humans. Oh, what delight I am going to have torturing the planet and all those loathsome creations that are so dear to your Father!"

Uriel knelt in front of her brother. She had no choice but to be bound in chains. Raphael led the bound and gagged Uriel. She was then attached to War's bridle. The mighty horse just stared at her, and she knew better than to try and battle with this stud. He went to bite her, and with a closed fist, she punched the horse in the neck.

Lucifer, taken aback, screamed, "Enough of this madness, sister! Do not touch War again." Lucifer threw a blindfold to Raphael and said, "Blindfold this disobedient angel. War, if you ever try to bite my sister again, the pain I will inflict upon you, you will beg for death to make a visit." Lucifer looked at Uriel. "Don't think you are special, dear, cunning sister. The only thing that saved you was your vagina. I will not kill a female archangel. Remember my slight mercy to you. It will not happen often."

Michael ran down the corridor to Uriel's bedchamber. He knew that part of the seraphim army had been there. He could see dead seraphim angels bloody and sliced in the hallway. He saw throats cut, wings hacked off. Among the dead seraphim were dead dominations as well. The hallway reeked of death. He couldn't wait to enjoy the killing as his sister did. His main purpose was to protect God. He would show brutality in the name of his Father. Sword drawn, he sidestepped the dead bodies that lay askew around the hallway. He crept, ever the warrior, closer and closer to his sister's door. He looked at her blood-splattered and splintered door, and a wave of grief fell over him.

He touched the knob; it was hard to grasp, sticky and slippery from the blood. His battlefield-ready mind sensed Lucifer. Beads of sweat began to form on his brow as he would finally be able to murder this dreadful creation of the Father. He slowly turned the knob and opened the door. One inch open, two inches open . . . his eyes met such a macabre scene.

Sword drawn up over his shoulder, he looked around the room. The dismembered bodies of angels lay around the room. He stepped closer and realized these dead angels were mostly dominations, dying from protecting his sister. He also saw dead and bloodied seraphim strewn about the room. A chill ran down his divine back as he searched for his beloved sister. He saw something shining in the sun, a glint of metal.

He walked over slowly, sword still drawn and up over his shoulder. He almost cried out when he lifted the sword and knew it was Uriel's. He searched his mind for her, yet he could not place her soul anywhere. He knew she wasn't dead; he knew she lived. But where? He looked around the room again for clues and saw hoofprints in the blood. This was not the work of Death; one's demise with him was instant. This was the handiwork of War. He knew this horse well. He knew how he took pleasure in seeing victims disemboweled, dismembered, tortured, and bloodsoaked.

Confusion entered his mind.

Had Ramiel joined with Lucifer and Raphael? He searched his mind again for his brother and again could not find his soul. He knew that pathetic Raphael was shielding them from him and from the Father. His cloak of invisibility would not last forever. He searched again in his mind for Saraqael and knew instantly that he and his seraphim had sided with Lucifer.

Now I must kill three of my brothers, he thought. He closed the door silently as he left to go see the Father.

He arrived back at the Father's chamber, went to a knee, and said, "Uriel has been captured, Father."

Jehovah clenched his fists, slammed them onto his marble tabletop, and screamed. "You, Michael, will now be the leader of the dominations. Who better to lead the mighty warriors than my very own warrior?"

Jehovah called out for Gabriel with his mind. Gabriel appeared before the Father, Michael standing at his side. They began to strategize about the upcoming battle. They all knew that the pain and death would be great on both sides.

Michael, with his teeth gritted, spoke first. "Father, Lucifer and Raphael have control of Saraqael and the seraphim army. The dominations are ready to lay down their lives for our cause, Father. I'm sure Gabriel and his newly acquired army are ready as well."

Gabriel spoke. "Indeed we are ready, Father. But may I ask a simple question? Please do not get angry with me. It is my curious nature as the angel of life and death."

Jehovah said, "I know what you want to know already, my son, but please, by all means, ask so your brother may know."

"Why can you not end all this? You are the Almighty, and with one giant sweep of your hand, you can stop all this."

"I want to prove a point. All the inhabitants of this world need to know that they cannot defy me. They need to realize the punishment for such betrayal. If I just sweep this away with my powers, what lessons are learned?" Jehovah stood and paced the floor. "There is so much deceit inside of your brother Lucifer that it needs to be seen eradicated. This domain must endure this gruesome lesson. They need to know that their lives are not eternal, that they all harness mortality. I created all life here in heaven and on the earth. I made everything have mortality. I had to do this so that they would cherish the lives I gave them. Humans can only live a little more than a century. However, my beloved children here in heaven can live for thousands of years. They must learn that all life is precious and should be protected."

Jehovah sat across his loyal sons and stretched out his arms palms up. The brothers instinctively put their hands in their Father's. He spoke to his sons.

"I am going to protect both of you from the ravages of the horses War and Death. I know this is a bit deceitful, but I cannot bear to lose either of you. Both of you have been ever faithful and loyal to me. I give you these protections so if War kicks you, it will hurt and it will dent your armor but you will not be dismembered. The protection from Death is that you can touch him and not feel his effect. However, the protection from Death dwindles every time you have to use it. So still keep a wide berth from that steed. Unless you need to pull Lucifer off him. Your brother has begun a transformation that was not foreshadowed. I feel his hatred and his evil growing inside him. When you finally do see your brother, you will be shocked, but do not get paralyzed by his new form. He will not hesitate to kill either of you. Don't give him any opportunity, as he will use it. I know you, Michael, you will be the first he goes after. You and he have had an ongoing battle since he was a child. He has a deep-seated hatred for you, Michael. You need to be careful of his intelligence and his cunning. He will use every means necessary to ram his sword into your heart. Raphael is with him and can heal the seraphim at will. I doubt very much that Raphael would heal either of you. I do believe he would stand over you and watch your life force drain. Lucifer is using Raphael for his psychic abilities. I have a feeling that he will even kill Raphael to get to either of you. I think he would sacrifice anything to kill you both. Raphael is Lucifer's little pawn, his lackey. After this war is over, and if Lucifer is victorious, I do believe he will kill all the archangel, one by one until only he is left. Please be careful, my sons. I will be watching, and with you both, but will not interfere. I love both of you, my loyal sons. Now go find Lucifer with your armies and finish this."

Both angels arose from the table and began to walk toward the door.

The Father said, "I know where Lucifer and Raphael are. I have just had a vision."

The boys stopped and turned around with shock on their faces. Michael spoke. "Really, Father? Please tell us."

Jehovah said, "I have seen . . . they are on the west end of heaven. Raphael is not as smart as he thinks. He broke his concentration for only a moment. They camp between the cloud layers. Be careful, my sons, as there are seraphim scouts all around the perimeter. If you catch them by surprise and dispose of them silently, you will gain access. Bless you both and your armies. Go with peace in your heart. Lucifer will hate that." Jehovah grinned. "And his hatred will unbalance him and make him vulnerable."

Michael and Gabriel nodded at each other and walked out the door.

CHAPTER 10

The War Rages

Lucifer, snug yet ever aware in his tent, could feel that he had somehow been betrayed. He sensed his brothers and their armies very close to them. He screamed, "Raphael!" and he appeared.

"Yes, my lord?"

Lucifer slapped Raphael across the mouth and said, "You broke your concentration, and the virtues and the dominations, along with Gabriel and Michael, are on their way. You fool! I told you to cloak us."

"Master, I never broke my concentration. No one can penetrate my mind. Not even him. Master, your effect on the west end of heaven has been dramatic. Your evil and hatred have blocked out most of the sun. The flowers are wilting and dying. Even the trees have begun to lose their leaves. Maybe he—uh, It has sensed the physical change occurring in his land."

Lucifer angrily paced the floor. "You may be right, but my gut is telling me we have a spy. I will make such an example of this deceiver that all of heaven will know of my cruelty." Lucifer sat in his chair and said, "I am going to go visit Ramiel. I want some torture advice from him."

Raphael said, "Master, Ramiel will never talk. He will not give anything to you willingly, but I am sure that once you begin to burn and torture him, you may break him and he may talk."

Lucifer rubbed his hands together, and sparks flew from between his palms. Shocked, he did it again, harder and faster this time, and larger sparks flew from his palms. "Oh, this is quite nice! What a wonderful new ability!" He rubbed them harder, and large blue and red flames came emerging through his fingers and licked at his palms. "I now own the power over flame. Just wonderful!"

Raphael, shocked, said, "Master, this needs to be harnessed so you can use it at your will. To be granted such an amazing gift is truly a mighty achievement." Lucifer grinned widely, showing his large fangs, his forked tongue lashing in and out of his mouth. "Ramiel will never see this coming. He will think I need to use an archaic form of fire like a torch. He is in for an amusing and terrifying surprise."

Lucifer left his tent and stared at every seraph he saw. He sensed no spies in any of them. He knew it was Raphael. "What a fool! I will deal with him in my own time. Right now I need him and his healing ability. Then I shall see what I will do with him."

He entered the tent where the bound and shackled Ramiel stood restrained against a pole. Throwing a bucket of water on his brother's face to wake him, Lucifer said, "Would you like a drink, brother?"

Ramiel shook his head, and Lucifer, angered, said, "You will look at me and answer me. Do not defy me, brother."

Ramiel looked up, hatred in his eyes, and said, "Yes, brother, I would like a drink."

"That's better. Now you may have a drink." Lucifer held up a ladle of water to his brother's dry and parched lips. Ramiel begged for more, and Lucifer said, "I need something from you, dear brother, then more water. As you know, I have no fear of you. I need some torture tricks, and I need them now. You can willingly tell your secrets, or I will take them by force."

Ramiel laughed and said, "Do you really think I would divulge any information to you?"

Lucifer giggled and began to rub his palms together. Large blue and red flames sprang from his palms and upward. Lucifer sneered, "Scared yet, brother? No? You should be. Actually, you should be terrified." Lucifer could feel his younger brother tense up, and smiled. He moved closer to Ramiel and said, "Do you ever want the ability of flight ever again?" Walking behind his bound brother, Lucifer started at the bottom of his left wing and began to singe the feathers. Lucifer took great delight in his torturing ability.

Ramiel screamed in agony and said, "Never!"

Lucifer went higher onto the wing, the smell of burning feathers and flesh filling the room.

Ramiel began to sob yet defiantly said, "Never!"

Lucifer went to the right wing and started at the bottom again. Ramiel screamed and begged for mercy. He had never been on the receiving end of torture. He always took great pride in his torturous work and was void of empathy. He was in complete agony, and finally he spoke. "I will tell you. Please spare my beloved wings and my ability of flight."

Lucifer smiled and said, "My, my brother, I thought you would've given me more of a fight. You are pathetic and useless. You were the great torturer? That amuses me. I see you can dish it out but can't take it. Pussy."

Raphael left Lucifer's tent and paced back and forth in front of it. He nervously thought about the enemy finding their hideout. "I did lose my concentration, and if Lucifer finds out, I am a dead angel." He thought for a moment of whom he could inflict his ability on to fool Lucifer. But what if the great leader found out? He couldn't risk it. He had to block Lucifer from his thoughts and only permit him to see what Raphael wanted him to see. Lucifer's power was becoming stronger daily, his psychic ability almost rivaling Raphael's. Raphael could not let him find out that it was his mistake that might cost him this war. He wanted to flee, but where would he go? Back to the Father? That was a death sentence too.

Gabriel set up camp about five miles from the seraphim camp. Gabriel could smell them. He wanted so desperately to eliminate the scouts so that Michael and the dominations could win the battle. He spoke to his army. "My brother Michael and I are your new leaders. I will choose six of my best killing machines to rid the perimeter of the seraphim guards. I want you to use the stealth that Ramiel taught all of you. Be extremely quiet. The seraphim will be able to sense you, but if they can't see you, you will be invisible to them. I will protect you six with my psychic ability as much as I can. Try not to engage in battle with them, as the sound of the swords clanking together will alert the others. I know that Ramiel gave all of you special weaponry. These must be utilized. Each of you carry piano wire and knives. I beg you to use them. A rear attack is your best bet. I know, with you being virtues, this goes against everything you have been taught by your beloved leader, Ramiel. This situation is much different and needs to be done as sneakily and underhanded as possible."

The six virtues looked at one another, confused by a sneak attack. The concept being foreign to them. Ramiel always taught them to confront their enemies to give them a fighting chance. To die protecting heaven was a beautiful death. Face-to-face, blade against blade, these were the tactics they were used to and knew well. Not facing one's enemy and looking in his eyes as they died was not a glorious thing; it was shunned. The six knew that this new maneuver was what was going to be needed and agreed with Gabriel.

Gabriel spoke to the six. "Now go and do as I've instructed. I want all of you to come back victorious. Be stealthy, silent, and deadly. Blessed are among the warriors that tread into battle." He lay his hand on each one of their heads as they nodded at him.

The first sentry seemed to know something was lurking about. He drew his long sword and took a defensive stance. The virtue was directly behind him. The seraph swung his sword widely, knowing that someone or something was there. In one quick and decisive move, the virtue wrapped his piano wire around the seraph's throat and removed his head. The other guards could feel the death of their compatriot telepathically, and they came toward their fallen comrade. Two virtues were lying in wait, hidden among the mist of the clouds, their white wings held tightly to their bodies. The camouflage was almost complete. The seraphim running to help their fellow soldier didn't even see them in the cloud layer. The virtues, swept at the ankles and both guards going down, immediately ate the knives of both virtues. The virtually invisible attackers knew that more would be coming and that they needed to regroup to surprise the new bait. Four seraphim guards came through the mist. Seeing the dead sentries, they drew their swords. Slowly they approached the spot of the guards and saw the beheading. They circled around the headless corpse, swords raised and in front of them.

The virtues stuck with such silence and stealth that the seraphim didn't even know they were there until they lay dead in the clouds. The virtues bent down and removed their blades from the backs of the dead and dying seraphim. One virtue even spit on a dying seraphim and said, "You make me sick, going against Father. May your soul rot for all eternity without a home."

One of the other virtues, with a look of shock on his face, fell to the cloud deck, bleeding profusely out of his side, a seraphim smiling behind him. But he didn't smile for long. From behind him, piano wire was thrown around his neck, and he was beheaded. The virtues grabbed their brother and carried him back to camp. They had done enough damage for one night.

They wished Raphael and his healing power were waiting for them, but only Gabriel with his ability to give life or take it away was there. Their virtue brother was badly wounded, and they knew Gabriel would not spare his life. Two of the virtues went back to the seraphim camp. They were looking for Lucifer himself. They crept through camp stealthily, almost invisible. Luckily, they spotted Lucifer coming out of the tent that they knew held Ramiel. They wanted desperately to save their leader, and a surprise attack upon Lucifer himself would be the end of this cursed war. They silently walked pass the tent and looked at Lucifer's back. His very large wings, no longer white and feathery, were now black and leathery. The one virtue gave out a gasp, and Lucifer smiled and stopped in his tracks.

"I can smell your fear. I can hear your hearts beating ever so fast." Lucifer sniffed the air. "Ah, and you are virtues."

Finally, Lucifer turned to look at the two virtue warriors and smiled. They both were shocked at the size of the fangs within his mouth. He hissed at them and came closer to their faces. He thought about taking them alive and torturing them, but he needed to release his rage. He was so angered that seven of his sentry guards had been killed. In one quick move, he grabbed them and rammed both his fists deeply into their armor. He pulled out their hearts and threw them to the cloud deck. Laughing heartily as life ran from them and they collapsed, Lucifer knew he was going to win this war. Triumphantly Lucifer began to stroll through the darkness and back to his tent.

The remaining three virtues carried their bleeding friend back to the camp. They went straight to Gabriel's tent. They lay his dying body upon the floor and called out for Gabriel. He appeared and went straight to the side that had the deep wound. The other virtues knew that Gabriel, being the angel of life and death, would soon put their fellow soldier out of his misery. They all bowed their heads and prayed together.

"Heavenly Father, please accept this soul into your bosom. He was a fierce warrior yet led a pure and righteous life. May he live forever within the special place in your kingdom reserved for dead angels. Thank you, Father, for this blessing."

Gabriel looked up and said, "What are you three doing? I will not take the life of this brave soldier. He will live to fight again. He is badly wounded, but I will be merciful and grant him life instead of taking it."

The three virtues, stunned, bowed their heads. "Thank you. You are as fair and righteous as Ramiel. We would have followed you anywhere as our new leader, but now we know that you are truly worthy of our loyalty and respect."

Gabriel, confused, looked about the room. "I sent out six of you, yet only four returned. Did the others fall in combat?"

The lead virte bent to one knee, his blood-spattered armor dripping on the floor. With the hilt of his sword against his forehead, he began to speak. "Commander, we ambushed and killed seven sentry guards. We regrouped, and the one that you so graciously spared was stabbed in the back. We carried our fallen brother, and two of us could not control our virtue reserve. They fled our group and went to find Lucifer himself to kill him."

Gabriel asked, "What happened to them? Do they live? Are they captive? Are they being tortured by my unfeeling brother? I want answers, and I want them *now!* These were not my instructions. In and out, kill the sentry guards as quietly as possible was what I commanded. Yet two of you defied me. You speak of trust with me. How is it I can trust all of you? If not total obedience to me, then to whom? I know that Ramiel was your leader and all of you loved him. However, he is not here. I am. You will obey me as if I were he." Gabriel moved to the other side of the room and said, "I need to step away from you, as your psychic powers interfere with mine. I will find my brother's mind and gain all the strategic and death thoughts that I can. I am going to find out exactly what happened to our fellow freedom fighters. Now leave me be. I will tell you what transpired. It will be no easy task penetrating my brother's mighty barrier in his mind. Now go. Take your comrade with you. He is already beginning to heal."

Gabriel lay upon his bed and closed his eyes. He searched the darkness and finally came upon Lucifer resting in his bed. His eyes closed, and Gabriel thought, *Good, he is asleep.* Gabriel tried to penetrate Lucifer's mind and was denied. He stepped back and tried again. Again he was denied. Gabriel was now sweating profusely and getting tired. With one last push, he was inside his cunning brother's mind. Searching the dark recesses of his brother's memories, Gabriel searched and searched for information about the dead virtues. Gabriel tiptoed through his powerful brother's mind. He didn't want to be noticed in there. He finally came to the memory of the virtues and was horrified at the brutality. Killing an angel was heartbreaking enough, but to do it with your bear hands . . .

What sort of monster had his brother turned into?

Gabriel then saw his brother and lost his concentration for just a moment. "I see you have seen my true form, brother." Lucifer's voice almost screamed in his head.

"You let me in, didn't you?"

Lucifer bellowed with laughter and said, "Of course I did. Don't you just love my true form? This is what I was meant to become. The frightening, newly crowned king of heaven. I was to be seen this way so all of heaven would fear me. Are you scared, dear brother? Does fear fill your heart? It should."

Gabriel tried to release himself from Lucifer's grip on his mind. It was a death grip. "Don't fight me, brother. It just makes it more strenuous on you. You will need every ounce of energy to even get close to me. You will need your strength to face me on the field of battle. Our swords will meet very soon. *Now get the fuck out of my head!*" When Lucifer screamed even louder, Gabriel's body was lifted and thrown through the back of the tent.

Gabriel lay in the clouds gasping for breath. Two virtue guards came running to his aid and touched the archangel to help him up. Defiantly, the once-gentle and always-fair Gabriel screamed, "Get your fucking hands off of me! Don't ever touch an archangel again."

The guards still helped him up and could see the panic in his eyes. Brushing off his armor and unsteadily standing, he spoke. "I have seen Lucifer, I went into his mind." Almost crying in fear, he continued, "I went in and thought he did not know I was there. He grabbed my mind and would not release it. I have never felt such helplessness. I can even overpower Raphael's mighty telepathy, but this was different. He baited me, he wanted me to see, he beckoned my mind to infiltrate his. His power is so great that I will never try and read him again. I may become his mental prisoner for all time. I do believe that Michael is the only chance we have against Lucifer's incredible psychic ability, as Michael never uses his. It's lain dormant for centuries. Michael would rather fight with his sword than his mind. That always benefited Michael as, even when Lucifer was a child, he played mind games with Michael that he didn't quite understand. Michael would become enraged at this and felt inferior to Lucifer. However, Michael's size was always a threat to Lucifer, so he never truly mentally infiltrated him. Michael has always been the largest and mightiest of all of us. Now I have seen Lucifer in his new form. His size is almost as big as Michael's, and he grows hourly. Now I need five of you to go seek out Michael and the dominations and get them here as quickly as possible. I want them to fly like the wind and be here in three hours. Time is of the essence. Lucifer's power is growing increasingly rapid."

The virtues soldiers bowed and said, "Yes, commander, we will have them here in two hours."

Gabriel said, "Wonderful. Blessings to you, my brothers. Be swift and cautious. My love is with all of you."

Gabriel thought to himself, *Please let Michael get here. I have no desire to deal with Lucifer and Death. I will deal with Raphael and War. The advantage is to Michael as the battle-hardened warrior he is. He has been fighting for Father and his laws for centuries. He knows how to wield a sword and take advantage of any weakness shown by an opponent. Father's gift to us against the apocalyptic steeds will definitely be Lucifer's downfall. He will not see that coming. Michael will be victorious, as always. Lucifer's size will mean nothing. Michael is the most fierce warrior in all of heaven.*

Gabriel reluctantly thought about his brother Lucifer. He didn't want to be mentally captured again. His experience as a fighting angel was adolescent at best. His greatest weapon in his arsenal was mind games, but Michael was almost immune to such pedestrian fighting. His childhood taught him long ago how to deal with Lucifer's mind games. He now had learned the ability to almost block his brother. It seemed like fate that they fought like this as children. Michael would need to harness his sleeping giant of physic ability. Lucifer would never see it coming. He was almost as strong as Raphael with his mind.

Lucifer sat upright in his bed, half-asleep yet very aware of his mind. He knew the dominations were coming. He knew that weak-minded Gabriel had warned them. He couldn't wait to behead Gabriel; actually, he would let Raphael do it. What sweet sorrow to witness on both sides. He could feel something different about Michael and sent his mind out to seek his weak-willed brother. He found him flying, with his beautiful white wings flapping and swooshing in the air. A twinge of envy filled his heart and enraged him. *My fucking larger leathery wings are faster and less destructible than measly feathers.* He sent his mind out to his warrior brother.

Michael landed in the cloud deck and said, "Hello, you fucking excuse for an angel. What the fuck are you trying to do in my head? Trying to read me, I see."

Lucifer, irritated that Michael knew he was there, said, "I'm here to read you, stupid."

Michael just shook his head and let Lucifer continue. Partway through Michael's mind, Lucifer encountered a brick wall. "This is new. Trying to build a wall against me, brother?"

Michael, in his mind, said, "No, brother, you built this wall yourself, with all the games and bullshit thrown my way through your mind over the centuries. I had no choice but to create this fortress from my inner thoughts. Now say hello to my wall."

The infinite brick wall began to slide forward, and Lucifer was abruptly thrown out of Michael's mind. Lucifer, enraged, threw a tantrum, while Michael only smiled and continued his flight toward the seraphim camp.

Lucifer screamed in anger and wanted nothing more than to capture the virtues. He sent out a mental message to all seraphim. "Capture the virtues. I have something special planned for them and Ramiel. If you kill a virtue, my wrath will be complete. Sacrifice yourself for the capture of the virtues. I also want dominations captured for my entertainment. I really don't care how many dominations you kill. Bring me two hundred captive virtues. I also want two hundred dead dominations brought back to camp. I have something terrifyingly beautiful to present to any enemy that tries to get into my camp. If you feel the need to bring a few live dominations, by all means, go head. Their death screams will be heard throughout heaven. I've changed my mind. I really don't care if the dominations are alive or dead, but a few live ones would please me greatly. Do not fail me, and again, do *not* touch my brothers Gabriel and Michael. An archangel is to be killed by another archangel. I intend to be that archangel. You pathetic grunts are not worthy of murdering a great being."

Michael's wings surged through the air when he got another mental message. He landed on the cloud deck and said, "Fuck off, Lucifer! I already told you I am basically immune to your games."

The voice inside Michael's head was the Father's.

"Oh, my Father, my Lord, I am sorry."

Jehovah spoke. "No need for apologies. All is fair in love and war. I have an image to send to your mind. This image is going to disturb you, as this is what Lucifer has become." God sent the transformation of his second-born to Michael.

Michael dropped to one knee in the clouds and said, "Heavenly Father, is this what evil does to an archangel? I would rather you cut my throat than become this."

Jehovah spoke, "My dearest of all my archangels, I wanted you to be aware of your brother's transformation so you are not caught off guard. I would never slice your throat, my ever-loyal son. Remember, you have my protection from the horses Death and War. Use it wisely and don't be foolish and rush at Death. My protection will diminish the more you touch him. I love you, my son, and be careful. Do not let your brute overrule your intelligence."

Michael again spread his mighty wings and flew as fast as he could to the seraphim camp. Oh, how he wanted to kill Lucifer, ramming his sword through his chest. Up ahead of him, he could see Gabriel and the virtue army waiting for their arrival. Gabriel smiled widely at his brother, and Michael could feel his brother's love and smiled back.

Lucifer, Raphael, and Saraqael, all atop one of the cloud peaks, watched as a fraction of the seraphim army began its exodus from camp. Lucifer sat upon Death, Raphael upon War, and Saraqael standing between them. Lucifer had granted him the same protection from the horses just as God did for Gabriel and Michael. Lucifer had no idea that the Father had granted the same protection to his brothers.

Saraqael asked Lucifer, "Shall I stay here with you, or shall I go with the rest of the army?"

Lucifer answered, "Stay here, as Raphael and I have some business to attend to in the main portion of heaven. We need to make an appearance to the civilians. They need to see who their new leader will be."

Raphael said, "I didn't know of this plan. You need to be kept abreast of what is going on, brother. I am not permitted into your mind without losing my own head in the process."

Lucifer sneered at his brother and said, "I'm glad you remembered my rule about my mind. But you disappoint me with your arrogance as to question anything I do. I do not need permission from you. As a matter of fact, I do not need anybody's permission. Now you will follow me. Our steeds could make the five-day ride to the middle of heaven. However, it will take them only a few hours, as we will help them with our aerial dominance. We can make it in a few hours. I can sense my brothers, and they are together. They are extremely close, but what we are about to do will distract them enough for the seraphim. They will be able to slaughter the dominations and capture the virtues. What I have in store for Its home is going to be grand and, may I add, very gory."

Saraqael flew down from the cloud peak and went to his tent.

Lucifer then spoke to both horses. "Raphael and I are going to help you both gain even greater speed. Our wings will allow you to have more power in your gallop. Now let's make our way to the center of heaven, and with any luck, It will be there. I will have my chance to end this war and become supreme leader of all of heaven."

With a quick kick to Death's side, they began the long journey back to heaven proper.

Raphael followed suit, except War tried to bite him as he kicked him. Raphael said to his stud, "Don't you ever try that again! You will not have to deal with Lucifer. I will get so far into your mind, you stupid animal, that your skull will explode from the inside out."

"I can feel you inside of my head already, and your power is mighty. I will never try that again."

Raphael's white wings spread out and flapped. War caught up with Death, and the four of them made their way to the center of heaven. Leathery wings along with feathery wings gave the horses a lift off the cloud deck so they could gallop through the air instead of having the clouds inhibit their speed.

Raphael and Lucifer arrived at heaven's main gates. They looked at each other, War digging a hole in the cloud deck. He was ready. Death, basically, was calm and collected. He looked at War and shook his head and said, "Fool, don't be so overzealous! You will warn the rest of those accursed angels inside. Do you not think our riders will fly us over this high but yet pathetic barrier? Calm yourself, and I mean right now."

Lucifer said, "I agree with you, my mighty companion. Raphael, control that horse. *Now!*"

With War finally calmed, the archangels easily breached the top of the barrier and landed softly like an angel feather falling to the clouds. The interlopers looked around and saw that there were no angels in sight. They began to stroll through the corridors, seeing all the subangel quarters, and noticed they were sleeping.

Lucifer looked at Raphael and said, "Watch this new power I have acquired."

With a mighty, high-pitched screech, one that would shatter a glass, he rattled all of heaven's suburb. The first angel to appear Lucifer recognized as a member of the jury. Lucifer said, "I recognize you, pig. Should I spare you? I knew your thoughts in the courtroom and knew you were with me. Either join my cause or perish."

The subangel said, "Never," and went for his sword. It was not there, to his surprise. He was rudely awoken and forgot his sword in his chambers. The sheer terror in his eyes made Lucifer giggle. Through a telepathic connection with Death, Lucifer sent him a message. With a giant grin on the horse's face, he rammed his head into the subangel's chest,

and immediately the angel wailed and was turned to dust.

Death said, "Master, my dear master, that was fantastic. Thank you. Thank you."

The next angel was Lucifer's prey. This angel was not caught off guard; he drew his sword against Lucifer. He laughed with delight and thought of the blood that was already soaking the upper layers of the clouds. It was about to get darker. Lucifer was not amused, and with one quick sweep of his broadsword, he beheaded the betrayer. Others emerged from their chambers, all with swords drawn. War ran past Lucifer and went into action. Kicking wildly with front feet and back, he dismembered angels in all directions. Raphael, with his sword swinging over his head and down upon the angels that avoided War, beheaded at his will, and his armor was covered in blood. Bodies of dismembered and beheaded angels lay everywhere.

Lucifer sat back and watched the mayhem develop in front of him. He finally called Raphael back with his mind, but Raphael was losing control of War. Death had to telepathically hurt the steed before it would relent and come back to Death's side. War was defeated in his mind by Death, who was more powerful. He was the greatest of steeds. Death was still controlled by the all-powerful Lucifer, and this terrified War. He thought in his head and sent the message to Death: "The angel that rides you scares me. I will never doubt you or your rider ever again. Please forgive my excitement at handing down a bit of war with the angels. It gets the best of me."

Lucifer spread his wings and knew what the horses tried to hide from him with their animal minds. He said, "Okay, we need to take a moment and look at the slaughter that War and Raphael has just reigned in heaven. I bet those fucking awful humans are being rained upon from the heavens with angel blood." He gave a hearty and gut-filled laugh and said, "Serves those motherfuckers right. I bet they are terrified and praying to him. A fruitless endeavor, to be sure. They should be praying to *me*! Then maybe, just maybe, I may spare them."

The four trotted through the suburb of heaven, blood splashing onto the horses' legs and onto their bellies.

Death looked at War and spoke telepathically. "Lucifer interferes in the conversation with the horses," he said. "Any survivors will be given a choice, side with us or die. Any dying survivors of your brutal yet beautiful attack are mine if they make the wrong choice. I will kill them myself. To join the victorious, then they will be spared. I want to feel the power to give life or take it away. Do you understand?"

Dismounting Death, he walked in front of their blood-soaked bodies and spoke directly to the horses. "You pathetic animals think I cannot penetrate your feeble minds?"

Knowing Death was the most powerful of the four horses, he said in his mind, looking directly at Lucifer, "They are all yours."

Lucifer could hear their conversation and just grinned. He was the most powerful of all psychics in heaven. He relished the power.

He mounted Death, all their armor caked in the blood of the innocent, and rode down the hallway. Death and War kicking and stepping upon dead angel bodies. The crunching of bones and popping of skulls made the horses smile. Blood spurted in all directions, and Lucifer's once-beautiful, shining silver armor began to change into black and became fused to his skin.

Raphael said, "Master, look at your armor."

Lucifer looked down at his chest, and his armor had become a part of him. He said, "Now I am protected for eternity. No weapon either forged by human or the divine shall ever penetrate my newly acquired power."

Little did he know that only an archangel's sword could penetrate another archangel's armor. Lucifer, in his arrogance, had forgotten the lessons he was taught in the fighting classes as a child. These classes were ones that It had made him take. He always knew in his heart he would never have the need for close combat or the use of his sword. He knew his armor would protect him, and he polished it daily. The fact that his armor was envied by the other archangels made him proud, and that was a sin in Its eyes. Even as an adolescent, he defied his Father with his playful mind tricks on Michael.

The four of them rounded the corner and went into another marbled corridor. Angels everywhere were bowing to Lucifer and said, "We are with thee. We hate the humans as much as you do."

Lucifer said, "Good, I will give you a mental image as to where my camp rests. And remember, if I find a traitor among you, I will inflict such torture and pain that you will not be able to endure." Lucifer sent the image, and the angels flew out of heaven and toward the seraphim camp.

Raphael brought War over to Lucifer, at his side. Lucifer, upon Death, rubbed his beloved pale horse with blood splashed on his side and said, "Master, you do have a traitor." He looked at the sky and pointed. "It is that one, sire." Lucifer rubbed his palms together, and a ball of fire incinerated the angel in midflight. "Any more that you can sense, brother?"

Raphael obediently said, "No, brother, just the one."

Lucifer bellowed, "Slaughter them all! Leave no one alive, not men, women, or even children."

They came back to the long corridor more bloodstained and tired from their battle. Lucifer strolled down the blood-soaked hallway, taking great pleasure in the crimson color of the clouds. He looked and saw the dominations; some were still alive and begged for mercy and prayed to God for help.

Lucifer said, "God? No God, only me, and I will be the new leader of heaven, and if any of you that survive call me God, I will kill you on the spot. You will call me Lucifer." The angel that begged and tried to speak to Jehovah, Lucifer bent down beside him and rammed his broadsword through the angel's neck.

Satisfied that he could hear the moans of dominations in the hallway, he turned back. He stood there in shock for a moment as three dead seraphim soldiers lay in a pile. Swords still clutched in their hands and still ready to fight, even in death. He thought of calling for Raphael to resurrect them but thought differently. There must be losses on both sides.

Lucifer looked at his mighty steeds and said, "The next hallway is all yours. You will have no riders. Release your rage."

Death spoke. "Master, I have never ridden without a rider. Thank you, this is going to be fun."

War said, "Indeed, my fellow beast of burden, this is going to be quite fun. Thank you, master."

Both mighty steeds went to one knee and bowed to Lucifer. He smiled, as he knew the mayhem he was about to watch was going to be extreme and exciting. The angels knew these horses and did their best to run away and hide. War struck first, but not with his mighty blow of his hooves; instead, he bit down on an angel's throat and ripped and tore at the flesh. The angel screamed in horror as his life was bled and onto War's feet. It felt like getting a warm bath from Raqael. Death played his own type of torturous games. He had three dominations cornered, and none of them dared try to confront Death. The pale horse was known throughout heaven. He snorted in their direction, and they all flinched. Death gave out a hearty, sadistic laugh. He then stood on his back legs. Towering over the terrified angels, he brought his front hooves so close to their chests. Again the angles flinched, and Death was beginning to tire of toying with these pathetic creatures. He turned his back on these angels, with confidence, knowing they would never get close enough to him. With a raise of his very long tail, he gave a slow and caring brush against all the angels' faces. Hearing their wails gave Death a sheer shiver up his back, as this was his favorite sound before they died.

The next wave that the horses unleashed was unprecedented even in Ramiel's dungeon. Death kicked and turned angels left and right into dust, their wailing sounding like a lullaby to him. War was kicking and dismembering angels at his whim. Some of the dismembered parts of angels still clutched their swords as their hands went flying. This amused Death. *Even in the face of my might and power, they still tried to get close enough to me.* Both horses triumphantly returned to their riders with large grins upon their faces.

Death spoke. "I do believe War and I have never had so much fun. Thank you again. We do love being riderless but enjoy having our masters with us during battle."

Raphael went to the sacred fountain in the center of the courtyard and dipped two buckets into the water untouched by any angel. This water was sacred and the Father's very own source to quench his thirst. Raphael, not caring, filled the buckets with the power of the restoring water. Then Raphael did something Lucifer didn't expect; he took a piss in the fountain. Lucifer tied the horses to one of the columns at the end of the archangel bedchamber hallway.

Lucifer spoke. "Raphael and I must do this alone. I want to kill It, and Raphael can watch as the life runs out of the Father yet does nothing to cure him or resurrect him once dead."

The horses drank deeply, and Lucifer spoke. "Nice touch with the piss, dear brother."

The horses, looking upset yet ever loyal, obeyed their riders and reluctantly stayed behind. Lucifer and Raphael, swords drawn, began down the hallway. Lucifer stopped and said, "What the fuck are you doing? Do you know nothing about war tactics? You need to get behind me, and we need to be wing to wing. You watch the back, and I will watch the front. Makes sense to you?"

Raphael said, "Of course, this is brilliant."

They walked past Michael's door knowing he was with Gabriel. They bypassed his door as well. Raphael and Lucifer knew their bedchambers were empty as well. Ramiel and Saraqael's were empty. The girls' rooms were also empty. Nobody was there to protect Its door. Before Lucifer could touch the handle, Raphael said, "This is an ambush, Lucifer. The virtues reside in his bedchamber, awaiting our arrival."

"Good," Lucifer said. "We will catch them off guard. Well done again, brother, with your incredible telepathic gift."

Lucifer grabbed the handle of God's bedchamber and flung the door wide open. The first two lines of defense closest to the door rushed Lucifer. With one sweep of the talons on his hand, the swords that the pathetic virtues held were instantly impaled to the hilt in the walls that surrounded them.

Raphael screamed, "Seraphim, *now!*"

The seraphim rushed into the room, swords drawn, bloody and reeking of death. Most virtues laid down their swords. The sound of the metal hitting the marble floor was music to Lucifer's ears. A few more, bold and defiant, made a move toward Lucifer, along with ten seraphim.

Lucifer said, "Do not kill them. Maim them, stab them, cut off their wings, as long as they live. I don't care what you do to them."

The seraphim took great pleasure inflicting pain on the virtues that had the nerve to go against Lucifer and Raphael.

Lucifer spoke. "I am going to chain all of you together single file. I will bind your wings under your arms as the thought of flight may get you killed. I will then chain your hands together, and if you notice, the chains are very heavy and harbor very sharp hooks in them. Do not try to escape—it will be futile. You will also be roped to the bridle of Death. I warn you, do not piss off this horse or allow a touch from him. You will be turned to ash. It's a very unpleasant way to die. Behind the line of you sorry excuses for angels will be Raphael and War. Again, I would not piss off this steed. It has no patience for stupidity."

Lucifer called for Raphael to come to the front near him, virtues tripping and falling as he made a semicircle.

"I have a very great gift to give to your leader, Ramiel. I am going to take such great pleasure making him watch as I murder each and every one of you. With the added bonus of having my fucking slut sister bound and made to bare witness to my debauchery. Raphael will hold her leash as I will make your fucking leader kneel before me. Any protests? Questions?" Lucifer put his blackened hand to his ear and said, "Oh, such silence! Nobody cares to challenge me? Fine, you are all cowards, and that's why you are virtues. Quite pathetic, if you ask me. Do you not think so, Raphael?"

"Master, I cannot normally read a virtue. However, with them being terrified, I can read their easily penetrated minds, and they are all extremely leery of you, me, Death, and War. It amuses me, as it does you."

Lucifer asked Raphael, "Did you bring the dead dominations with you?"

"Yes, my dear brother. I left a contingent to round up the dead virtues, the dead dominations, and our beloved fallen seraphim will be drawn in a hearse while the others will be dragged by horseback."

Lucifer smiled. "Oh, that is a fucking fantastic idea."

Raphael, confused as he could not read his brother without permission anymore, had no idea of this grand plan.

Lucifer spoke to everyone, turned around on War, and said, "Now, you scared bunny rabbits. That's why you are virtues. You may be the best in battle, but as far as torture or bloody massacre, it sickens you. You are all excuses of your name, virtue. You get to see what real terror is as we are making a visit to my sister Raqael."

Raphael spoke. "Brother, your brilliance never seizes to amaze me. Is she to ride one of the two left?"

Lucifer said, "I have no intention of leaving any apocalyptic steed behind. You will see what I am about to do."

They made a large detour to get to the stables. Lucifer dismounted Death and looked at his sister, her scar still visible, and she cowered under feathery wings.

"Do you fear me?"

"Yes, Master Lucifer, I do."

"Raise your head and walk with me. I am about to unleash the last two apocalyptic steeds. I want you to tide Pestilence, and we will take Famine to my loyal general, Saraqael."

Raqael, a bit confused, said, "Master Lucifer, these steeds will not permit anybody but you and their rider to mount them."

Lucifer took his sister's head in his hands. "Those fucking horses will do what I tell them. Got it?"

Raqael stopped at Famine's stall and unlatched the door. The horse, seeing Lucifer, bowed on one knee and said, "Yes, my master, time to ride?"

Lucifer said, "Yes. However, your rider is not to be woken, and I ride

Death and Raphael rides War. Raqael will ride you, and any problems with this, I will eviscerate you. Do you understand?"

Famine shook his head and said, "Master, I have loved Raqael for all time. It would be an honor for her to ride me. I would lay down my life for her."

Pestilence said, "Thank you, my merciful master, for allowing me out finally."

Lucifer said "See? This is the type of fucking complete loyalty I require from all subjects, four-legged or two, winged or not."

They exited the barn, and the virtues gave out a loud harmonious gasp.

Famine said, "Allow me to introduce myself. I am Famine, and it would be wise of you to not make me angry. Watch this."

Famine waited no time and went straight to the first virtue he saw. He touched this angel with his brow, and the angel began to grow pale and very thin."

Lucifer bellowed, "Enough, Famine! I want them alive."

Famine said, "Oh, he will live. It will be a miserable existence, but he will live. Any other of you fucking angels have a problem with my appearance and the fact that a female archangel sits upon my back? My deaths are slow and merciless. The four hoses have their own special abilities, and mine is to make you die of starvation no matter how much you eat. Understand me?"

Following Famine out of the barn, led by Lucifer, was Pestilence. This horse smelled of disease great and small. Lucifer handed Raqael Pestilence's reins. He could feel the virtue eyes on him. "Allow me to tell you about me. I cause death with sickness, I kill babies in their sleep, I slaughter cattle so then Famine can have some fun. Watch what I can do."

He grabbed the closest virtue by his hair with his teeth. The angel immediately became violently ill, and smallpox appeared upon his face.

Lucifer finally said, "Enough! They have seen your powers. Now we need to get back to camp."

Lucifer looked around for the virtue with the largest wings and said, "You there, virtue scum, sit upon Pestilence as he needs a winged rider. I will protect you from the many diseases he carries. This protection only lasts while you ride him and are my captive. Do not stray too far from me, as Pestilence will unleash such disease upon you. It will kill you slowly and painfully. Understood? Now we can be home even faster. I know that wretched Gabriel and that fucking Michael are close, and we have not much time to get ready and set up the surprise I have waiting. Let's fly and ride."

The horses let ride the virtue soldier, Lucifer, and the others to their destination. The angel that was riding Pestilence began to become violently ill and collapsed. Lucifer thought, *Guess you must have to be an archangel to be immune from the influences of the apocalyptic steeds.*

CHAPTER 11

Lucifer's Wonderfully Evil Surprise

Lucifer called out to Saraqael and Raqael, and both appeared before him. "You called us, master?"

Lucifer said, "Do you remember all the dead dominations that I commanded to be brought back?" They both nodded. "I have a very special and very gruesome task I want done with their bodies. I want them impaled around our perimeter to strike fear into the rest of that army."

Raqael and Saraqael looked at each other, confused, and Saraqael spoke. "Impale, master? What does this word mean?"

Lucifer, irritated at the sheer stupidity of his generals, pulled the knife from his belt and rammed it through the palm of his hand, coming out the other side. This blade was able to penetrate Lucifer's flesh as it was made from the same divine material that forged his sword. It was a special gift from the blacksmith to Jehovah's second-born. He had said that Lucifer was the most beautiful thing he had ever seen. The special forging of the knife was always a sore spot with Michael.

Without flinching, he said, "This is how you impale. But I want you to impale them through their bodies, up their privates and out of their mouths. As long as it's horrifying to the invading troops, do as you please. If you need to nail them to the spears for them to be five feet above the ground, then do so."

Saraqael said, "Master, that spot between our wings is tough and will hold a body. May we use that area as well?"

Lucifer smiled and said, "Indeed, I kinda like that idea. I just want them dead and about five feet from the ground. The perimeter must be first, but make sure a few make it out of the perimeter, just for the scouts, so they may see my uncaring for their dead. There is a platoon waiting for you outside, and they have the stakes that I want used. Have fun, because I know I would."

Waiting outside Lucifer's tent were ten seraphim guards. They looked at Raqael, knowing just by the size of her wings she was an archangel. She could sense the doubt in all their minds. One angel even said, "We have to take orders from this small and worthless woman?"

Raqael, without touching him, gave him such pain in his testicles he fell to the ground screaming. "Do any other of you doubt my power now?"

Still she could sense some still not convinced.

She conducted an even more torturous punishment. She went over to one of the guards and threw him to his knees. She slapped his face and bloodied his nose. He went flying to the ground, screaming in agony.

"Any questions or doubts now? Do not let my small stature fool you." She pointed out to all of them. "Do not push me. Remember, I am Lucifer's sister, and I ride the steed Famine. I will not tolerate any disrespect from any of you, because my wrath would be worse than my brothers'. Being female, we know exactly how to torture men."

After she had made her point, Saraqael appeared and could sense a change in his guards. They seemed to fear the fragile and gentle Raqael as well as they should. She had taken care of the apocalyptic steeds for all time, and although tiny, she was tough as nails.

Saraqael spoke. "Do you have the stakes asked for by Lucifer?"

They all nodded and began their journey. Arriving at the perimeter and unloading some of the dead, Raqael leaped off her steed and went straight to them. She was the first off her horse. Famine was given a bale of hay and bucket of water. The seraphim all looked at her, and she looked up with hatred in her eyes.

"Remember, you fucking morons, I can read your thoughts, and you won't even know that I did. I need not explain myself, as I am an archangel, so fuck you. Get the fucking stakes out."

She took two seraphim with her and pointed here, and here, there, and over there.

"Do not make it in a straight line. Scatter the bodies as if they died in battle. I can read you fucking pathetic excuses for warriors. I'll do the first one myself. Don't get used to me showing you the ravages of war. I will eventually have to tell my powerful brother of your incompetence. I was very gentle and kind at one point, and now with my master Lucifer's permission, I am changing into something truly grand, finally being unshackled from the divine. I am the harbinger of death and despair. I am relishing my new role, as my true nature is emerging."

Saraqael noticed a change in his sister; her wings were turning black and feathers were molting and falling off. He could see red leather emerging from inside. He shielded his mind as he thought, *By all that's merciful, she is becoming the female version of Lucifer.*

She grabbed a dead domination and threw it over her shoulder and began to walk away. The other seraphim thought she looked bigger, but how? She grabbed a stake, and with one mighty thrust, she rammed it between the toughest part that held the wings together. After he was impaled, she passionately kissed him and then spit on his face. The other seraphim, were horrified; some vomited, and one fainted.

Raqael looked at the one that passed out and took a piss on his face.

"Now, let's get this done. You fools best do it right."

She grabbed two more dominations and threw one over each shoulder. Saraqael could see her size and strength growing by the minute. She carried them about a mile out from the perimeter and skewered one through their privates and out of their mouth. She stepped back and thought, *This doesn't seem quite right.* She lifted the dead domination off and rammed the stake through the top of his head. She played in his gray matter till it sat just right. She saw how beautiful it all looked and did the same to the other domination. By the time she was finished creating her masterpieces, there were only two bodies left.

Saraqael stood there and said to his younger sibling, "Have you seen what you have transformed into? You are almost an exact replica of our brother Lucifer. However, being female, you will eternally be smaller. Yet I do have a feeling that your pent-up evil over the centuries has made you quite ferocious."

"Good brother, do you fear me? Do you want to fuck your sister and her beautiful leather wings?"

Saraqael, with no hesitation, said, "No, never. You are my sister, and the thought of that makes me sick."

Raqael continued, "You have no guts, no balls, no feelings, no glory. I can read you, my dear brother. Your mind is so weakened with your obsession of war that I just strolled in. It was so very easily done. I also have the ability of foresight. I see your betrayal of our brother, and he and I get thrown from heaven. I get tossed out for defending my beloved brother, courtesy of you and Raphael. But I am here to change the foreshadowed. It can be changed. Destiny is just a myth. You create your own destiny, and mine will be legendary. I never had the foresight of this transformation. I can tell you this much: these last two are mine, and I am flying to that ever-wretched and righteous Gabriel, and I am going to stake them at the front flap of his tent."

Saraqael begged her not to. As she flew away, a giant illuminated middle finger could be seen through her lathery wings. Raqael was connected to Lucifer; he only grinned at her devotion to him and her unwavering love for evil.

Raqael landed like a cat being tossed from a giant tree. Even the weighty spirits she carried with her made her look heavy, but she was not. She was quick in her action. She had no desire to be captured and tortured by the dominations. After this little field trip, she was certain she was to be Lucifer's second-in-command. The virtues could kiss her divine ass. She impaled the two angels, one through the wings and the other one through the brain. Happy with her work, she flew straight to Lucifer.

She entered Lucifer's tent, and he immediately noticed her transformation. He could see her red eyes, her wings, no fangs, yet he did notice her teeth. They shone in the moonlight and had become very sharp. Lucifer was excited at the sight of his sister. She was gorgeous. Then he realized that his eternal companion had to be his sister.

Lucifer spoke. "Motherfucker, motherfucking asshole, he gives you as my lifetime companion. A final slap in my face that you are so beautiful yet my sister. This makes me want to puke. You, Lord"—the word almost caught in his throat—"gave me the ultimate punishment. I fucking hate you! How dare you! Have you seen how fantastically wicked she is? I cannot bear this. When we rule your fucking kingdom, she will deal with the females and I with the men."

Raphael entered the tent and saw his sister Raqael standing at Lucifer's side. A twinge of jealousy ran through his heart. He spoke. "What happened to you? You are blood-soaked and . . . wait, I can see the brutal image. Nice work on the dead dominations. But remember, you stinking female, I have been on Lucifer's side from the beginning. You have been but a lowly stable maid. I love the transformation, but read me, sister. I am not afraid of you, and I can read you. You fear me as well as you should."

Raqael laughed and said, "You better read my thoughts again. I do not fear you. Do you think a lowly stable maid would have the power to transform like I did? I see you haven't transformed, brother. Is this because you still have love for Father? Or is it because you are weak and never had to restrain your feelings of inferiority. I have done it for centuries, and the seething anger that it left me with made me what I am today. Let's just say this is what I was meant to look like."

Raphael lunged at his sister, sword drawn. Raqael drew her sword. Lucifer smiled and loved that they were fighting over him.

Raphael spoke. "I am second-in-command, and you will treat me as such, bitch."

Swords at each other's throats, Raqael answered, "I have no doubt that in battle, the seraphim will listen to me and not anybody else but Lucifer himself. Read our brother, Raphael, and you will see who is second-in-command. Oh, wait, you aren't allowed into Lucifer's mind, but I am. I do believe I am the second-in-command now. You will have to take orders directly from me in Lucifer's absence. How does that feel, brother?"

Raphael, with a wounded look on his face, lowered his head and said, "I helped you throughout this confrontation in court, and this is how you repay me?" He then walked out of the tent, his sword dragging the clouds behind him.

Lucifer said to his sister, "If you ever speak to my brother like that again, you will feel my wrath." He took a deep breath and sighed loudly. "Yes, indeed, you are my second-in-command, but no need to rub it in."

"My next campaign in this slaughter is to send you, upon Famine, and your brother Saraqael on Pestilence. I need you to lead the seraphim army through the virtue camp. Your horses' powers will be at their height, I will make sure of that. I want the virtues taken alive. I want to torture them myself while Ramiel watches. Then I want you to ride through the dominations' side of the camp. Kill as many as you can, but try to bring me some alive, as I want my sister Uriel to watch as I personally kill her beloved dominations. Do not squabble with your brother. I need you both focused on this task. Do you understand me?"

Raqael said, "Yes, my dear king, I will do anything for you."

Lucifer grinned.

Saraqael appeared before Lucifer and Raqael and was shocked at his sister's appearance. She had grown so large her leather wings were large and bigger than his white feathers. He could sense the change in the command and said, "My sister, you have become quite large and beautiful."

She sneered at him and said, "Only Lucifer is permitted to speak to me in such a manner, but thank you."

Lucifer spoke. "You two will ride your apocalyptic steeds through the virtue camp and then the domination camp. Remember, the virtues are to be taken alive. Saraqael, you will ride into the virtue camp and spread a fast-moving disease of Pestilence's choice. Make sure it is swift but not deadly to them. You will need them sick to take the special forces of heaven's armies. Raqael, you will bind the virtues as they fall. Then you, my beautiful sister, will remount and take Famine and ride through the domination camp and begin to starve them, murder at your will. Saraqael, you will follow and bind as many as you can or kill them. I do want some dominations brought back alive. I have special tortures to inflict upon our prisoners."

The three mounted their beloved horses and walked up to the highest cloud point.

He then said, "I will watch from here. If it does not go the way I have instructed, I will take my anger out on you two. Do not fail me. Now go and have some fun."

CHAPTER 12

The Unleashing of Famine and Pestilence

Saraqael gave his gray-spotted stud a pat on the neck. The horse spoke. "I am ready to inflict such agony on these angels. I will not disappoint Lucifer or you."

They stepped down from the cloud peak and were lost in the mist. They waited for Raqael and Famine, and soon they appeared by their side. Saraqael couldn't take his eyes off his gorgeous sister. Her wings were outstanding, and her face had changed and was somehow less afraid and more aggressive. He thought of how sexy she would look naked with those wonderful wings.

She looked at her brother and said, "I know what you're thinking, and don't think of me that way. My heart and soul, my complete devotion belongs to another."

Saraqael read his sister and said, "Lucifer. I somehow already knew that."

They strode side by side through the mist and onto the cloud deck. Raqael looked back and up but could not see her beloved brother. She looked over at Saraqael, and he had a look of apprehension on his face. She reached out over between the horses, placing her hand on his shoulder, and said, "Brother, you must leave your fear behind you. Lucifer will be able to sense it just like I did. I may not love you as I love him, but you are still my brother, and I would sacrifice almost anything for your safety. I have such rage and hate in my heart for our Father leaving me to rot in those stinking stables for eternity. That is why I have changed. It's my hatred in its purest form. I can read you, and I know you are scared. Although it makes me sick that you fear the enemy, I will never let you fall. Feel better now, brother? I can sense that you are. You need not be afraid of anything. With me at your side and Lucifer at our back, we cannot fail. Are you ready, dear brother?"

Saraqael, with his soft eyes, looked at his sister and noticed her skin color had changed. She glowed like the fires at the camps yet did not illuminate. "Yes, dear sister, I am ready. Where has Raphael been? Do you know?"

From behind him Raphael spoke. "I'm right behind you. Lucifer has sent me to rage war against any of these pieces of shit that try to defend their fallen comrades." He looked at his sister and nodded.

She untrustingly read him and sensed no malice. Raphael had great malice and revenge in his heart for his sister but blocked her thoughts. He smiled at her and said, "I will follow you into the battle and will have both of your backs. No need for fear, dear brother. I ride upon War, the second most powerful apocalyptic steed"—he looked at his sister and grinned—"and he and I will never let you fail."

Raqael looked at both of her fellow warriors and said, "Let's do this."

Saraqael rode out on Pestilence first, trotting through the camp like he owned it. Every angel that came close to them immediately had an aggressively rapid form of smallpox hit them. This disease was Pestilence's favorite. They fell like stones within seconds, writhing in pain. The more he rode, the more he became aggressive and loved what he did. Although he felt Lucifer's power, this felt different, humiliating and disgusting with himself. He was sickened at the thought of inflicting such pain on an angel and vomited. He turned around and began shackling and binding the virtues that lay dying from smallpox. He had about seventy to take back to Lucifer. Raphael came bolting through the camp, and he and his steed, War, had a wonderful time dismembering angels and hacking off heads as they rode.

Pestilence and Saraqael began the journey back to the mountain-top. He hoped with all his heart that he did well enough for his powerful brother. Raqael strode through the camp of the dominations, and immediately they all began to shrivel and turn to skeletons with skin. Their wings began to fall off as they lay dying. She let her guard down for a brief second and was ambushed by four dominations. They seemed to be too large for Famine to affect them completely. She landed on her back, thrown and tackled from her horse. The dominations were so pleased at the chance to kill this bitch of an archangel. Swords drawn and up over their heads, they were ready to strike.

Suddenly, two were beheaded and two burst into pieces.

Raphael sprang from his horse and ran to his sister's side.

"Where the fuck were you? Conveniently late, I see. You fucking asshole!"

Raphael said, "I fucking saved you, you ungrateful bitch. Now get back on your stud. We have only a few captives. You killed too many. Lucifer will not be pleased. I can resurrect a few if you so desire."

Getting back up on her horse, she said, "Fuck you and your healing ability. Lucifer will always be pleased with his second-in-command."

Raphael felt like he had been slapped in the face, got back upon War, and helped his sister bind and bring the few dominations that were left alive.

The three were beside Lucifer upon the cloud peak. Lucifer saw his sister with her beautiful glowing yet unilluminated skin. He pulled her from Famine and kissed her passionately. He glared at Raphael. "You almost let her die. I am not amused by this at all. I am so grateful to you that you saved her and she is safe. Well done, brother, and well done, my beloved sister. How I wish we were born of different fathers. What presents have you brought me? Oh, my dear brother Saraqael, you gave them smallpox."

Pestilence interrupted and said, "No, master, that is my favorite disease to inflict, although I did make it a more rapid and more aggressive form." Pestilence bowed his head, and Lucifer rubbed his mane.

"Well done, my loyal and trusted mess-maker." He walked past all the captive virtues, and only one stared back at him. Confused by this disrespect, Lucifer pulled him out of the line of shackled slaves. "Why do you stare me in the eye? Are you just stupid or just too brave?"

The virtue spit on Lucifer's feet. Lucifer went into a rage and drew his sword. He cut off this bold yet stupid virtue's ears, then he blinded him with his talons. On his knees he begged for mercy.

Lucifer said, "Mercy . . . no, I don't think so." Lucifer then jammed his hand down this warrior's mouth and yanked out his tongue. Lucifer laughed as he said to the other virtues, "See what happens when you defy me? Not one of you is worthy to look me in the eye. That's why his eyes are gone. Defy me verbally, and I take your tongue. And finally, none of you are allowed to hear any response my rage gives you. You are all pathetic warriors fighting for a lost cause. Do you not see the four horses that I have released? You all know my power. I cannot read you, though, unless you are terrified. Your purity sickens me." When he said *purity*, he almost vomited. "Anybody want asylum and join us?"

No virtue took his offer.

Lucifer, fists clenched, said, "Fine. I will let this one live and stay in the stall with Death, who will toy with him for eternity."

Raqael was so enthralled by her brother's brutality that she wanted him even more.

This was the first time that Death had seen Raqael since he gave her a bite. He had sensed her but never looked at her unless necessary because she made him sick. The pale animal spoke. "Bitch, seems you have found your true calling. Huh? Kinda pathetic that you had this rage and pent-up anger in you for centuries but never unleashed it. You still make me sick."

Lucifer, losing his patience with his stud, said, "You better apologize, and I mean right now."

"No. This pathetic excuse for a submissive angel has made me sick for centuries. Now she is a mighty warrior for a few days, and I am to bow to her? Never! Master Lucifer, I would rather be put back in my stall than bow to this pathetic bitch."

Raqael leaped from Famine and went over to Death and said, "All these centuries, and now you finally see what I am capable of. You don't have to bow to me." After she said that, she put both her forefingers in the horses nose.

Caught off guard, Death did not see her shimmering, sharp white teeth, and she bit off half his ear.

She said, "Now we are even. Doesn't feel nice, does it?" Then she bent at the waist and hissed loudly, making the horse's mane blow back.

Unfazed, Death just stared at her. She turned and spit out his missing body part near his hooves. He finally bowed to her, his hatred seething through his stare. Pain was foreign to him, yet he could feel her power and connection to Lucifer. She was walking away when Death thought of revenge and how sweet it would be.

Raqael paused, knowing exactly what he was thinking, smiled, and continued to walk away.

Death knew that she sensed his hunger for vengeance; he just had to wait until the time was right.

CHAPTER 13

The Father Intervenes

Lucifer had the virtues and dominations together in a tent. The virtues were very ill and infecting the dominations, although not as quickly. They were all coughing and becoming ill.

The Almighty appeared in Lucifer's tent and spoke to his son, giving Lucifer a bit of a startle as he appeared. "I cannot help these sick and dying. They have already been exposed to Famine and Pestilence. You have not played fair, my son."

Lucifer drew his sword, and God, with arms open wide, said, "Stab me, boy. See what happens."

Lucifer rammed his sword into his Father's chest, and it felt like the best orgasm of his life. Jehovah looked into his deceitful son and pulled out the sword. "Boy, you cannot kill me. I am eternal. I am everything. I made everything. *I am the Almighty.*" He handed Lucifer back his broadsword and said, "Now may we talk like men, or may I hand down the judgment that was inevitable for you and your soul?"

Lucifer said, "What is in stress for my soul? Utter victory over your armies and eventually beheading you and becoming the leader of the new world order?"

Jehovah chuckled. "Yes, my son, but as always, you cheated. You brought the apocalyptic steeds Famine and Pestilence into your army. An unfair act, even for you. I am giving my armies protection from the effects of these steeds." With a divine sweep of his mighty hand, all armies had the resistance to Famine and Pestilence. "I will leave you War, as I have my War with Michael, and you may keep Death, as I have my own Death in Gabriel." Jehovah stepped back and sat at Lucifer's desk and put his feet up. "You have no idea that your destiny has been written by my Father's Father. I know what my own destiny is and yours. It's been shown to me with my foreshadowing ability. I know whom you can trust and whom you cannot. Will I reveal it to you? Never! Your brother Michael and you will finally have a personal battle that all of heaven and earth will feel."

The Almighty stood and paced in front of Lucifer's desk. "You think you are so powerful, Lucifer, yet you need to cheat. Cheaters never win, and winners never cheat. Lucifer, you are my son, but you and Raqael have become an embarrassment to your inner darkness and your evil being. Abominations, the two of you, untrusting and relentless. I do have a small bit of advice. Evil begets evil. Do not trust any of your generals. I am not trying to help you, just stating fact. They are conspiring to overthrow you and have become very evil, with the exception of Raphael and Saraqael, who still possess some good in them. It's apparent in their beautiful white wings.

"Raphael will never change fully. He is the healing angel as well as having the power of resurrection. Saraqael is terrified of you and your full potential for evil. He has been training his seraphim for all time. They are a mighty force and one that the dominations and virtues will need to be very careful with. You think that capturing and torturing these virtues and these dominations is going to fulfill any hole that you have in your heart? It never will. You will crave more and more of this as your power grows. I'm trying to tell you to just surrender and end this war. I cannot and will not intervene. This has to end up exactly as it has been planned since your creation."

Lucifer spoke. "Surrender? Are you in sane? I will never surrender. I plan on killing all the archangels with my own hands. Michael and I will indeed have a confrontation that he will epically lose. I will reign supreme over all that you created. I will desecrate every religious house that rests upon that planet. You destroyed it once with water. Now it is my turn to reduce it to ash and rubble. Your beloved humans will be my slaves. As for your angels, well, they either conform or die."

"Raqael will never leave your side, son. She adores you and will never betray you. However, you will need to make a choice soon, and very soon. A choice that will determine whom you will spend eternity with. Raphael has been by your side since he was first created. He also adores you. Remember that he holds the ability to enter other angels' minds and them not even knowing it."

Lucifer spoke and walked back and forth in front of Jehovah. "He will never penetrate my mind. I can feel you trying to right now. Are you weaker than him?"

Jehovah said with a smirk on his face, "No, son, I am the strongest of all. I am the Great Creator. You seem to forget that quite often."

Raphael entered Lucifer's tent and saw his Father. He couldn't believe that he was sitting there with Lucifer. "What is going on here? Hello, Father." Raphael, who always had resentment toward the Father, went to one knee and kissed the Father's hand.

Jehovah placed his hand on Raphael's head and said, "Hello, my son, it's been a long time since you have kissed my hand."

Lucifer, enraged, screamed, "What kind of treachery is this?" He ran over to Raphael and tackled him to the floor. "What are you doing? Are you trying my patience on purpose?"

Raphael whispered, "Get off me, brother. I am not betraying you. I am playing his game. If he trusts me again, I can read him easier."

Lucifer, with his hands around Raphael's throat, looked into his brother's eyes and could sense no deception. He doubted his feelings, as Raphael was very powerful as well. Was he only letting him see what he wanted to? Lucifer leaned down to his brother's ear, near his throat, and whispered back, "If you lie to me, you know what I will do. I will eat you alive. You will wish for death." He stood up and did not help his brother off the floor.

Raphael stood and spoke, "Brother, I have news about the latest campaign. I will come back later when you are alone. Send me a message, and I will come." Looking back at his Father, he said, "Goodbye, Father."

Jehovah smiled widely and could feel Raphael's sincerity. "Goodbye, son."

Jehovah winced as he could hear Gabriel screaming for him. He sounded like he was being murdered. His cries of anguish almost deafened the Almighty. Even Lucifer winced, as he could hear his brother's cries. Jehovah vanished, leaving a light mist behind. Lucifer grinned. He knew exactly why Gabriel was crying.

The Almighty appeared before Gabriel, Michael at his brother's side, sword drawn and held up, ready for battle. Gabriel was crying hysterically, pointing over the Lord's shoulder. Jehovah turned around and couldn't even believe what he was seeing. The sheer brutality of what he was seeing caught him off guard, and he stumbled back. He walked closer to the two dead domination soldiers impaled upon the stakes. Their ragged, decomposing insides already began to drop into the cloud deck. Giant globs of necrotic flesh hit with light, playful puffs of cloud. He sniffed the air. He walked around the abomination and back to the front.

He said, "Raqael was here. I can still smell her over the stench of these poor soldiers. Why she would perform such an act is beyond my comprehension."

He searched heaven for her and saw her. She spun around and screamed in her head at her Father. The high-pitched wail sent Jehovah flying back into his own mind.

Jehovah hugged his two sons and said to Michael, "I have scanned heaven, and there is this type of abuse of the dead across our home. I need some time to rid our home of this, before more cries are heard across our realm." He took Gabriel's face in his soft hands and kissed it gently. "My sweet gentle angel of life, such deaths and unholy sacrifices have never been seen in heaven. You are my gentle angel of death, my son. You have never handed down such tyranny. You are very merciful when you take a life."

Gabriel looked up at his Father, and he said, "I will not be merciful with Lucifer and his army when I get them, Father. They will pay for such disrespect for the dead and the living."

Jehovah stepped away from his loyal sons and said, "Stand back. I am about to remove the scourge of your brothers and unstable sister. This is just remarkable that an archangel is capable of such, such disgusting behavior. I can smell that she had no fear in her heart. I actually smell pleasure. It's nauseating."

He raised his hands, palms facing down. His eyes rolled over white, and although no breeze was felt, his hair and beard flew around his face in a whirlwind. He raised his bare foot and stomped on the cloud deck, large gusts of mist swirling around his feet and legs. Lightning streaked from his feet and rolled across the cloud deck. Thunder boomed shortly after. Michael and Gabriel were awestruck and could barely keep their balance as the Father raged. He stomped again, and the cloud deck began to turn a deep purple. Mother Nature appeared and grabbed Jehovah's hand, and together they once again would bring a terrific rain to the planet.

Mother Nature was floating above the cloud deck, her stark white hair that flowed and rose from her waist flying in all directions. She bellowed, "Where is your angel of water? Are we destroying this planet again?"

Jehovah screeched like an eagle. "No! I am ridding the clouds of the battle scars. There is too much carnage."

Together they released a worldwide torrential downpour of cleansing water. Mother Nature locked both hands with the Almighty, and they spun in a tornado. They had become one, god and goddess, bound by a common goal. The clouds visible to the humans turned black, the wind howled, lightning lashed at the ground, and thunder shook the very earth that humanity stood upon. Finally, Mother Nature released her grip and vanished.

Michael and Gabriel had never seen such a powerful being that was not archangel.

The Lord Almighty made the clouds fill with revitalizing raindrops. Michael and Gabriel went to their Father, who was fatigued, tears running down his divine face. He was barely able to stand, and his boys lifted him. He needed to complete the cleansing of heaven. Angel blood rained upon the planet, and the humans scrambled and prayed for mercy. Jehovah's mind was flooded; he sent the cries and pleading prayers to his boys. They both fell to their knees as the repentance of humanity filled their souls. He could see the blood of both armies begin to dissipate and hit the planet. The clouds were dark crimson and now a light red. He stomped again, and the storm raged, both in heaven and on the planet. Soon, they would be pink and then white again. The rain felt refreshing to all of heaven.

On the planet, the angel blood rained down in sheets upon the humans. The humans began to fear as they had only heard of rains like this before. That was the story of Noah and the destruction of the planet with water. They ran, panicked, fell to their knees, and called out to Jehovah. He had no time for them; he was too busy to show any comfort to the humans. The boys were getting the brunt of the repentant prayers. The blackened skies made it impossible for the covenant between God and man, the beautiful colors of a rainbow. The rains fell in great drops, both good and evil. As the angel blood fell, it soaked into the parched ground and pooled in underground reservoirs. Even though the blood fell mixed together, it separated like oil and water. Wicked and righteous blood could not mix. Even though removed from angels, the drops knew whom they belonged to in heaven. The droplets began to seek one another out. They slid and came together. The larger the pools became, the more the blood droplets felt as one. These pools would be sought after in the years to come by both the sinner and the saint.

Jehovah, exhausted, went back to his bedchambers, and as he lay in bed, he could smell angel piss. He sat up in his bed and sniffed the air. He began to laugh as he realized his amazing fountain had been pissed in by Raphael. He shook his head as he thought of Raphael standing on the edge, his wings touching the ground, relieving himself into his fountain.

Boys, he thought and, in his mind, cleaned his fountain and went to sleep.

CHAPTER 14

The Great Deception

"My beautiful mess! What the fuck happened? All the fucking clouds are white again."

Lucifer paced back and forth. He could feel sheer hatred for Gabriel. He knew this was his doing. He knew that he wasn't directly responsible but was somehow involved. Lucifer began to sweat and swoon. This feeling was foreign to him. He went back to his tent and spoke to the empty room.

"What is happening? My head, my head feels like it's going to explode."

Enraged by the feeling of helplessness, he began to drool and fight it. He rose and screamed. The angels, arch and normal, could all feel what Lucifer was feeling. Some smiled at his agony, and some wept.

He spoke again to the empty room. "I am Lord Lucifer! I will *not* surrender to anything or anyone. I am to lead this fucking place. Be rid of me, spirit."

In his own thoughts, he wondered if this was divine or something else.

Death began to grin widely as he ate his hay in his stall. He knew exactly what was happening to this being known as Lucifer. Death's grin widened as he could feel the remaining archangel being expunged. He kept eating and grinning, and a large blue glow began to emit through the boards of the barn. Death had finally had the appropriate rider.

The troops began to circle his tent, feeling an inevitable battle. Raqael tried to enter the tent but was denied by an unseen hand. The troops and generals all looked at one another nervously, not knowing what was happening to their leader. He stumbled around his tent, screaming.

Raphael appeared beside Raqael and said, "Let me try, sister."

She nodded.

Raphael entered the tent and screamed as well. He could feel the presence of pure evil in the room and thought his best friend, his leader, his brother was being attacked by something. Raphael ran to his brother's side, and Lucifer couldn't even hold his head up.

"That fucking Father of yours cleaned up my wonderfully terrifying scenes."

He pushed Raphael away and staggered out of his tent, Raphael close behind him. He was there to hold the lord up if he was to swoon; they could not afford to have Lucifer pass out in front of his troops. Blood dripped from Lucifer's hands as he held his head. Raphael finally got to him, holding his brother under the arm.

"I don't need your fucking help! Don't fucking touch me!"

Raphael didn't listen; he helped his brother, lifting his head, and this sight that met his eyes was surely fantastic. Raqael ran over and tried to release Raphael's grip on Lucifer's jaw. She again was denied by an unseen entity.

Raphael, still holding his brother's face, went to one knee and said, "My beautiful brother, you should see what I see." He drew his broadsword and said, "Look at yourself, my brother."

Lucifer grabbed at the blade of the broadsword, no care of the slicing consequence of grabbing the divine, mighty instrument of war. He pulled the sword toward his face and could see for the first time the symbol of what he would be known for throughout time. Past, present, and future generations would fear him even more. His lovely, gorgeous, wonderfully fantastic ram's horns burst through his skull. Lucifer was shocked at the display before him and gave a boot to his brother Raphael in the middle of his chest.

He called for Raqael and said, "This is finally my crown for my kingdom. I will be called Lord Lucifer from this moment on by all. Anyone who defies this order will be promptly beheaded. Behold, my kingdom and my queen."

Raphael, down in the cloud deck, thought out loud so anybody listening could hear. He said, "Queen? Fucking shit. Queen? Fucking little whore. Angel of perdition."

He plotted in is mind with the unseen entity that was surrounding their brother only moments before. This spirit told him about a great deception. It would be by this great psychic that he would learn of the spirit's name.

The spirit spoke again. "You four archangels are always so worried about one another you never gave us a second look. You may be Father's last-born, but remember, we, other archangels, wield special powers as well, brother. Search your thoughts and think, brother. I am the angel of the oceans and waters of the earth. I am the one that released the great flood. I will always protect thee as you protected me from Michael's abuse as children. Thank you. Hear my name. I am the great betrayer of Lucifer. I am your unknown ally. It is I, the one you never expected, the ever loyal. I am—"

And the psychic connection was broken.

Raphael screamed in the darkness, "Fuck!" Calming himself, he began to think about who it could be.

He could feel the presence of two, maybe three, that could be possible candidates. Raphael held these names close to his inner mind, his inner core. If Lucifer would get any indication of betrayal in his armies, it would mean the end of them all. Raphael closed his mind to everyone except himself for two days. He kept a slight opening for his mysterious visitor. He searched his mind and couldn't quite remember the archangel that released the great flood under the Father's command.

Raphael could feel somebody trying to enter his mind. Normally, he wouldn't let them in, but he knew it had to be from the entity that kept Raqael out of Lucifer's tent. This had to be the most he'd been excited about an invasion of his mind.

The spirit spoke. "So, brother, have you figured out who I am?"

Raphael spoke, only in his mind. "I think I have an idea. You spoke of me protecting you from Michael when you were a child. Only one other archangel was born near me. We would be about five years apart, am I right?"

The spirit spoke and said, "Yes. Hello, my dear protecting Raphael. I do love thee more than you know."

Raphael said, "Hello, my sweet brother Saraqael."

"My, most loyal armies are leaving this battlefield and defecting back to Father."

"Why?"

"Have you seen what he's become? He is truly evil in its purest form. That bitch sister of ours that he calls his queen is only after his power. Lucifer is a blind fool when it comes to her, and this unsteadiness with his distraction with her is going to be his downfall. I beg you, my dearest Raphael, to come with us and defect. I can feel your fear for him since his transformation, and I know deep within your soul you want to see him fail."

Raphael said, "I must think about this. How do you know that I won't tell Lucifer myself about this to fuel my greed for power as well?"

"Oh, brother, do you not think I read you before risking my life by contacting you? I knew that ever since he chose our sister over you, you harbored thoughts of taking your beloved steed, War, to Father and ask for his forgiveness. You are quite easy for me to read, brother, as I am a great psychic as well. You taught me how to harness it as children. Even as you were only two and I only seven, you were very strong, and you perfected your gift at an early age. How I used to laugh when you would mess with Michael's mind on my behalf."

Raphael spoke and said, "You must keep this secret with you at all times and never let anyone read you and find out. You must keep your walls up and guarded."

"Dear brother, you didn't even know that I was in your mind. I think I will be safe. I will leave a spot open for you always so we may talk, and I ask you to do the same for me."

Raphael, shaking his head, said, "I will, brother. Just be careful. I will have to think about defection with you, though. I have been with Lucifer from the beginning. I love you, dear brother. Bless you, and we will speak again very soon."

With that, Saraqael left Raphael's mind, giving him a lot to think about.

Raphael sat in the clouds for a moment and thought about Saraqael's offer. He could hear Lucifer calling for him and chose to remain seated and ignore Lucifer. The feeling of being independent felt wonderful to him. Lucifer bellowed again, and Raphael reluctantly disappeared and stood before Lucifer.

"What the fuck took you so long?"

"Sorry, brother, but I was in the middle of speaking to one of my commanders."

Lucifer stood and went over to Raphael, grabbed his shoulders, and said, "You will kneel before me, always, when you speak to me. I am more important than any of your commanders. When I call you, you better come immediately, understand?"

Raphael said, "Yes, Lord Lucifer."

Lucifer grinned and let his brother stand. "What do you want?" Raphael, keeping his mind closed off to Lucifer about his conversation with Saraqael, could feel his brother probing around in his thoughts.

Raphael spoke. "I was coming to make sure that you were all right after your ordeal this morning. Also, I wanted to ask what the plan was for the virtues and the dominations held captive."

Lucifer sat back down on his throne. "First off, there was nothing wrong with me. It was my final transformation. Second, I have plans for Uriel and Ramiel and our captives. We are going to take the battle to what you call Father. I am tired of these small insignificant battles. I want something grand to remove any hope that they may have. I want to smash their morale. Then I am going after Michael himself."

Raphael looked at his brother and said, "You and Michael? Can't wait to see you kick his ass. I will be feeding the steeds. When you want to have the meeting about the upcoming battle, just call and I will be here. I will not hesitate this time."

Lucifer nodded and motioned for Raphael to leave the tent.

Raphael stood in the barn and thought as he fed the horses. He confided in War what Saraqael was planning. War whispered, "What are we going to do, Master Raphael? I will go where you tell me and never speak ill of you, ever."

Raphael already knew this as he read the horse's mind before he confided in him. Raphael scratched the steed's large neck and whispered, "I'm not quite sure what we will do. I'm still trying to figure out what Lucifer will do if he finds out about anything that I've done. I wanted that fucking Raqael to die in battle. I did take my time getting to her. I don't know why I saved her. I should've let those soldiers tear her apart. But I acted as a brother should act and protected my sister. I also let my guard down, briefly, and that was how they found our camp."

War spoke softly and said, "I can't get close enough to Raqael, but you know who can? Death. Let me speak to him, and I will let him know when she is alone. Like the angels, we, too, can communicate with one another through our minds. He loathes her sheer presence around him. He only bowed down to her because Lucifer was there and he didn't want to provoke him and his anger."

Raphael said, "Perfect."

He began to brush the horse's mane, and War's eyes closed and he enjoyed every second of the sweet care.

When Raphael left, War began his conversation with Death. Their minds connected. He didn't tell him about Saraqael's plan to defect, only that he needed to get even with Raqael.

"She totally disrespected you, Death. You really need to find that fucking filthy angel alone and teach her a lesson."

Death completely agreed and said, "How will I know when she is alone?"

War answered, "Raphael and I are always roaming around camp, and when I see her alone, then you can move in. Unless, of course, you are with Lucifer. I can even open your lock if you are stuck in here. I am War, after all. You know, all's fair in love and war." War chuckled. Death just shook his head. "Maybe even convince Raphael to allow the rest of you to go out and walk through the cloud deck in that fenced-in area. Why it's fenced in, I don't know."

Death said, "Yes, yes. I like this plan. Oh, how I can't wait to get that fucking bitch alone. I know Lucifer gave his archangel generals protection from me. That means I can get close, very close. Thank you so much, War. This favor will never be forgotten."

Both horses smiled secretly inside their respective pens, and War couldn't wait to tell Raphael.

Walking back from the stalls feeling that he had planted a volatile seed in War's head, Raphael began to hum a song. Instead of walking back, he decided he would fly. It had been a long time since he was able to spread his beautiful wings and let the wind lick at them. It was fantastic. He soared like an eagle. Just outside of camp, he landed and tucked his wings back tightly against his body. Lucifer never wanted any of the archangels to show their white feathers; he seemed jealous of their beauty. Raphael walked slowly across camp and made sure the perimeter guards were all performing their duties. He also stopped by the tent that held the captive virtue and domination soldiers and gave them water. They begged and pleaded for Raphael to heal them. Although the thought did cross his mind, he could never get away with such a deception. Surely, Lucifer would be able to smell his healing on them. He had no choice but to refuse their begging cries. Before he left the tent, he peeked out between the flaps and scanned the camp with his eyes and his mind. He didn't want to be surprised by Lucifer or Raqael.

He could sense an intruder inside his head as he made his way to his tent. He spoke with his mind and said, "Who the fuck is in my head? Identify yourselves, or I will kill you where you stand."

The voice of Saraqael answered him and said, "We are leaving in twenty-four hours. I beg you, dearest brother, come with us."

"I cannot, and you know why."

Saraqael began to sob and said, "Please, Raphael, Lucifer will eventually sacrifice you on behalf of our cunt sister."

"Please, I must stay, dear brother, and as a gift to you and your armies, I am going to grant you a cloak until you are miles away from here. Lucifer will never know you are gone until it's too late."

Saraqael said, "Brother, if he finds out, you are surely dead. My gift to you is complete devotion, and I will speak to Father myself of how you are also a captive of Lucifer and helped us."

Raphael began to feel anger. *"I am no fucking captive!* I knew what side I chose. I am now beginning to wonder if this was all worth it. Safe travels to you, and let me know when you make your exodus. Then and only then will I grant you the cloak. Goodbye, brother. I love you."

Without hearing Saraqael's response, Raphael shut him out of his mind and began to cry.

Raphael knew he wasn't going to be able to sleep and made his way back to the stables. He had no desire to fly this time; he slowly walked with his wings dragging behind him and his head hung low. He just wanted to be near his beloved steed, where he could be himself. He just wanted a friend, and he knew War was his only one left here.

As they exited the barn, War began to trot toward camp. Raphael pulled the reins the other way and said, "Not tonight, my friend. I just need to clear my head and ride."

War was thrilled to hear that he would be away from the smell of that camp. "Indeed, sire, let's ride."

Raphael and War rode hard, and with his wings out and flowing behind him, he felt like a new angel. He remembered the days of cruising the corridors of heaven with his wings partially out as the constant breeze played with his feathers. They paused just outside of the camp, and Raphael dismounted. He came to the front of the steed and held the horse's head in his massive archangel hands. He hugged the horse's giant neck and snapped back, a look of confusion filling his eyes.

"What are you doing? You are up to something. With our minds so close, I could actually sense something in your mind."

War's eyes were closed, and he did not hear Raphael. He was too busy sending all his telekinetic energy to the barn to release Death. When the latch was released, War opened his eyes and said, "Raphael, my rider, my best friend, my confidant, look to the left and tell me what you see."

Raphael scanned the left side of the perimeter, and to his shock, he saw Raqael alone and keeping a vigil over the camp's torches. Raphael spoke to War. "Where were you in your mind? You left briefly. What happened?"

War began to grin a very human grin and said, "I have just released Death to seek his vengeance on that masquerading ally of Lucifer's. That bitch bit off part of his ear. She needs to learn a very painful and very needed submissive lesson. She forgets that we are the four horses of the apocalypse. Lucifer himself begged Father to create us. She has no idea that with embarrassing Death as she did, she only awoke a sleeping giant within Death. He is never merciful, so I don't even know what he has planned. I do know that she cannot kill him and he cannot kill her. They would have to explain their actions to that pathetic Lucifer. I know that we were not granted the second-in-command. I also know that it pisses you off. I also know—sorry for sounding so arrogant with you, my master—that you hate her as much as my more powerful brother. He and I are the greatest of Lucifer and Father's bringers of doom, yet we were treated poorly by that fucking excuse for an angel. She only took care of Famine because of the way he looks. He, in turn, returned her love, and that is why that is her steed. How ironic that the weakest angel and the weakest stud are together. I am scanning my feeble-minded brother as we speak."

War closed his eyes, and when he opened them, he was laughing. "You'll never believe where his is."

Raphael began to smile, a smile he hadn't had on his face since this mess all started, and said, "Tell me now!"

"The fool is standing by the window of his stall and looking at the fucking cloud deck. He is wondering what stars are. Ha ha ha ha ha! He never even noticed Death leaving, and that giant brother of mine shakes the deck we stand upon as he walks. What a fool! They deserve each other."

As War was speaking, Death appeared beside them, and Raphael went over and scratched the horse's nose and said, "Hello, Death. Why are you out?"

Death was taken aback by the kindness shown to him. Never in his centuries had anyone touched him except Lucifer, and it felt wonderful. Death looked at Raphael with a bit of concern in his eyes from the affection shown to him by an archangel. War spoke telepathically to his brother and said, "No need for concern. He is privy to our plan in part. But again, with our being horses of the doom of mankind, he doesn't know the full agenda."

Death spoke aloud and said, "Where is the cunt? I can smell her . . . oh, wait, there she is." A huge almost-childlike glint in his voice, he said, "I'll be right back. Please stay and watch. This is going to be fun." Death looked at the archangel before him; although not Lucifer, he knew of Raphael's power and bowed his head slightly to him as he trotted by him.

Death almost floated over the cloud deck. He was stealthy in his movements. He didn't want one sound to come from his hooves. He found a nice, dark spot beside a tent where the torch had gone out. This tent was three tents away from the outskirts of the perimeter. He needed more darkness. He quietly went to the other tents and puffed out those torches as well. A sideways smirk came across his face, and he knew that she was his. Although an archangel, she could not produce fire with her hands. That luxury was only granted to Lucifer. He made his way to the middle of the darkness and waited silently beside one of the tents. Her scent filled his nostrils, and he wanted to vomit. Yet he held on to his constitution and did not. She drew closer and closer, lighting torches from one to the other. He thought he was going to burst; he controlled his breathing as he could feel the anticipation of confronting his centuries-old adversary. The excitement that filled his body, he could barely wait. He had to bide his time and wait for the right moment to strike.

An unforeseen nuisance became apparent to Death. The bitch was relighting torches with the one she carried. He spoke to War telepathically and said, "Do you think your rider, your best friend, and dare I say, a brother to you can help me out and douse the flame from the torch she carries and the ones on either side of the one she stands before?"

The answer he got was incomprehensible to Death; it was the voice of Raphael. "Steed, I am the great psychic of anything ever created, and yes, I will help you, but I am going to have fun with this as well. Be patient. You will get your vengeance, and I know you are wondering why I could penetrate your mind as I am not an animal. I will explain it all upon your return."

Death was annoyed by the winged interloper into his mind, but help was help. Anything to achieve his ultimate goal of confronting Raqael. He would deal with the intrusion of Raphael when he was done with his target. He thought, *These fucking angels are such easy targets.*

Raqael lit the next to last torch, and as she went to light the last of her duties, her torch went out, as did the one she just lit. Confused and a little scared, she looked around and then stopped. She could feel somebody or, better, something around her. She anxiously peered through the darkness and around herself. She saw two glowing eyes emerge from the darkness. All fear and uncertainty left her heart, and she said, "Lucifer, you gave me such a start."

Death grinned and said, "I'm not Lucifer, *bitch*! I have been waiting centuries to find you alone." He spat out his own dismembered ear part that she had bit off, and it landed by her feet. Death hissed, "Is this what makes you feel powerful? Is this what makes you think you think you are superior? This fucking part of my ear, *cunt*? Let me show you superiority. You are about to learn a very painful lesson, you power-hungry excuse for an angel! You should be human."

Death emerged a bit from the darkness, and she could see the humongous head of a horse she never thought to see face-to-face again alone. Death spoke. "Oh my, without your beloved Lucifer by your side, you are just that fucking miserable excuse for a stall mucker, aren't you, bitch?"

Death victoriously sniffed the air and came closer. His massive pale first half of a body became visible to the terribly frozen Raqael. She was trembling, and Death just grinned even wider. Before she knew it, Death lowered his large head and was nose to nose with the angel he had always wished to confront.

"How does it feel, bitch? I know you are in total fear of me." He snapped at her face and nose. He obviously gave her time to react.

She began to lose it and grabbed at her face and neck and cried out, "My face, my beautiful face! You better never bite my face, you fucking animal!"

Death said, "Oh my, courage all of a sudden. Raqael, you are truly an enigma. But I do feel your shroud of confidence beginning to fade." He snorted onto her face, and snot and hay went flying all directions. She winced and wiped from her face quickly the glob of goo. She was about to vomit. Death let out a large laugh and said, "Did I just make you almost vomit, cunt? I can feel the bile in the back of your throat. Let's see what else I can inflict upon you but not really give you much marking. Lucifer would skin me alive, as well as you, if we left any marks on each other. I am not afraid of you, whore. You can mark me all you want."

He began to circle her like a shark. His large haunches were at face level to Raqael, and he flicked his tail at her. A stinging sensation began to fill her psyche. She reached up and could feel the warm, pulsating blood spilling from the open gash on her cheek.

Death spoke. "It's just a flesh wound. It will heal by the time the sun rises. Oh, how I want to inflict such damage to you."

He began to circle again. He could feel Raqael's fear and fed upon it. He grinned and saw her gorgeous, leathery wings. He reached his gigantic head up and bit the top of her wing by her shoulder. She recoiled, fell over, and screamed in agony.

She bolted upright and screamed, "I will tell my brother of your insolent behavior!"

"Really, bitch? You would risk being unmasked in front of your master? You disgust me! Your threats mean nothing to me."

Raqael looked at Death and knew he spoke the truth. Lucifer would surely impale her, as she did so many, if he found out her true loyalty. Although she loved him, she wanted his power and his glory. She wanted his children to be in her womb and have him subservient to her.

Death began to move again. He was as swift as he was giant. He was at the other side of her face in seconds. He had his head down and looking at her feet. The armor the archangels wore forgot about the feet. They were as bare as the day they were created, and Death took full advantage of that. With his mighty size and weight, he stomped on her foot, and a spark of fury left his hoof. She screamed again, this time sobbing and begging for mercy.

Death said, "That's a good girl. I always knew you were nothing but a slave to me and my brothers back at the barn. Now that I have achieved this small but so satisfying piece of victory over you, I will sleep well tonight. Lucifer will think I am a new stud. He will wonder why I am looking like the glorious Death steed again. I will close my mind to him, as you better do as well. You don't want another visit from me, do you?"

Raqael, bruised and battered from her confrontation with this mighty steed, just nodded.

"Good, now remember this, bitch, I am Death, and no one—and I mean no one—is more powerful than I." Chuckling, he slowly backed into the darkness, his fiery eyes never leaving the sneaky Raqael.

CHAPTER 15

Another Deception

Death sprang from Raqael's shuddering and terrified body and went for the cloud hills. Sitting up there was that fucking archangel that invaded his mind and his beloved brother War. Death thought, *Hope they saw everything I just did. It was fantastic, a true testament to my power.* Death sprinted up to the hill and was abruptly confronted by his brother. Death slid on the cloud deck. Sparks and fire flew from his hooves as he tried to stop from crashing into War.

Behind War stood Raphael.

Death spoke. "You are blocking me from my prey, brother."

War reared up onto his back legs and said, "You will *never* touch my rider!"

Death stood with his head cocked sideways and was in complete confusion. He spoke to his brother aloud. "What the fuck?"

War spoke and was on all fours again. "Brother, we have been together since the womb. I love you more than you know. However, my rider, Raphael, just helped you. This how you repay him? He needs to explain a few things to you. Do not touch my rider, brother, as we are connected more than you know."

Death spoke, sarcasm in his tone. "Tell me what I don't already know, brother."

War turned his back on Death and said, "You will listen to this archangel whether you want to or not. He will explain."

Raphael came around his trusted steed and rubbed his mane. He began to speak, crossing in between War and Death. Pacing back and forth, he wove his tale, one that would leave Death's head reeling.

"I know you hate me, Death. Quite frankly, I don't care. I am the one that just helped you get your sweet vengeance. If you want to test me, then go ahead. Before you do, remember, I am an archangel and I am Raphael."

Death lunged forward a bit to scare Raphael. The archangel stood his ground and, to Death's surprise, grabbed the steed by the ear and twisted his head around. Death shouted, "How the fuck can you touch me? You should be dust. What is going on?"

Raphael chuckled and spoke. "Lucifer didn't tell you? He gave all of us archangels on his side and his generals on the field of battle immunity from you."

Death spoke through gritted teeth and said, "Liar! Release me now and let me see your face."

"I will release you. Remember, Death, you are a mere horse and I am an archangel. Learn your place." He released Death's ear slowly and met the horse's eyes. The fire in the steed's skull would kill an angel or human on sight. Raphael just stared into them. He spoke. "See, Death? I am not dead. Now will you listen to what I have to say, or will you run with your tail between your legs?"

Death snorted and nodded. Although very annoyed, he wanted to hear this tale that this brave yet stupid archangel was about to weave.

Raphael grinned and sat upon an uprising in the clouds. His large yet bloodstained white wings played with the breeze. Death sneered at him; such a display of self-serving made Death ill. He rolled his eyes and listened to Raphael.

"You want to know why I can read you? I can feel the question ever present in your mind. See? I am very powerful with my psychic ability. You didn't even know I was in there. I can read you for two reasons. One, because I have the strongest mind in all of heaven and, two, I ride War."

Death was about to charge the archangel again when Raphael stood and said, "Go ahead! Do it! I am not afraid! You will lose."

Death backed down and stood beside his brother. Raphael stared in Death's eyes and said, "I thought not. I want you to know I have no ill feelings toward you and you should have none toward me. You think I invaded your mind. I did not. I ride War. Without Death, War is minimal, and without War, Death is minimal. Do you understand?"

Death did not quite grasp what the archangel was saying.

Raphael sighed and said, "Let me explain. Without Death on the planet, War is imminent. Without War, Death is minimal, a mere side effect of life. Gabriel could handle that."

War and Death looked at each other in amazement. Death thought this angel actually had a brain and was quite intelligent.

"I ride upon War. This makes me very attuned to his mind. As the greatest mind in heaven, it was easy for me. As you two are connected, we three are connected."

Death spoke. "Whoa, whoa, Lucifer rides upon my back, and I have yet to feel him in my mind. Will he try to read me? What if he finds out about what I did to Raqael?"

Raphael felt what he had not expected, a twinge of fear in Death's heart. "Lucifer is immune to my power. I will have no defense against him. Sweet Father of all created, put me back in my stall. I want no more part of this."

Raphael began to giggle internally and walked over to Death. He put his hand on the mighty steed's mane and stroked it kindly. "Death, you need not be afraid, as I am with thee. We three are connected. There is no room for a fourth. Do you understand?"

Death shook his head in an irritated manner and spoke. "What do you mean *we three?* I am fucked. Lucifer himself had Father create us upon his request. We are all the same mare. He will sense that I betrayed him. I am a bit apprehensive of the thought of confronting him, but I am not afraid."

Raphael spoke, walking around the two brothers. "You need not feel apprehensive at all. I will help you so my brother will not be able to penetrate your mind fully. He will think he has gotten all he can from you, yet he will not be able to penetrate the barrier that I will teach you to build."

Death looked at the archangel with unforgiving eyes, yet he was vulnerable and spoke. "Please teach me. I would like to enjoy the inevitable apocalypse to come for mankind."

Raphael showed Death how to build the wall inside his mind. He showed him brick by brick how it was to be done. While building, Raphael said, "Now I will give you a blessing of each brick and the mortar that holds them." Raphael raised his hands, his eyes closed. He was inside Death's head. "Fear not, dear brother of the resistance. I grant thee immunity from Lucifer's mind. I give thee the power over the probing influence that is known through the land as evil. I am the archangel Raphael, and I grant these to you, one of the apocalyptic steeds. I grant this to you, Death, the brother of my steed, therefore, my brother as well." Raphael lowered his hands and said to War, "You two four-legged beasts are more brothers to me than my own flesh."

War said to Death, "Your wall is complete, blessing and all. We need to get back to the stalls. Your rider will be coming for you soon. We do not need any unwanted attention as to why you are out. The scrutiny would be severe from your rider, and it would put both of our lives in jeopardy. Lucifer is not a stupid angel. We both know this. Please be careful, brother. I will die for you and take my rider with me if necessary."

Death just looked over his great shoulder to his brother and, with his head hung low, entered his pen. He had never felt such a pang of regret in his life and did not embrace it. He knew that he needed to put this out of his mind on the other side of the wall.

Raphael, feeling better than he had in weeks, began his stroll back to camp. He had a lightness to his step. He could feel his brother's presence around him. He looked behind him, and there stood Lucifer, arms crossed, and read his brother. He spoke. "Where have you been? On one of your walks to clear your mind, brother?"

Raphael answered, "Yes, brother. I was just out thinking and checking the forest for intruders."

Angered, Lucifer slapped Raphael across the mouth and hissed, "You will call me, Lord Lucifer, understand?"

"I understand, but I will never call you Lord Lucifer. Your power has gone to your head. I'm your brother. I was your second-in-command and your biggest confidant. I see this title of mine has been given to another. Yes, I was angered, but I remembered the ultimate goal of all this. To see you sit upon the throne of heaven and rule."

Lucifer scanned his brother again. "You need not call me Lord. After all, you're right, you are my brother and I do love you."

Inside Raphael's mind as he stood beside Lucifer, he could hear Saraqael's voice. "It is time, brother."

Lucifer could sense something as he said, "Did you feel that? Like a strange feeling in my head."

Just then, Raqael appeared, and Raphael said with a glint in his voice, "Well, there's your odd feeling, brother." And he secretly laughed to himself.

With Lucifer distracted, he could answer Saraqael. "No, brother, you do this alone. As I said, I will give you a cloak of invisibility to disguise you from Lucifer. Let me know when you reach the outskirts of the forest, and your cloak will be gone. I am descending the cloak as we speak."

Raphael closed his eyes, and a light mist began to engulf Saraqael and his defecting armies.

Lucifer walked with Raqael toward the camp and left Raphael where he stood. Lucifer stopped and squeezed Raqael's hand hard enough to make her wince. "Tell me what happened last night. I can read you, bitch, and something rattled you. Tell me, as you know of my punishments. It will be brutal for betraying the crown."

Raqael spoke through tears. "He said he would kill me, my lord. I tried to build a wall around the memory to keep you out."

Lucifer, enraged, slapped Raqael over and over across her face. "You wait till I get you to my chambers, you conniving little cunt! I knew I should've chosen Raphael as my second."

With that, Lucifer dragged Raqael toward his tent. She was resisting and crying the entire time.

Once back at Lucifer's tent, he lifted Raqael over his shoulders and threw her inside. He stomped over to her and grabbed her by the hair. "Ready to tell me yet, bitch. Let down that unforsaken wall and let me in. I am lord and master to you. You will keep no secrets from me."

Raqael shook her head. "I will never speak of last night. Ever."

Lucifer calmly said, "Fine then, cunt, I will beat it out of you until you lie unconscious and I can stroll right through your mind."

Raqael began to shiver.

Lucifer spoke. "Oh my, are those horse hooves I hear in your head? Which one, bitch?"

"He said he would kill me in battle and make it look like an accident. Please, my lord, I beg you, please do not make me reveal the assailant."

With that statement, Lucifer leaned back and, with one mighty backhand, threw Raqael across the room. Blood stained the walls of the tent, and she screamed in agony.

"You think that hurt? That was nothing compared to what your defiance has brought out in my rage."

Raqael cowered in the corner and begged Lucifer to be merciful.

"Mercy? What in the fuck is that, bitch?" Lucifer went over to his hanging torture devices and grabbed a large flogger. He walked over to Raqael, slapping it on his thigh as he went. He beat her and whipped her until she finally relented.

"I will tell you! Please, lord, please stop."

Lucifer smiled and beat her a few more times. "Tell me, bitch, tell me now!"

Raqael tried to stand, and Lucifer kicked her in the chest and said, "Have I given you permission to stand?"

Raqael shook her head.

"No, I didn't think so. Oh, my ever-loyal steed, Death, did this to you?"

Lucifer beat Raqael five more times, and she begged, "Why, master, why?"

"Because you, ungrateful bitch, you deserve it for trying to keep something from me. I know all and will always know all, even if I have to beat somebody to get it. Understand, you filthy cunt?"

She tried to rise again and again.

Lucifer said, "You will stay there until I deem you worthy of standing again, understand, whore?"

Lucifer went over to his large desk and put his feet up, satisfied with the day's events. Now what to do with Death? He pondered the question in his mind and decided he would do nothing for now to his ever-loyal steed. He needed this horse in battle. He possessed great power over life and death. He would pay for his insolence eventually. When this war was over, he would geld this mighty male steed. How ferocious would he be with no balls! Lucifer grinned and was completely satisfied how the war was going.

Chapter 16

Unforeseen Allies

Inside God's bedchamber, he could sense an intrusion beginning into his homeland. He spoke to the virtue guards and said, "I do believe that my son has lost his mind. Lucifer's arrogance with his power has finally made him a bit insane." God bellowed, "Michael, Gabriel, here now."

His loyal sons appeared before him and bowed their heads. "Yes, Father?"

"I want you to order the virtues to outflank the seraphim army that is coming our way. They have already breached our territory. I want you, my ever-loyal sons, to protect the very wall of heaven itself. You need to hang back and protect all that live here." God paused and said with a wrinkled nose, "Your brother Saraqael is with them. I want him taken alive." He looked at his mighty Michael and said, "Understand?"

Michael bowed his head again and said, "Your wish is my command."

"I want the virtues to be silent and deadly as they outflank the seraphim. They must start at the back and take as many as they can. Their numbers are great indeed. I do believe it is almost two-thirds of their army. I sense two regiments of six hundred each. They need to dwindle as they get closer. You have your orders, now go, my sons, and all my blessings to you and your fighting forces."

God sat back and thought, *That number, I always knew, would come into play. Two regiments of six hundred each and six hundred back at camp. Three sixes, 666. My vision is coming to pass.*

The virtue army set out, their wings strapped to their sides, their swords ever at the ready. The piano wire they all carried was wrapped around one hand. Tactics that Ramiel had taught them only to be used in extreme circumstances. Being angels of virtue, they were God's special forces. They were honed as stealthy and lethal predators. Ramiel taught them to face their enemy and draw swords. This situation, however, called for different tactic, again ones that Ramiel had taught them. They stopped and gathered in a circle before they outflanked the intruders. They bowed their heads and said, "For our leader, will we save you our lord and teacher."

With that being said, they went silently in different directions, some at the back of the seraphim, others at the side, to protect their brothers. Piano wire drawn taut, they began their assault. One by one the seraphim fell dead silently and without one pang of surprise. They advanced their assault, leaving dead seraphim soldiers behind them. Not caring of the mayhem they left in their wake, they continued their assault until a virtue had a wing almost amputated by a very aware seraphim soldier. They were trained not to cry out and ask for help; however, another virtue saw this and ran to his side. This was an abomination to the virtue code. They had been discovered. They were at blade tip by the seraphim, and rather then being captured, they rammed their swords into themselves and had a "beautiful" death.

The other virtues could feel deep in their souls the death of two comrades. They vowed no seraphim would live to see the dawn. The battle that ensued was bloody and brutal. Wings here and there, heads strewn about, once-white wings stained with the blood of the fallen. Swords ramming in, and the seraphim were losing at an alarming rate. The virtues finally killed all seraphim except the ones surrounding their leader.. He was engulfed in seraphim soldiers, yet Michael was there behind their leader.

What is this treachery? Michael has forsaken God? Let us kill him where he stands!

They were confused, and in that split second, they were vulnerable, until Michael stepped down and spoke. "Ramiel's beloved army, I assure you this traitor is my captive and we will have fun torturing him."

Gabriel appeared beside his mighty brother and said, "Brother, no torture. He came to us for a reason. Remember, my brother, this is God's plan, not yours, not mine. You are not the divine, only Father is. Your brawn has gotten the best of you. Resheath your sword, my brother, and let's go talk to Father, with Saraqael in chains, of course."

His very mighty and large hand at the hilt of his sword, ready to strike at a moment's notice, Michael said, "You may chain him as much as you want, but my broadsword will be at his throat at any sign of betrayal. You make one move toward Father, and my divine weapon will impale you."

Gabriel smirked at his brother Michael, staring at Gabriel, and grabbed the hilt of his divine weapon. "Michael, please, you really have no power over me. I am the angel of life and death." Gabriel chuckled.

Michael drew his broadsword and put it to Gabriel's throat and said, "Really, motherfucker? If I kill you, you will die. Remember, I am Michael, and I kill everything in my path."

Saraqael said, "Go ahead, you big dumb sword-wielding moron! Kill him and see what Father does to you."

Michael, growing more impatient, said, "Shut your fucking betraying mouth before I ram my sword down your throat! My presence will be with Father at all times. You try anything, and you will perish by the tip of my sword."

They entered God's chambers, and the Almighty was sitting with his back to the door. "Hello, my sons."

Gabriel unchained Saraqael, and he rubbed his wrists in pain. Saraqael went for the hilt of his sword, and Michael moved with the swiftness of a jaguar and threw Saraqael to the floor, his mighty broadsword at Saraqael's throat. "I will fucking behead you. How dare you draw your sword against Father? Do you not realize I will kill everything and everyone that threatens Father?"

The Lord spoke. "Michael, let him finish. Put down your sword."

Saraqael, with a small gash in his throat, began to speak. "My mighty yet stupid brother, I was surrendering my sword to Father. However, I do admire your loyalty."

Michael, with a sneer upon his face, said, "Loyalty? You speak of loyalty, yet you sided with Lucifer?" Michael stepped back, his eyes never leaving his brother Saraqael, and went back to the Father's side.

Saraqael approached with Gabriel at his side and presented the Almighty his sword. He gave it to him hilt first. Michael only sneered at the meaningless gesture. He still didn't believe his brother. "I have news from the front, Father. Lucifer is planning to bring the battle to you. He has lost two regiments of six hundred each and only has six hundred left. He knows of Raphael's betrayal, and Raphael and his stud, War, are on their way here as well. Lucifer found out that Raphael cloaked us so we could make a clean getaway to come to you so we could join you." He bowed his head, and sweat dripped onto the floor.

Michael noticed it immediately, and his distrust only grew stronger.

The Lord spoke. "Michael, I want you to go meet your brother Raphael as he emerges from the forest. I am giving you a direct command: do not harm him at all. You will need Raphael and his powers more than you think."

Michael, ever loyal, bowed his head and left God's chamber, only before kicking Saraqael in the ribs as he left.

Michael mounted his horse and set out for the outskirts of the forest. He sent out a mental message to his brother. Raphael, a bit confused by hearing Michael's voice in his head, spoke telepathically to his brother. "What the fuck do you want? Is this one of your pathetic traps for me?"

"No. Father has sent me, and we know of your deception toward Lucifer with the cloaking of the seraphim army. We need your powers, brother. You will be able to let us know when and where the enemy makes camp."

Raphael answered, "No repercussions from the pain I inflicted upon you as children? And no punishment for my deception and siding with Lucifer?"

"We will get to that after the war, dear brother."

Raphael made War race as fast as the horse's feet could carry him. Raphael's wings were out to help the propulsion. Flames sprang from War's feet as he knew the importance of getting there as soon as possible. War heard the entire conversation between the brothers as Raphael allowed him access. They emerged from the forest, and there, waiting, was Michael on his massive steed.

War thought, *Wow, that horse could be one of the apocalyptic steeds. He is huge! I have never seen an archangel that large in all my centuries. He must be the greatest warrior in all of heaven.* War wrinkled his nose and thought, *I know that horse, that is my brother of the womb.* War was so confused he swooned and almost fell over.

Raphael kept his steed upright and rubbed his neck. "I'm sorry, my ever-trustful friend. Yes, that is your brother that my brother sits upon. Father made five horses, four for my brother and one for himself. You know Father. It's a wings-in-the-air and fly-with-the-eagles life. He had to make him. Let me introduce you to your brother. His name is Rapture. Michael is the one that has taken care of your brother for the centuries."

War began to rear and buck against Raphael in a defiant move; Raphael had to use a strong hand and restrain War.

War began to resist Raphael, who was his friend and mental love. War was confused and blamed it on Rapture. Raphael was also present in War's head and could hear the conversation between the two horses.

Rapture spoke. "My friend, my love, one of the apocalyptic steeds, how I envied the four of you for centuries. Alone in my stall, knowing you all had one another, I had but Michael. Although he was a wonderful master and rider, I longed to be with my brothers. This is not easy for either of us, brother. Are you really that unsure that you don't trust me?"

War spoke. "Of course I trust you—no, really, I don't trust you. I trust your rider, Michael."

War went over to Rapture, not caring of the archangel that rode him. He spoke out loud as he didn't know this horse. But before he could speak, Rapture entered his mind and said, "I am the firstborn of quintuplets, and Father took me as his own. I have longed to meet my brothers, yet my rider, Michael, kept me silent with his mind."

War reared up in front of Rapture and tried to intimidate him. Raphael leaped off his mighty steed and said, "If I can be on the same side as my brother Michael, you can be on the same side as your newfound brother, Rapture. Do we not agree?" Raphael was nose to nose with his ever-loyal stud. If War was to be defiant, Raphael would mount him and go with it. But luckily, they were in accord.

"Father wants to see you, Raphael."

"Yeah? No shit. You forget of my ability to read minds, fool."

Michael irritated at his smarter brother and, jealous of his ability, only made Raphael smile.

"Hello, Father. I am here to surrender to you. My brother Lucifer is drunk with power and has become an abomination of an angel. Raqael has also transformed into a smaller female version of him. His hatred and rage have grown by leaps and bounds. He grows stronger by the day. I am truly frightened that heaven will fall to him, and that is why I am here."

The Almighty chuckled and said, "Heaven will not fall to my son. I will destroy all of it before that happens. I now have my four angels that I have seen in my prophecy. Saraqael, bring me your seraphim, and, Michael, as the temporary leader of the dominations, I want them in my chambers now. Understand, boys?"

They both bowed their heads and did as told. "You, my every-loving and tender Gabriel, bring me the remaining virtues to my chambers as well."

Gabriel spoke. "Father, they all loathe one another, and there may be a bloody confrontation."

"Not in front of me, there won't be. Now go."

Raphael was alone with the Father. "Raphael, I know, with your stealth and ability to cloak yourself, I want you to go and release Ramiel and Uriel from Lucifer's prison. Bring my children back home to me. You can do it. I have complete faith in you."

Raphael bowed his head to the Father and said, "Yes, my Lord, I will do as you wish."

Raphael mounted War, and the horse did not want to go back to Lucifer's camp. Raphael patted his mighty companion and said, "Remember, I have the ability to cloak us."

Raphael could hear War's voice in his head. "Why, sire, are we going back?"

"We are to rescue my brother and sister Ramiel and Uriel."

War shuddered all over and spoke telepathically, a sense of fear in his voice. "As you wish. I am War and nothing scares me, but I am a bit concerned if Lucifer finds us."

Raphael smiled and said, "Easy, my friend. He will never know we are gone until it's too late."

War and Raphael sprinted back to Lucifer's camp, fire at War's hooves and Raphael's wings out. They were at the edge of Lucifer's camp.

Raphael cloaked himself and War. He began to tread lightly to the prison tent. He entered, and Ramiel said, "Lucifer, you pathetic excuse for an angel, you wait till I get out of these chains, and you will be mine."

Inside Ramiel's head was a voice he hadn't heard since his capture. "Sshhh, it is I, Raphael, and I have turned against Lucifer. I am here to save you and bring you back to Father."

As soon as the chains were broken, Ramiel grabbed Raphael by the throat and read him. He sensed no deception and said, "What of our sister?"

"She is next, brother."

Raphael went over to Uriel. Her massive breasts and large arms were chained even tighter than Ramiel's. She spoke. "Who the fuck are you? You sent one of your pathetic minions to rape me, you fucking coward! Lucifer, when I get out of these chains, my dominations will dismember you!"

"Shhhhhhhhh, it is I, Raphael, and I have become a soldier for Father. I am here to rescue you."

With great effort, he and Ramiel were able to loosen her chains. She immediately went to Uriel, reached out, and grabbed his balls. "I will castrate you where you stand. This better not be a fucking test."

Raphael said, "I have my trusted steed, War, cloaked and waiting for us."

Ramiel smirked. "He will never be able to carry us all."

Raphael smiled and said, "He will if we help him with our beautiful, feathery wings."

He tiptoed out of the prison tent and went directly to War, still cloaked. Ramiel and Uriel were both wounded and couldn't fly. War said, "I am to carry all three archangels? Are you insane?"

Raphael rubbed his beloved horse on the nose and said, "They will help you with the power of their combined wings. I will fly beside you. Fear, not my friend, we will make it back to Father."

War was exhausted upon his return to heaven. Raphael, with his healing powers, made War feel like a new horse. He felt like a colt out to stud and smell the ladies. He bent down to Raphael and ever so gently rubbed his soft nose against Raphael's cheek. "Thank you. In all my centuries, I have never felt such devotion, not even from my rider"

"I am your rider for the rest of time. Your rider that lies in the dirt will never come to you." Raphael kissed War between the nostrils and hugged him deeply.

Ramiel, the hardened general, said, "This makes me want to vomit ... this display of emotion, really? Gross. May we see Father now?"

Raphael triumphantly entered the Father's chambers, and behind him were Ramiel and Uriel. Ramiel pushed to the front and bowed before the Father. The Almighty said, "I hate to tell you this, Ramiel, but you will take orders from Raphael. Uriel, you will take orders from Gabriel."

The two powerful archangels were not amused but would not protest as this was the Father's command and law. Not happy, Ramiel went over to Raphael and gave him his broadsword. Raphael said, "By the power of the Almighty, I grant you second-in-command."

Ramiel rose, not happy but must obey. Uriel went to Gabriel and gave him her sword, and Gabriel said, "By the power of the Almighty, I grant you second-in-command."

The Lord spoke. "However, all of you, general, archangel, second-in-command, will answer to Michael. Do we understand? He has the final word as my warrior-angel. If not, be gone from my kingdom, and I will strip you all of your power and banish you to the planet. I will burn your wings off myself. Although I have found my six warriors and I do not wish to inflict such punishment against my loyal angels, I will not tolerate insubordination."

Michael, ever loyal and ever at the Father's side, did not even break a smile. He knew the power he owned and did not want to flaunt it. All battles would go through him. He was the most hardened warrior of all of heaven and all of time. He knew his battle skills and tactics would come into play within the next few days.

CHAPTER 17

Lucifer's Beginning of the End

Lucifer exited his tent and looked down at his armies. He was shocked at the low numbers. He searched his mind. How? Why? Who? No answers came to him. He spun around and stormed back into his tent. He lifted Raqael up by the hair and said, "What happened, bitch?"

Raqael was shivering and terrified. She could just look at him with tear-filled eyes.

He read her mind and knew that she knew nothing. He thought, *My prisoners, my prisoners!* He grabbed his pathetic, battered, and bruised second-in-command and sprinted for the prison tents.

He entered the first tent that held the virtue prisoners, and all were still there, dying of smallpox. Lucifer's heart made a leap, and a rush of relief ran over him. Smiling and not in a rush anymore, he went to the second tent, and the dominations were all there. He smiled at his small yet significant victory. He could sense an archangel presence and drew his broadsword. The divine steel felt like an extension of his very soul. Every archangel had the same connection with their weapon. Lucifer, having two blessed weapons at his disposal, ran a cool finger over his knife blade.

He cautiously went to the tent that Ramiel was in. He entered into the dark tent and sniffed the air. He thought, *Raphael, that motherfucker. He was here. No Ramiel.*

He screamed into the darkened tent, and the remaining alive seraphim guards ran to his aid. Angered and annoyed, Lucifer ripped the heads off the first three guards to come into the tent. He bellowed, "What the fuck? Where are my brother and sister?"

He knew if Ramiel was gone, so was Uriel. He needed not go to her tent. He began to think of ways to kill his beloved brother Raphael. An unusual feeling of despair filled his heart at the thought of his beloved brother betraying him. Why did he protect him as children? Why did he provoke the wrath of Michael for him?

A long bloodstained tear ran down Lucifer's face. He thought of the love and the betrayal, and the thought of getting even made him smile.

Lucifer was swinging his sword wildly and screaming in the tent. He exited the tent, his hair stuck to his face from sweat. Raqael was there, and he kicked her in the chest. "Get the fuck away from me! You make me sick with your compliance and submission. I do not need that now. I am plotting my revenge, cunt. I can only trust me and only me. The only soul in this realm that I can totally count on is my own. When I rule heaven, all will bow to me, and I will be able to count on others. Right now? No one!"

Raqael, emotionally and physically wounded, couldn't believe Lucifer's words. Why was she with him? Her brother was a maniacal brute who needed to be taken down.

Lucifer spun around in his rage and said, "Really? You think I'm a brute and maniacal? I should kill you right here and spare myself from further betrayal."

He began to draw his sword again and go toward Raqael. He could feel a shudder of defiance roll through his body, and it stopped him in his tracks.

"Who has the nerve to read me?" he said aloud.

Death was shocked that Lucifer felt him in his head. He recoiled his mind, but Lucifer knew who the intruder was and what hy wanted in his memory. He was not a fool, and Death would pay for his insubordination.

Death, in his stall, was taken aback by the power of his rider's mind. He knew Lucifer was the one to ride him, as he gave him and his brothers life. The mighty steed was shivering in his hay as he knew that Lucifer knew that he was in his mind. He wanted news of Raphael and the resistance. Now he put his own mortality at risk. He would try to rationalize his intrusion to Lucifer when they would meet. He would try to tell Lucifer that he was wondering when he was going to be ridden again. Because an apocalyptic steed without a rider was just a fucking horse, and Death was just not an ordinary horse.

Lucifer lost interest in the intrusion with a new and provocative thought. *I'm going to end this. They are going to see and respect my power.* Lucifer had a large smile across his face as he passed Raqael lying in the clouds and cowering. He didn't even notice her and the horrified look on her face as he passed. His smile was so broad and fang-filled it terrified her.

He entered his tent and called for his sergeant at arms. A seraphim soldier appeared by his side. He wearily went to one knee. "Yes, Lord Lucifer?"

The sergeant was battle-worn and tired. His wings were soaked with the blood of many battles. He had large dark circles around his blue eyes.

Lucifer went outside and said, "Follow me. I have a task for you and your soldiers." Lucifer pointed up to the cloud hills and said, "I want you and several of your quickest craftsmen to go up there and make me spikes for impalements. I also want several crosses."

The sergeant cocked his head to the side and said, "Crosses, sire?"

Lucifer looked at his loyal angel and said, "Yes, you fool, like a letter *t*. I want several of them as I am going to crucify some of our prisoners."

The sergeant didn't know what *crucify* meant, but he knew it was something awful. He rolled the concept through his mind, and a large shudder ran through his body. The sergeant turned and had begun his descent down to the camp when Lucifer put his hand on his shoulder. The sergeant stopped and turned his head. "Yes, Lord Lucifer?"

"Remember, we are ending this soon, and you definitely want to be on the side of the victorious. I have complete faith in your ability as a ruthless predator. I have seen you in battle. Now go and fulfill my needs."

With that being said, he gave the sergeant a slight reassuring squeeze on the shoulder.

Lucifer called for Raqael in his mind, and she reluctantly appeared. "Yes, my lord?" she said.

"Sit."

He was sitting behind his desk, and she sat in the chair directly across him. He spoke. "You need to be the fearless warrior that I recruited in the beginning. You even changed into a female version of myself. Now look at yourself. You are pathetic. Get your shit together. I need you for this upcoming battle. We are ending this, and Michael's head will dangle on the tip of my sword. You are my second-in-command, but lately you have been nothing but a thorn in my side. Do you not remember impaling the seraphim in front of Gabriel's tent?"

She shook her head, and a smile began to emerge.

Lucifer continued. "See? You do remember. Did it make you feel superior that you could infiltrate one of the greatest archangel camps? I know it did. It made me proud of you, not just as my sister, but also as my greatest general. I know I've been anything but civil to you, but you always hurt the ones that are closest to you."

He stood and opened his arms to her. She was stunned. She went over and gave her older brother a huge hug, their leathery wings brushing against one another.

Lucifer said, "Now I need you to go to the cloud hills and oversee the construction of the spears and crosses."

She pulled back from him and said, "Are you crucifying the prisoners?"

He looked at her, confused, and said, "How do you know what a *crucifixion* is?"

She looked at him and smiled. "I am one with you, brother. I could see it in your mind, and it is a beautiful, miserable idea."

Lucifer grinned and thought, *She is falling for this. She is truly as pathetic as I thought. She will learn just like the rest of them. I am not to be trifled with and certainly not to be underestimated. She is definitely needed, but she will never know my true intentions. I want to be the last of the archangels standing when this is over.*

She smiled at Lucifer and began her journey up to the cloud hills.

Raqael appeared on the cloud hills. She was ready to command again. She had begun to bellow out orders when the sergeant at arms came to her. "What are you doing here? This is my command, not yours. Lucifer himself gave me this job, and I fully intend to see it to the end."

Raqael felt like her old self and grabbed the sergeant by the throat. "Do not take that fucking tone with me. I am Raqael, the second-in-command. I will oversee the construction of Lucifer's ultimate endgame. You will answer to me. Understood?"

The sergeant bowed his head and said, "Of course, M'Lady.."

The mahogany that the soldiers were using was heavy and strong. The stakes looked fantastic; however, the crosses were top-heavy and could not be anchored. The sergeant made this clear to Raqael, and she said, "So what? Put them inverted then, moron. They will be bottom-heavy then, and they will stand the test of time."

CHAPTER 18

God's Beginning of the End

Michael was in God's bedchamber, speaking with his Father. "Father, we need to end this. My brother is growing stronger by the day. We need to move now." As Michael said *now*, he punched the desk and put a large dent in the oak.

"Calm yourself, son. This is your ultimate decision, not mine. I have foreseen this and cannot interfere. You need to be extra cautious of your brother. Trust no one, my son. I know what you have planned, and I can't tell you yes or no. The only thing I can tell you is, this will be heartbreaking on both sides."

Michael called for Raphael and Gabriel. They appeared beside his chair. "We need to strategize on just how we will destroy our brother. We have very few at our disposal."

Gabriel spoke. "Brother, we are archangels and can crush normal angels under our bootheels. I know that our brother is a very powerful being, but we must be victorious and not let Lucifer win. Father will destroy heaven if we fail."

Raphael began to speak, and Michael glared at him and rose. "What exactly do you know about it? You were on his side, remember?"

Raphael smirked and said, "Exactly, brother. I know the lay of the camp and where Lucifer is vulnerable. You can use my expertise to our advantage. I know that he always sits atop the cloud hills, looking down on his army. He sits there at dusk with the sun at his back. We should strike then. We must also be very aware of where Raqael is at all times. She has become very powerful as well."

Michael laughed out loud and said, "The barn girl? Really?"

Raphael said, "Yes, the one and the same. She has become almost the same as Lucifer, but female. She is not as large or as cunning, but she is very dangerous."

Michael was confused and said, "How did I not know of this transformation?"

Raphael said, "Lucifer has kept her cloaked from all of you on Father's side. Now I am with you, and my knowledge is now yours. Ramiel and Uriel probably have seen her yet didn't realize it was her."

Gabriel interrupted. "She is the heinous creature that left the impaled seraphim at my door. I could smell her but thought it was a trick of Lucifer's. She is very dangerous indeed."

Michael began to pace the floor, his large wings raised up from tension. He was shaking his head and said, "This makes no sense to me. The barn girl? Unbelievable!" He closed his eyes, and Ramiel and Uriel appeared in the room, went to one knee, and bowed before their generals and their commander in chief.

Saraqael appeared in the room and bowed as well. He spoke to Michael and said, "I and the remaining seraphim are at the ready for you, sire, for heaven, for victory."

Michael didn't trust his brother and said, "How many?"

"There are seventy-five left. They are my personal guards and will lay their lives down for Father and heaven."

Ramiel spoke and said, "My virtue army was virtually wiped out. There are only fifty of them left. However, fifty virtues are mightier than seventy-five seraphim."

The two brothers glared at each other, hands on the hilts of their swords.

Michael yelled, "Enough! No pissing contest. I'm sick of the bullshit.

No more. We will fight together or we will fall. A united front is always best. Uriel, how many dominations are left?"

Uriel spoke and said, "There is a full regiment of domination soldiers. They number three hundred and ten."

Michael said, "Okay, this is good. Even without their beloved leader, the seraphim army numbers six hundred. Their commanders are scattered, and they are in need of guidance. They will be easy to take. Saraqael, will you be able to go sword to sword with your own soldiers?"

Saraqael looked around the room and said, "Of course, brother."

Raphael shouted, "Bullshit!! I just read you, and you are a liar. He cannot be trusted. He will betray us all."

Michael stood and drew his broadsword, went to Saraqael, and put it to his throat. Gabriel began to cringe and said, "Please, Michael, don't."

Saraqael, unwavering, spoke. "I am no liar. I am very upset about going against my own men. But for the preservation of heaven, I will lay down my own life. For the righteousness of Father and my homeland, I will dispose of my past comrades."

Michael looked over his shoulder at Raphael, and Raphael said, "He speaks the truth, brother."

Michael withdrew his sword from Saraqael's throat and resheathed it. Saraqael looked at Raphael angrily and said, "Get the fuck out of my head! How do we all know that you can be trusted? You were Lucifer's second-in-command."

Gabriel, with his soft and loving voice, spoke. "Brothers, please. There is too much distrust among us. Like Michael said, we need to be united. We are all in this together. We don't need to love one another, but we must have some respect for one another. Uriel, what do you think?"

She said in her deep voice, "I think it's amusing watching my brothers fight with testosterone when the real enemy lies within the forest. We need to concentrate on Lucifer and not one another. My loyalty lies with Father and heaven. I don't care if you kill each other, but I will not let heaven fall."

They all nodded and looked at one another. The tension in the air seemed to dissipate. Uriel's words struck each of her brother's hearts, and the battle was imminent.

Michael scratched his forehead and wiped at the sweat of his brow. He spoke. "We have over four hundred angels at our disposal. We also have two apocalyptic steeds, Pestilence and War. Plus my beloved Rapture. We are also five archangels. Our numbers may not be as mighty as Lucifer's, but we are strong and we will triumph."

Raphael responded, "Brother, we have three apocalyptic steeds on our side."

Michael was immediately angered at being corrected. "What are you fucking talking about? We have two."

"No, brother, I know for a fact that Death is on our side as well. I personally have had contact with this mighty stud and know that he fears and loathes Lucifer."

Michael raised an eyebrow and said, "Really, brother? That's fantastic news! We are all immune from the effects of the steeds. However, I'm sure that greedy Lucifer did not grant his armies the same courtesy. Raphael and Gabriel, come up with a blessing for our armies so that the apocalyptic horse named Death will have no effect on them. Lucifer will never see that coming. Raphael, you must hone your healing abilities and your resurrection abilities for the battle, for heaven, for Father, for us all. I don't mean the armies, I mean the family. Do not let any of us fall. Only spare the archangels. I know that sounds heartless and battle-worn, but that is my law and my command. After we have won and Lucifer is banished, you may use your healing power to help the wounded. We will need an army to guard heaven even after this is over."

Raphael nodded and thought, *Moron, I already have my skills honed.*

To Raphael's surprise, he heard Michael in his head. "Shut up, fool, and do as I command."

Raphael was taken aback and smiled at his older brother and bowed his head.

Raphael said in his mind just so Michael could hear, *How are you able to be inside my head? Did you breach my wall?*

No, brother, I did not breach your wall. There is always a way around a barrier for a warrior of my stature.

With that being said, a loud roaring laughter ensued in both of the archangels' heads.

Seriously, brother, how are you in here? I taught Death the same trick. I hope he is not in peril. If you, my moronic brute of a brother, can breach my wall, Death is in danger.

Fear not, my cunning and sneaky brother. Lucifer needs Death in the battle to come, and it would be foolish for him to harm him. He has too much in his mind right now to worry about a four-legged beast. Unlike you and me, brother, Lucifer is a self-serving asshole and will not see the deceit of Death coming until it's too late. This is our unexpected advantage over Lucifer and his very strong will.

C<small>HAPTER</small> 19

The Greatest Battle

The righteous armies had a long journey to Lucifer and his armies. They gathered at the gates of heaven. Over four hundred strong. Raphael and Michael at the back on their steeds, Gabriel absconded Pestilence from Saraqael and rode the steed like he was born to. The rest were in front of the mighty archangels, ready to die for heaven and the Father. It was time to show the rest of the residents of heaven who was really in charge. Some cowered and some cheered, the righteous armies of heaven. The inhabitants of heaven were split with their loyalties. Michael had never released his power among the masses, but Lucifer had. The houses that were spared from his initial assault were homes of Lucifer, not of the resistance. Michel knew of these homes and the insurgents. He paid no mind to the feelings of despair and fear. He actually fed off it.

Ramiel, Uriel, and Saraqael were frontline. They knew their spot; they were to die for heaven and the Father. They had no problem with this order. They knew of the sacrifice needed to overthrow an evil sibling. They could feel the eyes of the betrayers on them.

Michael bellowed so all of heaven could hear, "CONQUER YOUR FEARS. PRESS ON. FOR FATHER, FOR HEAVEN, FOR VICTORY!"

This was what they needed, a gift from behind. The front forces pushed through their collective fear and went for Lucifer and his mighty army.

Uriel's only thought was, *I hope Raphael's cloak of invisibility has worked, or we are fucked.*

Michael said to Raphael, "Take yourself and your steed and go to the front. You know this territory better than any of us do."

Raphael agreed and rode War to the front, ready for battle. War stopped, and Raphael lifted his arm, bent at the elbow, fist raised. A sign for the armies at his back to stop and be very aware. Raphael spoke to his friend and steed in their minds. *You felt that too, didn't you? Its something awful.*

War was a battle horse and nothing really bothered him, but the sight he saw in his mind made a tear run from the horse's brown eyes. He spoke with Raphael in his mind. *Yes, my rider, I did see, not all of it, but I saw blood flowing from the cloud hill like a waterfall.*

Yes, I felt and saw the same thing, except I could feel the terror and anguish of the victims. My brother has finally lost his control. I don't know what he is doing, but I know it will rattle our army.

Raphael mentally went to his brother Michael. *Brother, War and I both sensed and saw an atrocity of such greatness that it will promote fear in the ranks. Fear is a killer in battle. It will take the morale of our soldiers completely away. Let me show you what we both saw.*

Raphael sent the gruesome image of the blood flowing down the cloud hills and running across their path. Michael wrinkled his nose and spoke to all the archangels with his mind. *Keep your armies close. Our insane brother is doing something so horrific. They might run when we come to it. Here, let me show you what Raphael and War showed me.* Michael sent out the mental image to all the archangels, and a loud cry came from Gabriel. He knew exactly what was happening: more impalements. He had to show his brothers and sisters the memory of the impaled soldiers he discovered in front of his tent. All the archangels—except for Michael, who had seen it with Gabriel—all had a shiver run across their souls.

War spoke to Raphael, blocking out all the other archangels. "My brother is with Lucifer. Lucifer sits upon his back. I have just spoken to him, as Lucifer is busy with whatever task he is performing right now. He is with us as part of the resistance. I told him to wait for the right time. He will know when that is. I, being War, am just as knowledgeable as your mighty brother Michael is with battle tactics. You said he wasn't very smart. Don't underestimate his intelligence. He lets you see what he wants you to see. As an apocalyptic steed, I do have a bit of foreshadowing myself, and I see him needing you desperately in the near future. I will tell you the same thing I told my brother: you will know when the time is right."

Sitting atop the cloud hill, Lucifer proudly rested on War's back and watched as each and every domination prisoner was impaled alive. Some through the tough part at their back where the wings attached, others with the stakes slammed through their bottoms and out of their mouths. The blood flowed from them down the hill, and it made Lucifer smile with victory. He thought, *Just wait till they see my display of power and mercilessness. They will surrender immediately.*

Raqael was especially having a good time torturing and impaling the angels. She was almost aroused at the sight of their white wings turning crimson with blood and their faces turning pale as the life ran out of them.

Now it was the virtue prisoners' turn. The crosses lay on the cloud deck, and one by one they had their arms stretched out, large spikes hammered into their wrists. Their feet were placed one on top of the other, and another, even larger spike was hammered into them. The screams of pain echoed off the cloud deck. Again and again, each virtue met the same fate. They would live, for now, and Raqael was not happy about that.

She went to Lucifer and said, "My lord, why must they live?"

His blood-spattered face and armor shone in the dwindling sunlight. He said, "Because that is what I want. Do as I command. The sight that you will see soon will be even better than the impalements. Now go back and get these crosses anchored into the deck."

Raqael bowed her head and looked up. "My lord, we have to invert the crosses. They are top-heavy and would not anchor."

Lucifer smiled and said, "That's fucking perfect! Even better than what I had planned."

Lucifer was shocked to see Raphael upon War emerge from the mist. He patted Death on the neck and said, "Look at that. The betrayers have returned. What do you think should be done with somebody that betrays?"

Death began to sweat and became a bit unnerved. "I think they should all be destroyed, Lord Lucifer."

Lucifer smiled and said, "Interesting . . . that's exactly what is going to happen to all that have betrayed me."

Lucifer could feel the horse tense underneath him and was satisfied with his sarcasm. To Lucifer's surprise, Uriel and Ramiel emerged, Ramiel on Pestilence and Uriel flying beside him. Behind the three archangels was an army that Lucifer could not see the end to. He could feel his brothers Michael and Gabriel but couldn't see them.

"Oh, it has begun, and I cannot wait to have them bow down to me after I murder Michael."

The seraphim began their assault. They struck toward Raphael, and War kicked and dismembered each angel that came within feet of his master. Some made it past War and Raphael, and the carnage began. Domination armies struck first at the oncoming seraphim. Sword to sword, feather flying, and heads rolling on both sides. Ramiel dismounted Pestilence and began to help the virtues. He taught them well and had no fear of putting his life in their hands. Uriel landed and gave a battle shriek. Her dominations came from every direction. The defecting seraphim got involved in the folly. Gabriel was sickened by the mass destruction of life that was occurring in front of him yet drew his sword and flew into battle.

Michael was watching this happen and saw his disgusting brother on the hill. He must get to that fucking Lucifer. He began to hack and chop his way through the battle. He was the largest and the fiercest of all the archangels. His anger did not unbalance him; it only made him stronger and more determined. The other archangels could see their mighty brother making his way through the battle. They knew exactly where he was going. The brothers and sisters came to his aid to help him get to his ultimate target. The defecting seraphim were dying and surrendering at an alarming rate.

Death could see the archangels trying to make their way to Lucifer. He bucked and kicked and threw Lucifer from his back. Death went racing down the cloud hill, and every angel he passed within feet died instantly. They fell dead without even a sigh or a scream, just dead. Both sides felt the power of Death until he came to his brother Rapture. Death spoke. "I knew you were real. I knew in my heart there were five of us in the womb. Now we finally meet and I am safe with you."

The two horses stood and watched Pestilence come over to meet his brother. They all knew War had already met Rapture. There were still two apocalyptic steeds out there, War and Famine. War was still with Raphael and would never leave his rider unless the horse died in battle. Famine was with the Raqael, and their bond was great, and the horses wondered where their brother was.

Uriel was on her way to help Michael when she was ambushed from behind. They tumbled across the cloud deck, mist flying up. Leathery wings and white wings in a blur. Raqael went after her sister. They finally found their footing, and Uriel was almost as large as Raqael.

"What happened to you, sister? You have changed so. What happened to the quiet, sweet sister I once had?"

Raqael screamed, "Quiet and sweet? How fucking dare you! You were in the palace, and I was stuck with the fucking horses. You, the princess of heaven, and I forgotten in that cursed stall. The only one that ever showed me a little kindness was Lucifer, you bitch. How I have longed to go sword to sword with the great Uriel. Now you fucking die, sister."

Famine could feel the pull of his brothers and one other horse he did not know. He went to his brothers. Uriel said, "Princess? My ass! I was made a general of an army. Do you think I lived in luxury, you spoiled bitch? No, I was made to stay with my armies. You have no idea how hard it is for a female, archangel or not, to command men."

Their swords began to clank together. Uriel's beautiful, shining armor was bloodstained, and Raqael's had the stench of dried and decaying flesh on it. Raqael lunged for her sister, but Uriel, being the trainer and general of the dominations, knew tactics that a mere barn girl couldn't even dream of. Uriel had Raqael on the ground in no time, sitting on the small of her back. She wrapped chains around her and bound her leathery wings to her legs. Uriel flipped her sister over so she could look her in the eye and relish her victory. Raqael continued to fight until Uriel, still holding her sword, took the hilt and hit her in the face with it. She was immediately rendered unconscious. With no respect for her sister, she dragged her body by the hair over to the horse and said, "If she moves, stomp on her."

Death grinned and said, "With pleasure, your highness."

Michael and the rest of the archangels made their way to the top of the cloud hill. The abominations that met their eyes were too much for Gabriel. He went over to each of the impaled and dying dominations and gave them the gift of death. Lucifer was enraged. He went over to the inverted crosses that held the virtues, crying and in pain. He took his broadsword out and began to slice throats as he walked and talked.

"Michael, my brother, do you like my mess? Do you like seeing how powerful I have become?"

The blood spilled over Lucifer's feet and onto the approaching Michael's. Michael spoke. "You have become insane, and now this battle ends here and now, between you and me. I have been waiting a long time to kill you."

Lucifer grinned and said, "You have no idea how long I've waited to hear those words. You are the one that is dying today, not me."

Raphael still rested upon War and could sense he would be needed soon.

Michael turned his back on Lucifer to address his brothers and sister. "Please do not interfere between this pathetic brawl. I am Michael. I will not fall. I have a deep-seated resentment for Lucifer, and you all know this. I have wanted this since childhood."

Lucifer said, "Michael's gigantic feathery wings will have no power but to burn."

Michael's back was exposed as he talked to his brothers and sisters. This unfocused behavior gave Lucifer his chance; he lunged at his brother, sword over his head. Michael, being the ever-aware soldier, felt Lucifer behind him and, with both hands, slammed his broadsword behind his back to protect himself.

Michael said, "Always the fucking sneak. You can never meet your foe on common ground?"

Sparks and lightning emitted from the strike.

Lucifer stepped back and said, "Lightning? Really? Is Father here protecting you?"

Michael spoke through gritted teeth. "I need no protection from Father or anybody else. You forget that I am the firstborn and I am the greatest warrior of all time." Michael sidestepped, the perfection of a fighting angel, and faced Lucifer face-to-face, sword tip at sword tip.

Lucifer began his assault, two-handed, powerful broadsword movements, and struck and struck again at Michael, every strike above. Michael had his sword over his shoulder to deflect the fatal blow. The sweeps under his feet for Lucifer to remove his legs at the knee were met by gigantic feathery wing eruptions. Michael, feeling like this was a sparring contest with an unschooled foe, realized the sheer brutality of reality. Lucifer stuck again, trying to decapitate Michael, and again a defense move pushed away Lucifer's broadsword held at his throat. Michael pushed Lucifer's blade point down into the cloud deck.

"I need not wield my weapon with two hands, brother. You think you are so quick-witted and smart. How very pathetic."

Michael grabbed Lucifer's blade by the sharp tip. Not caring of the pain the divine weapon would inflict, Michael grabbed Lucifer by the hair and brought him face-to-face. At this point, swords meant nothing. Yet

Michael, being the ever-virtuous follower of God, pushed Lucifer from him. Lucifer slammed into the cloud deck with a giant woof of mist. Michael went to his brother and extended a hand. "Rise, brother, there is no honor for me to kill you like this."

Lucifer hissed, "I will not show you the same courtesy, brother. If I have you down, you can guarantee your life will end."

Lucifer pushed Michael's hand away and rose on his own. He went over to his broadsword, the hilt barely visible in the clouds and mist, grabbed it with both hands, and made a move toward Michael. Lucifer's anger and emotions were getting the better of him. Michael knew from all his battle training that this was exactly what he wanted to happen. Lucifer had forgotten the lessons they were all taught as children. Michael practiced daily and was just waiting for the right moment to strike. His brother was losing his energy and becoming tired from assault after assault.

Defensively, Michael moved around Lucifer and deflected every deadly blow his brother could throw at him. Now Michael was on the offensive, holding his broadsword with one hand and using the other for balance. He struck at Lucifer, blades sliding off each other, with sparks flying around. Michael lifted his sword to the side and swept across Lucifer's chest. A loud screech was heard as the weapon scratched at his armor, denting it but not penetrating Lucifer's vulnerable chest. Michael returned to his battle-ready stance, both hands on the hilt of his sword and the blade in front of him, ready for the next clash. Lucifer began to beat his feathery wings to get an advantage over his brother. Michael, seeing Lucifer rise, began to beat his even bigger feathery wings. The battle now was to take place in the air.

Lucifer rose first, Michael close behind. They began to race at each other, their wings flapping and the winds blowing back the hair of the angels watching. They clashed into each other with a thunderous boom, spinning, leather, then feather, leather, then feather. Michael kicked Lucifer in the chest to separate them. Lucifer came at Michael with his sword out and wings flapping behind him. The propulsion itself was fantastic; Michael flowed away just at the right moment, and Lucifer's back was at him. Michael took the hilt off his sword and slammed against where his wings anchored. Lucifer let out a yelp and began to fall to the planet. Michael grabbed his brother by the throat, and with a gigantic thud, they hit the cloud deck. A blinding mixture of clouds and mist engulfed all that were around. The two brothers rolled around on the ground, exchanging punches and kicks.

When the mist was cleared, there was Michael sitting on top of his brother.

Michael spoke. "See? Good always triumphs over evil, and you, my brother, are evil."

Lucifer's sword was only feet from him, yet he could not reach it. Michael had Lucifer's wings pinned to the cloud deck. Michael, with tears running down his, face said, "I do not want to kill you, brother, but it is what Father and heaven need."

Michael, with both hands on the hilt of his sword, point down, raised his divine blade to finally impale him and finish this. Lucifer grinned at his brother and, with his divine knife, thrust it into Michael's chest through his armor and into his heart. Michael gave out a slight sigh and fell, mortally wounded.

Lucifer bent over his brother and said, "See? I always told you that you would never get close enough to me to kill me, brother. Now I will rule heaven, and the rest of these pathetic archangels will fall victim to my reign of terror here."

Raphael, sitting upon War, screamed, "NO! Michael!" He leaped down and went to his already-dead brother.

Raphael, with extremely emotional tears, ran to Michael's side, covering him from head to toe with his giant white wings. The only parts of Raphael that were visible were his back and his wings. The other archangels rushed Lucifer and, finally, after some struggle, subdued their powerful brother and had him in chains, his large wings tethered to his thighs.

Lucifer kept saying, "Raphael, please, brother, don't do this. Heaven is better without that cursed Michael."

Uriel, hearing enough from this excuse of an archangel, took the hilt of her sword and knocked Lucifer's fangs out of his head. She said, "Now, try and talk with your mouth busted up. I've heard enough of your bullshit."

The archangels had never seen Raphael use his resurrection powers and stopped in awe and watched. A soft neon-blue hue came from beneath Raphael. Beams of light were only visible through his wings. They could hear the humming of a prayer being said in Raphael's voice. The light went out as quickly as it lit up. Raphael rolled off his brother, gasping for breath. Lying beside his brother, Raphael could feel Michael's hand grab his. Raphael, spent from releasing such an enormous power, could only lie there. Michael sat up from the clouds, and the archangels all gasped.

Lucifer said, "This is not what I wanted. You fucking Raphael and your powers! Of all the angels to save, you save him?"

Michael stood and went to Lucifer and slapped his face. "You had to cheat to beat me? How typical! You always were a coward when it came to battle. You think you're smarter than the rest of us. I have news for you, brother, we are all smart in our own way." Michael spat at Lucifer's feet and added, "Now fuck you, brother! It is time to get your just rewards. Father will take great pleasure in seeing you in chains."

Michael's focus now was on his savior as he looked at the cloud deck and saw his youngest brother in a heap. He rushed over and lifted the lifeless yet still breathing Raphael. He carefully carried him over to War. War went down to his knees and allowed Michael to place his rider upon his back.

War, with tears in his eyes, said to Michael, "Is he dead? Please, if he is dead, I want you to ram your sword through my broken heart."

Michael smiled and patted War on the neck. "He lives. But his sacrifice was great and will not go unnoticed. Father will be so proud of him. It is time to begin our journey back to heaven and Father. We need to collect the rest of the horses and go. I feel time is of the essence to save Raphael. Father will know what to do to restore his powers and help save his life."

They began their journey down the hill, Lucifer in chains, Michael's armor still showing the hole from Lucifer's blade, and Raphael across War's back.

They made it back to the rear of the line, picking up the wounded as they went. The ones that were too far gone to save, Gabriel had mercy and ended their suffering. Gabriel was sweating and crying until he saw Raqael lying on the cloud deck with Death sitting on the small of her back. He gave a victorious grin, knowing that it was finally over. He couldn't wait to get back to the Father. Death, Famine, Pestilence, and Rapture were all waiting for instructions. The sight of Raphael strewn across War's back made Death run over to his brother. He sniffed at Raphael, and a wave of concern washed over his face.

Death spoke aloud, and the archangels were all taken aback. "We need to get Raphael back quickly. He is fading fast. I know, as I am Death. One of you angels needs to fly him back to heaven and back to your Father."

Michael scooped Raphael's limp and cool body up, and with a large gust of wind, he was off the deck and into the air. He was gone from sight in seconds. The few survivors that were there were placed upon the horses. Each steed was large enough to carry five soldiers at one time. Lucifer and Raqael went to get upon one of the horses and were met with the tip of Uriel's sword.

"You deceitful pieces of shit will walk. Ramiel and Saraqael will carry the most wounded back to Father."

Each of the huge archangels grabbed three soldiers and flew off. Uriel and Gabriel could handle Lucifer and Raqael. They had begun to walk them back to the Father and heaven when Lucifer began to whine. Uriel struck him between the shoulder blades, where his wings were anchored, with the hilt of her sword and said, "Shut your betraying mouth before I smash you again." Uriel turned and looked over her shoulder. She said, "Death, come closer to this fucking whore."

No angel, wounded or not, could ride Death. He was taking the wounded and the prisoners back. He stepped closer and walked beside Raqael. Lucifer said, "You better get the fuck away from us."

Death trotted behind Lucifer and said, "Or what? You are in chains, I am not. Just keep walking. Your stench makes me sick, and always has. There is no honor in your scent, and it took all my strength not to vomit every time you came near me."

Lucifer lunged at Death, and with a quick yank, Gabriel had Lucifer on his knees in front of him. "Don't test my patience, brother. I will allow death to make a visit to you, and I don't mean the horse. As the angel of life and death, I can kill you with only my will if I so want to. I, however, do have respect and honor."

Uriel had heard enough from her deceitful brother. She pulled some feathers out of her wings and fashioned a gag. She went to Lucifer and shut him up once and for all. He began to struggle against the gag, and smoke began to rise from his parted lips. Uriel stepped back and said, "Oh, how the evil has fallen! Mere righteous feathers and you almost burst into flames."

She grabbed Raqael by the hair and pulled her close to her face. "You want one too, bitch?"

Raqael couldn't even look her sister in the eye.

Uriel, laughing, pushed her sister back and made her stumble.

CHAPTER 20

Raphael's Fate

Michael burst open the doors of the Father's chamber and startled God. Michael was out of breath and rested his brother's limp and lifeless body on the Almighty's desk. God was shocked and said, "What happened to my son? How did he get like this? What happened to your armor, Michael?"

God was full of questions.

Michael could barely breathe yet went to one knee and spoke. "Father, my armor was pierced by a hidden blade of Lucifer's. He actually killed me, yet Raphael resurrected me. He used too much of his power to help me. I don't know why this has affected him this way, but, Father, please help him."

God knew exactly why Raphael was like this. "With you being my firstborn, my most powerful son, the leader of everything I hold dear, it was almost too much for your brother to bear. He may be the angel of healing, but he is not as strong as you, Michael. He is also my last-born and not as mature as you and the older angels. He almost took his own life giving you his life force and energy. It is a great testament to his loyalty and love to you, my son. The healing of normal angels or humans is easy for him. You, being the great warrior and having a strong will, sucked him almost dry. It's not your fault, Michael, it's just who you are. We must move quickly to save him. Where is Gabriel? He should be the one that brought your brother. His abilities and gifts over death are needed right now. I need him and his mind as a conduit between the worlds of life and death."

Gabriel heard the Father, and in Michael and the Father's mind, they both heard him. *Listen to me and follow my instructions. Only then will Raphael have a chance. Death is at his doorstep, yet his will to live is strong.*

Walking the prisoners and wounded back, Gabriel was shocked into a trance. His eyes closed, and he swayed back and forth.

Uriel, with concern, said, "Brother, are you okay?"

Gabriel just nodded. He spoke in his mind. *Father, Raphael needs the very essence that he gave Michael. I am not there, but I am sending my mind to you. We need stardust and ash from Mt. Vesuvius on the planet. With these and my instructions, we will heal Raphael together, Michael included.*

Michael said, "What can I do?"

Gabriel said, "Raphael needs strength, brother, and with your brawn and might, you can spare a bit."

"I don't know how to do that."

Gabriel smiled and, with his soft voice, said, "I've already taken it from you and have given it to Raphael."

The Father and Michael looked at Raphael, and the pink tone of his cheeks was beginning to reemerge.

Gabriel said, "Michael, I need you to go to the planet, *now*. Father, get your canister of stardust. We must move quickly, as the strength I gave him from Michael is dwindling fast. I will even send some of my strength to him right now. Please, this is vital to save my little brother."

Michael, with a large gust of wind, was gone. He was back in minutes with a large container of sacred ash from the mountain. Gabriel began to chant, and the Father sprinkled stardust onto Raphael as Gabriel chanted.

"Dust to dust, we reclaim my brother Raphael from the grip of death."

Michael began to spread the ash over his brother.

Gabriel chanted again, "Ash to ash, we reclaim my brother Raphael from the grip of death."

The Father's hands began to glow, and he placed them on Raphael's forehead and said, "I reclaim my son Raphael from the grip of death. Ashes to ashes and dust to dust, live, my son, live."

Like being hit by a bolt of lightning, Raphael's body began to jolt and convulse. He began to breathe deeply, and the Father could hear his son's strong heart get louder and louder. He looked at Michael and, for the first time in centuries, saw his eldest son crying.

Gabriel opened his eyes and saw Uriel's eyes, full of tears, staring at him. "I'm fine, baby sister, I'm fine. Raphael lives. All is right with heaven again."

Uriel, extremely angry, went to Lucifer and began to beat him mercilessly. "This is all your fault! You fucking greedy bastard! You caused all this, acting like the spoiled child you are." She was punching and kicking, spittle dangling from her chin.

Gabriel came over and grabbed his sister's wrist and said, "That's enough. Leave some for Father. He will want Lucifer alive when we bring him back."

The first to arrive in the Father's chambers were Ramiel and Saraqael, both carrying wounded. The angels that fought this great battle, that fought to the death. There were few survivors that could be saved. The soldiers on both sides were scattered on the floor as more and more were delivered. Rapture, War, Pestilence, and Famine all arrived. The angels that needed attention were ones that Gabriel chose to save. Some were beyond saving, and Michael made them comfortable until the inevitable end came. Even without Gabriel's presence, some angels still perished.

Finally, the rest of the wounded and the prisoners arrived. A hush fell over the room as Lucifer entered the room. God went to his son, and to everyone's surprise, he hugged him. Then he stepped back and looked at his son. With a giant hand, he backhanded the ungrateful, spoiled Lucifer.

He said, "Why, my son? Why did you cause all this misery?"

Lucifer turned his reddened face, a hot handprint beginning to appear, and said, "You know exactly why I did this, Father." When he said *father*, he hissed it at the Almighty. "You love those pathetic creatures on that disgusting planet more than your angels. It makes me sick that we must obey every law that you set yet you allow the humans to defiantly break every law that you have handed down to them. Thou shall not kill? Really? Thou shall not steal? Really? Shall I continue? You maimed a beautiful being in the Garden of Eden yet did minimal punishing to Adam and

Eve. You destroyed this planet with water, and yet here they are. The twin cities? Any of this rings true to you?"

A large blood-filled tear began to roll down Lucifer's face as he became more and more emotional.

"You have given us powers over the humans, yet we may not use them. I am the angel of light, but when I shine an accusing eye upon your beloved humans, you look the other way. You won't even let Gabriel take a life of a man you call righteous even when he openly defies you. There needed to be a battle over these creatures. This will be remembered by all, and they will know that my love was with heaven at one point. I loathe mankind because of your unwavering love for them."

Jehovah looked at his sweating and crying son and said, "I created you eight as an example for the humans to follow. Lead by example, wouldn't you say, Lucifer? I make you and your siblings obey my laws to the letter for the sake of mankind. It's not that I love them more, son. They are my greatest creation."

Lucifer lunged at his Father. "Greatest creation? Fuck you!"

He was met with the tip of Uriel's sword, and he said, "Go ahead and kill me! I'm dead inside already. We, as archangels, are your greatest creation. We are the mightiest of all of heaven and of the earth. You just choose not to see us for who and what we are. I love the fact that I was able to transform like this. Raqael and I are your greatest creation as we show the ability to evolve into something even greater than our brothers and sister."

God spoke. "My archangels live in heaven, and this is your home. The humans need to prove that they belong among the angels while they live. I need to give them my forgiveness for them to be allowed entry."

Lucifer was screaming now. "Earn your right? Come on, all they have to do is repent on their deathbeds and you welcome them in our home! Murderers, rapists, thieves all welcomed. It makes my skin crawl at the fact that we have to live by your laws yet all they have to do is call out to you when they are dying."

Jehovah took his son's face in his hands and said, "I don't care what your thoughts are on the humans. I am the Almighty, and I will do as I please. It would've served you well to remember who exactly is in charge. Now I must make an example of you to all the angels that are left and the humans. I need them to know that there will be another place for your murderers, rapists, and thieves. You want to rule? Well, I have made a special place just for you, my son. You loathe the humans so much you will smell them for all eternity. I am banishing you to the center of the planet. You will be beneath the humans. You will be with the fire and brimstone that I once carried in my heart. They will walk above you every day, and you, my son, will rule over the sinners. Do as you please with them. Just for company, I am also banishing this whore of a daughter." He turned to Raqael, a stunned look on her face, and said, "You chose the wrong side, sweetheart." He turned and looked at Lucifer. "I am removing your chains, if you want to live. I suggest you not do anything stupid."

Lucifer's chains melted away, and he rubbed his sore and swollen wrists. Raqael's chains melted as well.

Jehovah said, "You will be in a place not fit for angel feet. This is the last favor I will ever grant you, my son."

With a wave of his hands, Lucifer's angel legs began to transform into goat legs. His angel feet became cloven hooves.

"You, Raqael, I will not grant the same gift. You don't deserve it. I can feel that the only reason you were with Lucifer was so you could feed off his power like a parasite. Now you can feed off him for eternity. I hope your feet will blister and burn as you so deserve. Lucifer, if he so chooses, will have to carry you forever so you don't burn. I am sure he will grow tired of this in no time, and it will give me great pleasure to hear your screams of anguish seep into my mind from the middle of the planet."

Raqael spoke. "Father, please."

God had no patience for such insolence and slapped her in the face and grabbed her by the hair. Her face turned up to his, and he said, "Get the fuck out of my home!" He threw her through the clouds and down to the planet. His attention was now all Lucifer's. "I am stripping you off your name, Lucifer. For the rest of time, you will be known as Satan, the great deceiver, the adversary of mankind, the accuser, and finally the fallen one. You will be loathed by mankind. Hunted down by my churches. Enjoy your new role, my son, as I do not have the heart to just kill you. I want to see you suffer for the rest of time. I cast thee out."

With that, God lifted his leg and, with one great kick in the middle of Lucifer's chest, sent him flying through the clouds. Banished for all eternity from his once-beloved home.

Lucifer, with one last defiant speech, screamed as he was falling, "You gave them dreams! I will be the essence of all their nightmares! I will taste the sweet victory of revenge!"

CHAPTER 21

Lucifer's Hell

The two fallen angels landed on the planet with a giant thud, and dust and debris flew everywhere as they were engulfed into the abyss of the deepest recesses of the center of the planet. Lucifer was amazed at how beautiful the fire was. Raqael was crying out in agony as her angel feet began to blister.

Lucifer spoke. "Listen, bitch, I will not fucking carry you for all time."

With his hands lowered and fists clenched, he changed her legs, fashioned like his with cloven feet. She went to her knees and grabbed her lord's hands and kissed them and licked them with her cold, forked tongue.

Lucifer slapped her away and said, "He has his Ten Commandments. Time for me to create seven deadly sins that will be my laws. They cannot ask for forgiveness, as once they partake in breaking my laws, they will spend eternity with me." Lucifer was so angry at being cast out that he thought of the most common of sins for the humans. He began to write his manifesto.

One, lust. Anyone that looked upon a female with a throbbing in his pathetic excuse for a penis had already committed it. Oh, he would make

Raqael in charge of this and give her access to succubus. There was a new thing for him to create. To come from his beautiful hell and temp the weak male humans with sex and their fantastically disguised bodies that they could temp Michael himself. Lucifer would make sure that Raqael made them the most beautiful human females on the outside yet a demon inside the disguise. Lucifer chuckled as he was enjoying this work.

Two, gluttony, reserved for drunkards and overeaters. He would have his demon Beelzebub handle the most extreme cases. Lucifer thought, *Yeah, he thinks he's so smart with his Ten Commandments. Just wait till he gets a copy of this.* All he could do was smile, his fangs dripping spit off them as he wrote.

Three, greed. Easy one, given extensive sensuality to indulge in all forms of impurity.

Four, sloth. This one might be a tough one as the humans worked the land in his Father's name. Some had to be lazy.

Five, wrath. This was Lucifer's favorite, uncontrollable anger and a strong vengeful anger or indignation.

Six, envy, another of Lucifer's favorite. He knew this feeling well as he always envied the humans. He himself would handle these souls. It was a painful awareness of the advantages of others, just like the Father and the fucking humans.

Finally, he wrote the seventh, pride. This one would be fun to torture as this law was broken by going before their ultimate destruction with a haughty spirit before the fall.

Lucifer was pleased with his new laws. *Let that fucking piece of shit in my former home write laws to counteract this fantastic deadly sins.* Lucifer knew that God would try, and thought, *I rule hell now. Go ahead and try!* He laughed heartily, and the souls of the twin cities stuck in purgatory and the fallen army soldiers all appeared and knelt on both knees in front of him.

Lowering their chests to the floor, all said together, "Hail Satan!"

This gave Lucifer a great feeling of power, and he relished it.

His loyal sergeant that had fallen in battle spoke to Lucifer. "Lord Satan, may I suggest you run hell like an army? I have been loyal to you from the beginning. I can run your armies for you and answer to you."

Lucifer sat on his throne, legs crossed, and jumped up. "That's a fucking fantastic idea! Are you volunteering to fill that position?"

The sergeant, knowing Satan for centuries, spoke very carefully. "It is you ultimate decision, Lord Satan. I am but a mere slave in your grand scheme. I would love to help you, as I have been your complete servant. How do you want to handle the damned?"

Satan sat back down onto his throne and thought for a moment. "I am going to make several levels of torture in this forsaken yet wonderful place. The two lowest yet highest in sin levels will be reserved for the most heinous of the humans, the mass murderers and the suicidal. The quality of sin as the levels rise will become stagnant. The ones that rule each level will have their own ability and powers. They will answer to you, understood?"

"Yes, Lord Satan, I will make sure it all goes according to your plan."

Lucifer spoke. "Sergeant, I don't know what your angel name was, but for all eternity, your name shall be Baal. You are the first of my princes. I give you the power over the ash and size of flames. There will be eight levels to my domain, and I shall create other princes to handle each level."

Lucifer began to stand. Fire surged around him, and six other demons appeared behind him. He began to introduce them to Baal.

"This is Asmodeus. He will handle level 1. This one is Belphegor, and he will be on the second level. Welcome your brother Mammon, third level. This is Astaroth, in charge of level 4. Now, my first prince, Baal, the next two have powers like you as they will be dealing with levels 5 and six, you having seven, and eight will be my throne room."

Two brothers stepped forward and bookended Satan.

He spoke. "This is Leviathan. He has the power of transformation. He can shape-shift for more brutal torture. His powers will come in handy when I bring hell to earth and he transforms into the seven-headed serpent. Belial, he is my angel of light, so to speak."

Satan gave out a shrill laugh.

"Funny, he will be in charge of my seven deadly sins and deciding who ends up in what level. You, my first, Baal, will be in charge of level 7, the murderers, molesters, and rapists. Have fun torturing them as you wish. I myself will move my throne to the last level, reserved for the most cruel and disgusting of mankind. How I will relish in meeting them! That fucking thing that rules heaven will expect them to ask for forgiveness, but these souls will be the worst of the worst. I may even grow to like some of them."

Baal went to one knee, his hand on his still-bloodstained sword, head bowed. He said, "Lord Satan, what about your sister? Raqael will need a rule, will she not?"

Satan sat back down and studied his princes. A look of thought crossed his face, and he called for Raqael. She appeared beside her lord and knelt. He spoke. "You, my sadistic queen, shall be in charge of all the succubus. It's the perfect job for you."

She wrinkled her nose.

Satan said, "I know, my queen, none will rival your beauty, ever."

She smiled and rose, kissed her brother on the cheek, and went to meet the princes.

Lucifer chuckled as he looked around. "Now this is beginning to feel like home. I am quite enjoying myself with the ability to create such beautiful demons. I wonder if that cunning god knew about that?"

CHAPTER 22

The New Archangel

Lucifer's expulsion from heaven left the rest of the angels stunned. Michael broke the silence with an inquiry. "Father, there are only six of us archangels left. You have said that we need seven to fulfill your visions. What are we six to do now if your vision comes to fruition?"

The Almighty looked at his firstborn, looking older and more tired than Michael would like to see. He answered, "I will make a new one. Gabriel, Michael, and Raphael, I will need your powers and strength. I am going to make a new female angel. She will have the ability to speak to animals. She will be a new angel of light."

Michael shivered and spoke. "Another angel of light, Father? Are you insane? Lucifer was your angel of light, and we all know how that turned out."

God, growing ever more impatient with his firstborn, screamed at him, "Light over the fucking creatures of the planet, not the humans! Did you not just fucking hear me?"

Michael lowered his head and, in a whisper, said, "Yes, Father."

Raphael, Michael, and Gabriel all went with Jehovah into the birthing chamber and began to create the new archangel.

The birthing chamber was made of an alloy of metal that only God knew the composition of. Heaven's blacksmiths repaired and maintained it but still had no idea what type of metal it was. (In today's age, it would be known as titanium.) They entered, and a light breeze blew back all their hair.

Raphael entered after the Father and said, "Father, why am I here?"

The Father spoke. "If this angel struggles when it is born to grasp its first breath, I need you to heal her."

Gabriel and Michael entered after Michael spoke. "Father, I understand why Gabriel and Raphael are here, but why am I here?"

The Lord went to his firstborn son, his general, and stroked his face. "My son, I want you to give her part of your loyalty to me. You possess the most fidelity to me. I need to make sure that I do not create another spoiled and powerful angel."

Gabriel went to the Father, went to a knee, and said, "Shall we begin?"

The Father responded, "My sons, when I was a younger god, I needed no help in creation. As the centuries have passed and my wrath has calmed, I now need my archangels' help. Yes, I am the great Creator, but even gods need help at times. Do not confuse this with weakness. I can still destroy planets at my will, but my passion for it has diminished." He went to Gabriel and said, "Yes, my son, we are ready. Here are the canisters that we need. You and I need to lock hands with your brothers and begin the chant of creation."

The canisters were opened and poured in the center of the circle of archangels and the Father. They began to sway and chant, Gabriel leading the words, the others repeating.

"Dust to dust, ashes to ashes, we bring forth a new life, a new beginning. We bring all our powers and the power of Father to induce flesh. Flesh of our flesh and blood of our blood, we bring forth a divine being. With Father's blessing and power, we create a new female archangel. With the loyalty of my brother Michael, the foresight of my brother Raphael, the love of myself, Gabriel, and the divine power of Father, the Almighty, the Creator of everything upon heaven and earth. We call upon the powers of wind, earth, fire, and water. Make my sister live."

A large glow began to form from the stardust and the ashes of Vesuvius. It swirled and rose and fell in the air. It pulsed and grew red, then blue, then green, and finally gray. Gabriel began a different chant as the gray mass fell to the floor, shaking the angels to the core. They kept the circle together. He began to chant again.

"The powers of earth, wind, fire, and water."

Gabriel kept chanting this over and over. The Father was stunned as a great wind tried to knock him from the circle. He could see across from him Michael engulfed in water. Gabriel looked as though he was entombed in earth, and Raphael was on fire that did not burn. They were creating life, an archangel, a new beginning for heaven.

The gray ball began to glow like the sun, and the angels and the Father were released from their grasp of the elements and they began to hear a soft cry. They all collapsed in a heap of feathers and sweat. The Father went over to his new daughter and lifted her over his head.

"I name thee Francis. I give you the power of light over animals. I will love thee as my daughter and as my warrior."

The infant began to scream and cry. A large tear ran down the Father's face as a great hurricane hit the planet.

The four of them emerged from the chamber with a newly created baby angel swaddled in cloth. The other archangels gathered around, curious to see their new sister. She was smiling at them and cooing.

The Almighty spoke. "This is Francis. She is the new angel of light."

Uriel wrinkled her forehead and said, "Father, another angel of light? Are you insane?"

The Lord chuckled and said, "You sound just like your brother Michael. She is the angel of light for the creatures on the planet, not the humans. She will be a gentle soul, and I will not banish her to the stables. That was my mistake with Raqael. I will require the surviving enemy soldiers to make sure the horses are taken care of." He looked at Michael. "Except, of course, your beloved Rapture. You and that exceptionally white steed have a bond that no god, angel, human, or creature can break."

Francis began to squirm and wriggled out of her swaddling clothes. She was now a toddler. Archangels grew at an alarming rate; they needed to be mature in a short time. This unusual growth was to ensure that the Father was always protected by seven archangels. Michael was the only one that kept growing after maturity. His size was massive.

He went to a knee to his baby sister, who now was six years old, and said, "I am your eldest brother, Michael. I will teach you loyalty and respect for Father and his rules."

Raphael approached his sister. "I am Raphael. At one time, I was the last-born. I am here to teach you the ability to heal a wounded animal."

Uriel approached now the eight-year-old and said, "I am your sister Uriel, and I will teach you the skills needed for battle."

Ramiel came closer and said, "I am Ramiel, and I will teach you stealth in the skills that Uriel will teach you."

Saraqael approached. "I am Saraqael, your brother, and will teach you to lead."

The last to approach the now almost fully grown Francis was Gabriel. He knelt on his knee and bowed his head. "I am Gabriel. I am the angel of life and death. You will need to call on me more that you would like. I will teach you the difference between a mortal wound and just an injury." He kissed her hand softly, rose, and stepped back.

Francis spoke. "Hello, my brothers and sister. I look forward to the teachings that you all have so gracefully granted." She walked past her brothers and sister, making her way to the five mighty steeds that were in the corner. She touched the black horse known as Famine. "You are so thin, my friend. I feel your name is Famine. I understand now." She went to the spotted mustang and stroked his mane. "Hello, War, I feel that you helped my brother Raphael in a great time of need. You certainly are beautiful." She then touched Pestilence. The horse cringed and backed away. She held out her hand. "Come now, I will not hurt you, and none of you can hurt me." Pestilence allowed her to touch his brown nose and snuffed at her. She went to the beautiful spotted horse and knew that this was Michael's stud. "Hello, Rapture." She stroked his mane. The last was a pale horse with his back to Francis. She touched his haunches, and his tail flicked at her. She giggled. "You must be Death. Such a beautiful pale coat you have, sir." She went to the front and petted him softly. She turned to all the angels and said, "Father, who is Lucifer?"

The Almighty, at the sound of his son's name, turned his back on his children. Francis went to the Father and put a soft hand on his shoulder. "Please, Father, I must know. I could sense him all over Death's coat."

The Father turned and took his daughter's hand in his and said, "Allow me to tell you a story, my dear."

The Father began his story. He told her of the betrayal and the war. He began to speak of an angel she had never heard of. She interrupted her Father and said, "Raqael, Father?"

He said, "Yes, my very empathetic daughter. At one time in heaven, there were eight archangels. I only needed seven to fulfill my vision, but I knew that the prophecy that was handed to me upon creation of the planet was that one of my children would betray me. I didn't know which one, so there were eight of you. Your brother Lucifer has been banished from this home along with your sister Raqael. If it weren't for their betrayal, you would have never been created, my dear."

Francis stood and said, "They betrayed you? They betrayed all of heaven? Good, I'm glad they are gone. I may just have to thank them when I see them. I may be merciful to the creatures on the planet, but nobody shall betray my Father or my siblings ever again. I will show no mercy."

Michael turned to Uriel, nudging her with his forearm, a gigantic grin on his face "A warrior already. I love it!"

Uriel nodded, and another gigantic grin was visible among the archangels.

The Father said, "I am very tired, my children. Time for me to sleep. Not like I did after the great flood, but I need some rest."

God left his chambers, and the archangels followed suit. Gabriel and Raphael granted one of the righteous virtues a bit of power and left him in charge of the wounded. Michael took Rapture with him and instructed the other horses to return to the stables.

Heaven was eerily quiet. After a great battle, there was no noise, and it was easy for all the angels to become comfortable in their beds and sleep. Jehovah was lying in his bed, almost asleep, his mind wandering down to the planet, and he sat bolt upright in his bed. He called for his archangels. The first to arrive were Michael and Uriel. The ever-vigilant warriors went wing to wing, back to back, swords drawn.

Michael spoke. "What's going on, Father?"

He and Uriel scanned the room, swords unsheathed and at the ready. The other angels arrived and, seeing Michael and Uriel, all drew their swords, even the new one, Francis. Her armor was brand-new and was blindly shining in the moonlight.

The Father said, "Thank you, my protectors, but this threat is not in this room. Please resheath your swords and come sit on my bed. I have something to tell you about that bastard son of mine."

They all sat around the Father, except for two. Michael stood sentry at the Father's door, his hand on the hilt of his sword. His sister Uriel stood beside the Father's bed with the exact same stance as her brother.

"Your cast-out brother has created seven princes of hell, only to rival my loyal seven. He also created a manifesto containing seven deadly sins. Lust, greed, gluttony, sloth, wrath, envy, and pride. He thinks he is so clever. However, I have given each of you the power over these seven deadly sins. In extreme cases, you may interfere. Michael, you will counteract wrath with forgiveness. Gabriel, you will counteract envy with your extreme kindness. Ramiel, you will counteract gluttony with virtue and temperance. Raphael, you will counteract lust with chastity. Uriel, you will counteract sloth with hard labor. Francis, you will counteract pride with humility. And finally, Saraqael, you will counteract greed with charity."

The archangels that were sitting on the Father's bed, plus Michael and Uriel, went to the foot of the bed. They all went to a knee and said in unison, "For Father and the preservation of heaven."

Michael stood and spoke. "The seven princes, Father?"

The Lord responded, "You will meet them on a great battlefield that will take place on the planet, yet that vision is centuries from now."

CHAPTER 23

The Birth of Greatness

All the angels began to leave God's chamber, and he said, "Gabriel, wait. I need you for something."

Gabriel held the door for his brothers and sister and began to walk toward the Father.

The Father said, "I need you to harness your psychic ability for me. I don't need you to cleanse it afterward, as we know how that worked. Satan will try and pry at your mind, but if your abilities are harnessed, he will see nothing. I need you to go to the planet and seek out a woman named Mary. She is married to a man named Joseph, yet they have yet to consummate the marriage. She is a virgin, my son. I want you to visit her and plant my seed in her womb. It's time for my visions to finally begin to become reality. Too much time has been wasted already."

Gabriel nodded and bowed to Jehovah. He vanished, and a small mist was left behind. He returned in seconds and said, "My Lord, I have found her and planted your seed. Are we to have a demi-archangel in our midst?"

Jehovah just chuckled and said, "No, my son. I created this boy to become a martyr for all of mankind. Your banished brother will never see this coming."

Gabriel lowered his head and said, "Luci—I mean Satan was unable to read me while I was on the planet. My intuition is telling me, and I fear he may be planning something just as grand."

The Almighty just glared at him.

Lucifer was sitting on his throne, watching the drawing and quartering of the damned in his realm, when he felt a presence he hadn't felt in years. He stood and lifted his hand. "Stop!"

The demons continued.

"I said fucking stop! I need to leave, and I don't want to miss one second of this fantastic show."

With a strong smell of sulfur, he was gone. He landed in Israel, cloaked by his immense power, and spotted Gabriel entering a tent. He waited till that fucking wretched Gabriel left, and entered the tent. He sniffed the air.

"That bastard is having a kid with a human woman? What the fuck? That fucking Almighty thinks he's so smart! I will outmaneuver him and create my own boy."

With that, Satan was back on his throne, watching the drawing and quartering of Ramses over and over. He called for Raqael. She loyally appeared beside him. "Yes, my lord?"

"I need you to go to the planet, disguised, of course, and find me a human woman worthy of accepting my seed. Be gone and do as you are told and with great haste."

She jealously looked at her brother and disappeared.

The birth of Jehovah's son did not quite go as planned. He made sure they guided them and made sure they made it to Jerusalem. However, being that Jehovah could not really interfere in the real lives of humans, Joseph and Mary were poor. The donkey they rode was old and frail. Gabriel made himself shine in the night sky as a star for them to follow, yet there were no rooms for the destitute and poor couple. They located a barn. Among the animals and the magi that were summoned to follow the star, Mary gave birth to a son. Unbeknownst to anybody present, Lucifer himself was there. Disguised with white wings and all—even the cursed Gabriel didn't notice him—he was just another angel. Lucifer thought, *Magi? Really? I have several in my sixth, seventh, and eighth levels of hell. How ironic.* He disappeared before any angel noticed him.

He appeared in his throne room, still disguised, and was met by Baal's sword. "Who the fuck? What the fuck? I will kill you now for my lord and master, Satan."

Satan turned, and as he turned, he became himself again. He went to Baal and said, "Your loyalty to me has just been proven. I make you my second-in-command of all hell. You have proven yourself to me with your actions. I also have a gift for you. I have created four hellhounds, two for you and two for me." The being appeared beside Satan, crouching and snarling. He snapped his fingers, and the hounds went to each side of his throne. Foam and snot ran from their faces, large fangs visible even when their mouths were closed. The other two went to Baal.

"Thank you, Lord Lucifer. These hounds will do some of my torturing in my level 7. Sir, have you anybody in the final level?"

"I have a few, but the only great one is that pharaoh." Lucifer's wide fang-filled smile made Baal smile as well. He screamed for Raqael. She appeared, and he said, "Well? Where is my human whore?"

"Master, I have found none that are worthy. Why can I not carry your seed?"

Satan, angered, stood and slapped her face. "Even here in hell, incest is forbidden. We do have laws here. Incestuous behavior lands you in either my level or level 7. Never mind, cunt, I will find her myself."

Raqael, with tears in her eyes, just vanished.

Satan looked at Baal and said, "Women, huh?"

Lucifer asked Baal, "Where does one go to find a woman that deserves to carry my seed?"

Baal thought for a bit and said, "Sire, there is one city on the planet that will serve your purpose. We have several of the inhabitants here in hell already. It's a city of pure sin, like Sodom was. The name of the city is Thebes. It rests on one of several islands named Greece."

Satan looked confused and said, "How do you know of this city?"

Baal went to his knee and looked down. He did not want to correct the lord of darkness but had to. Without looking him in the eyes, he said, "Lord Satan, as I have stated, we have several of the souls of that city here in hell."

Satan leaped from his throne and said, "Fan-fucking-tastic! That's where I'm going, and you are in charge in my absence."

Satan vanished up to the planet. He was perched on the top of the temple of Hades. He blended so well with the gargoyles that he went unnoticed. He spread his wings and floated down, cloaking himself as he walked among the inhabitants of Thebes. He could smell the sin all around him. He breathed deeply and knew he would find whom he wanted there. He spotted a very beautiful, curvy young woman, and he followed her for the day. He got close enough to smell her virginity and purity. He brushed past her to touch her hair, and she spun around, looking for the source of the brush. Lucifer, standing right in front of her, cloaked, almost touched her nose with his. He was hunched over and down to her level. His wings were wrapped around her like a shroud without touching her. She looked around and only saw the street with the vendors and the shoppers. She thought that somebody had to have accidentally brushed against her. She knew no man would come close to her as her father was a powerful sultan. He could behead a man at his will. Satan sensed his power within her genes and began to focus only on her. She kept walking, picking up flowers and smelling them, unaware that she was prey. Lucifer was evilly skipping beside her, just waiting for nightfall and the fun he was going to have with her.

She finally made it back to her father's large estate and relaxed down in the grass to watch the clouds. Satan spread his wings, still cloaked, and hovered over her. He was level with her prone body. Floating above her, he began to become aroused. She could sense something but thought her mother was watching her. She knew any minute that she would be called to help prepare the evening meal. He began to flap his wings, and a cool breeze played with her hair. Satan made his move. He began to flap harder, and his invisibility began to dissipate. She could see a being hovering over her that she had never seen before. She tried to scream, but her voice would not come. The winged beast above her had his hand across her throat. The smell of the claw around her neck made her gag and almost vomit. Satan gave her a gigantic smile as he lowered himself onto her. She writhed and tried to shake this hideous creature off her. He was just too strong. Her skirt began to rise higher and higher until her entire torso was exposed.

Lucifer saw the beautiful scrub of hair between her legs and her bountiful breasts. She was magnificent. He whispered in her ear, "Beautiful, simply beautiful."

She was crying and trying to scream the entire time he was raping her. Over and over he raped her. She was bleeding badly from her throat and from her vagina. Her neck had claw imprints on them that oozed blood.

When Lucifer was done, he stood and held out a clawed hand for her to take. "Take my hand, my dear. You belong to me now, and my twins will tear your insides out. You better take my hand, bitch. I will be the only one that will be able to save your life when the births begin."

She was rolled on her side in a fetal position, crying, and looked up at Satan and took his hand. Her voice came out in a hoarse, raspy whisper. "What are you? Why me?"

Satan grinned and said, "I am the fallen angel. My name was once Lucifer, but you know me better as the great deceiver, Satan."

She swooned and fainted. Satan, cradling his prize, began to flap his wings, and with a cloaking, they disappeared into the dusk. In his mind, he instructed his demons to clear an acre of land of the fire and brimstone at the edge of hell. The obedient demons did as instructed and built her a grand home. Satan encased her estate in a bubble that would keep her safe from the sulfur scent. She had servants and anything she wanted. As the mother of Satan's boys, she was treated like a queen.

Raqael hated this and hated her.

CHAPTER 24

Life and Death

On the planet, Jesus was growing and learning. He followed in Joseph's footsteps and became a carpenter. He excelled at his profession but knew he had a gift. Jesus always seemed to know when the rains were coming or when the livestock were pregnant. Joseph's life was even saved by his son by his pulling his father from danger as planks of wood began to slide off a roof. He was in his early thirties and was known throughout the land as a great prophet. He was soft-spoken but strong voiced with his devotion to Jehovah. He would tell his followers during his speeches that he was the Son of God. He preached the Word of the Almighty to all that would listen.

Pontius Pilate sat on his massive throne in a land known as Rome. His long blonde hair swayed playfully in the breeze. A scantily clad servant girl knelt beside him, washing his feet. He snapped his powerful fingers and called for his messenger. Ruthless and showing no mercy, he had full control over his citizens and armed forces. The Roman messenger came into the emperor's chamber, went to one knee, and with a fist balled up, bent his arm at the elbow and hit his armor at the shoulder.

Unfazed by the complete devotion, Pilate barked out an order. "Take four men with you, Lieutenant, and travel to Nazareth. I want information about this so-called Son of the God named Jesus Christ. The foolish Jews will believe anything. One god? Ha! He is becoming anything but too powerfully influential for my liking. *My* Rome will never follow such tripe."

In Nazareth, Jesus was known as a faith healer and the Son of the great Jehovah. He always felt that something was spiritually missing from his soul. During a dream, Jesus was visited by an angel, and the giant magnificent creature spoke to him. "How dare you have a missing in your heart! How dare you doubt our Father! I am the angel that upholds his laws and protects them, yet here you are, the Son of Father and ever full of apprehension. You will obey Father at all times. I am known as the great torturer in heaven, but to you I am uncle, brother, archangel, protector of Father's laws. If you are that unsure of your destiny, seek out a man named John. The locals know him as John the Baptist. He will dunk you in the blessed waters. Do not make me call upon you again. My next visit will not be so polite."

The next day, Jesus went and saw the Baptist and was baptized in the pure water of a lake that sat upon a gigantic pool of righteous angel blood.

Mary was a beloved apostle of Christ. She and her brother Lazarus followed his every Word. Walking through the marketplace, Lazarus was struck dead from an unseen force. Mary threw herself to the ground, convulsing in complete sadness. She started chanting to Jesus's uncle Gabriel. He appeared before Mary in her mind and said, "Sshhh, the miracle of the rift between life and death will embrace thee."

As the funeral was coming to a close, the Almighty could feel her pain and sent Raphael to the planet to resurrect her brother. Jesus, some of his followers, and the Roman guards were at the tomb. Jesus promised Mary that her brother would walk among the living again. He told her that being the Son of God, he could breathe breath back into his lungs and he would live. Unknown to Jesus, Raphael was in the tomb, resurrecting her brother. He was bringing him back from the grip of death. Gabriel allowed Lazarus's soul to return to the planet. Between the two brothers, they released Lazarus's soul, and he was alive again. Jesus, outside the tomb, said, "Lazarus, arise!" The large boulder covering the grave began to roll away. Out of the mist came Mary's brother, alive and well. The crowd that witnessed this was completely thrown to their knees. The Roman soldiers couldn't believe what they were witnessing. What would the emperor think? What blasphemy! This must be eradicated.

As Jesus, Mary, and Lazarus were walking away, Christ heard a voice in his head. *Please, Son, come to this palm tree. I need to speak to you alone.*

Jesus was in a trancelike state and arrived at the palm. Jehovah stood there and proudly looked at his Son. He hugged him tightly and spoke. "You have some trepidation in your heart, and doubt. I can sense it. I am the Almighty God, and I am your Father. I have a task for you, my Son. You must wander the desert for forty days and forty nights. This will be a loyalty challenge for you, as you must fast. You may drink water, but no food. Without food, you will become one with your soul. Remember that you have free will, and if you choose to become mortal, I will grant your wish."

"You really are my Father, aren't you? This is how I can heal the sick, make the cripple walk again, and make water into wine. Was the ability of resurrection also granted to me, Father?"

Jehovah lowered his head and said, "Yes, my Son, but the power of resurrection is not you. That role was of Gabriel and Raphael. Now go, my son, and blessed be the travelers."

Jesus wandered with no real destination or plan. He looked up at one of the dunes and saw a man standing there. He thought, *This is where the bonding of my soul begins. I am having hallucinations.* Jesus went to the figure at the top of the dune. Standing there was Satan.

"Hello, my nephew. You probably have no idea who I am." Satan once again became himself, losing the disguise. Revealing himself and expecting his nephew to run.

Instead, Christ said, "I know exactly who and what you are, Uncle Lucifer."

Satan was taken aback; he hadn't been called by that name in centuries. "Yes, I am. I am here to show you the bounty of the planet and what can all be yours. Come, you look tired and need to rest."

With a wave of Lucifer's clawed hand, a large oasis appeared in the middle of the barren desert. He took Jesus by the hand and led him to the clear, cool water in the middle. "Drink, nephew, and get your fill."

Jesus bent and drank. As he began to look up, a large sheik's tent appeared at the edge of the pool. Lucifer said, "See, my nephew? I could grant you all this at your disposal. Money, power, women—I could have fresh virgins delivered daily from the four corners of the planet!"

Lucifer clapped his hands twice, and a plethora of women exited the tent. Women of all shapes and sizes. Some belly dancing, others coming to Christ and removing his clothing to bathe him. Two naked beauties took his hand and led him to the center of the pool.

One cooed, "Let us wash you and remove all desert sand from you and refresh you."

Christ allowed this and was in pure relaxation. The two women dressed him in fresh linens and fine silks. They brought him inside the tent and laid him down. Christ could smell the lamb on the spit; his mouth began to water. He saw the rolls, the fruits, and the dates. There were several women serving him and tempting him with food and wine, yet he refused. Lucifer was growing ever more impatient.

"Dance, bitches."

The women began to striptease in front of the weakened Christ, rubbing their beautiful bodies on his. They showered him with gold pieces, dancing and writhing.

Jesus just kept his Father ever present in his mind and said, "Lucifer, you cannot tempt me with any material possessions of this planet. I am but a poor shepherd and have love for only one woman."

Lucifer leaped down from receiving oral sex from one of the women and said, "Fool, I could burst you into flames!"

"Go ahead. If you could do that, you would've already done it. You make me sick with your deception of Father. Your war cost many angels their lives. You are the great deceiver, and I will never trust you and never be on the side of evil. I have made up my mind. Thank you for your hospitality, but I have only ten more days to wander the desert. You have kept me here as a prisoner long enough."

As Jesus was speaking, Lucifer was getting angrier and angrier. With a high-pitched scream, the tent, the food, the women, and the oasis disappeared. The barren desert was all that remained. Jesus now knew his destiny and visions were to come true. He needed to get back to his apostles after his journey and speak to all of them of the visions and realization that he would become a martyr for mankind. He would have a great supper for them and speak to them all as they broke bread. He thought of his friend Judas; his visions told him that he would have a pivotal role in what was to come. He would speak with his old friend, and together they would figure it out.

In hell, Satan returned to find that the twins were being born. The beautiful young girl was now a haggard and worn old woman. The babies that she carried fed off her life force. She died during labor, and Satan allowed his boys to claw their way out of her lifeless body. To help his newborns, Satan took one long claw and sliced open the dead woman's abdomen to make it easier for his boys to enter the realm of hell. They were out, and the proud father held both his babies. He turned and burst the woman into flames and burned her estate to the ground.

They grew at an alarming rate. They lived and played in hell. The first of the born twins, William, was loud and obnoxious, like Satan when he was a boy. The second-born, Mathew, was soft-spoken and intelligent. They both possessed the power of telepathy. They had such fun torturing the damned souls. Mathew especially enjoyed running from level to level. He would start at the top, and by the time he reached the bottom, where his father was, he had aged by three years. They didn't grow as fast as an archangel did but still grew faster than any human on the planet.

They both had their father's temper and ability to cloak themselves. William had large fangs in his mouth, yet his brother, Mathew, did not. The boys always fought over who had the bigger fangs. The boys weren't quite as large as their father, and their wings were smaller, but they were more ruthless. They seemed more determined to prove their cunning and intelligence. When Lucifer was a boy, he could harness his temper and his anger. He knew exactly how to push his brothers and sisters to the point of rage. The twins knew how to push each other. Some of their fights would end in bloodshed. Satan would even provoke them against each other. He loved to watch them fight, their beautiful claws and wings. Their muscular builds reminded him of his early days protecting Raphael from Michael. He spoiled his boys and gave them whatever they wanted. Their psychic abilities were almost as strong as his. All they had to do was think it, and it would appear in front of them.

Satan could sense that the Almighty's Son was in danger and wanted to go watch. He landed in Rome and saw his nephew in shackles. He went to the Roman guards—cloaked, of course—and whispered in their ears, "Torture him ruthlessly. It will be fun. Son of God? Nobody should make that claim."

The soldiers thought these ideas were their own and relished in the thought of torturing this pathetic prophet.

Satan continued, "A prince? Make him a crown of thorns. That is fitting. Use the whip with the hooks on the end. I think you should crucify him."

The Roman guards drank wine and took turns making this false prophet pay for his claims. The laughter that came from the courtyard was riotous and infectious. The people that stood around also thought it was funny. All Christ could see and hear was laughter as his back spilled his blood onto the sand. Satan floated above the scene, a large grin on his face. He though, *That fucking ruler of heaven cannot interfere as they all have free will. Oh, the laws I will turn on him will be endless. I need to call my boys.*

In his mind he called, and William and Mathew appeared, cloaked and floating beside their father. They wanted to go participate but could not. Their presence would be known soon enough. Their Father always taught them that the less the humans see them, the better. *You may do polite suggestions of sin and give them ideas, but you cannot control their free will.* The boys completely enjoyed the show of the torture, and the sight of the blood splattered on the walls of the courtyard gave them ideas for hell.

Satan and his boys decided they would wait and watch the crucifixion and enjoy themselves completely. They hovered over the city and watched the workmen build the crosses. There were only two, and they wondered where the last one was. Satan looked at his sons and said, "Y'know, this was my idea to nail beings to a cross. But it looks as though they are doing it wrong. They have the holes ready to put the wrong end in. Those crosses are going to be top-heavy. I cannot wait to see how many of these fools get killed doing it wrong."

He began to laugh, the boys laughed with him.

William was full of energy and was swooping down and back up again, soaring through the air. He flew back to his father and bother, and with one long pointed claw, he said, "Look, over there."

They all looked at the crowd that was beginning to gather. They could see a badly beaten and bleeding man carrying a cross over his shoulder. They began to fly over to get a better look. They hovered over him, laughing and shrieking. They relentlessly dived down at him, pulling up at the last moment to avoid contact. Jesus carried his cross to the top of the hill. He set it on the ground and waited. The guards were already crucifying the murderer and the thief. They saved Jesus for last.

Satan and his boys hovered above, watching as the Romans pulled Jesus's arms taut. They hammered spikes into his wrists. They put one foot atop the other and drove a spike through them. They made sure that the bodies were anchored well. They began to raise the three crosses together. Satan spread his wings even wider and began to shake in anticipation of the failure about to come.

When the guards used ropes and spikes in the ground to hold the crosses upright, Satan began to scream in anger. He was flying and swooping, screaming, "They are making a mockery of my beautiful creation!"

He was about to reveal himself when Jesus began to speak, "Father, why have thou forsaken me?"

The Roman guards were in tears as he said, "Forgive them, Father, for they know not what they do."

He was struggling for breath when a guard came and stabbed him with his spear. Jesus wept and died upon the cross between a murderer and a thief.

Satan, William, and Mathew all were shrieking and laughing, flying and soaring with the death of Jehovah's son. They had begun their descent back to hell when Satan stopped and said, "Why would he allow his only begotten Son to die upon the cross? I would never allow any harm to come to my boys."

Mathew went to his Father's side and spoke. "Father, maybe he didn't want him anymore. He did cast out the greatest of his angels in you, Father."

Satan just shook his head and thought, *Curious, very, very curious.*

As the trio landed back in hell, Satan could feel a righteous presence around him, and it made him almost gag. The hounds of hell began to bay, and the boys drew their swords and stood around their father. They could sense the intruder as well. Satan called his wonderful four-legged creations to his side. They snarled and sniffed the air.

Satan said, "I know you are here. I cannot quite place your scent, but I know you don't belong here. Reveal yourself! I can sense it is a great angel, and how dare you, Michael, come to my domain?"

Jesus Christ said, "It is not Michael, Uncle Lucifer. It is I, Jesus Christ. I have come to barter with you for the souls of the ones that you have in the top three levels of your hell. What do you need with petty thieves, unbaptized babies, and blasphemers?"

Satan spoke, "I have need for all the souls that belong to me. They are my property. What do you bring to replace them? Do you bring the Son of God to replace my bounty? Oh, how he that lives in that wretched heaven would try to get you back! Are you willing to sacrifice yourself for these pathetic creatures?"

Jesus spoke. "I already sacrificed myself on their behalf." He turned his arms palm up and showed his uncle the holes in his wrists. He bent forward and lifted his shroud and showed him the holes in his feet. "Do you think the great battle for earth is to happen now? You could not be more wrong. I am here to pluck at the remaining archangel in you and make him sing like a fine violin."

Jesus went over to Satan and placed his hand upon his shoulder. Satan began to smoke, and a look of confusion filled his face. He was convulsing, and for a split second, the beautiful white archangel known as Lucifer was visible.

Satan shrugged it off and said, "Don't do that again." His singed wings and shoulders were smoking. The stench of burned hair filled the room.

William and Mathew were crouching in the darkness, not believing that this human was transforming their beautiful father back into that abomination he once was. Again, Jesus placed his hand on Satan's shoulder, and again he convulsed and Lucifer, for an even longer time, was visible.

Satan said, "I fucking told you not to do that again!"

Jesus Christ said, "If I do this a few more times, the end of days may not come to pass."

Satan recoiled from Christ's hand and said, "Fine, take three hundred souls from the top two levels and get the fuck out of my home."

Jesus, with a smug look on his face, said over his shoulder as he was leaving, "I knew you'd eventually see it my way."

Satan sat on his throne and said, "Oh, by the way, does your Father know you are here?"

Jesus stopped and turned. "He knows. He said I was foolish. However, I know, being the Son of God, I am and always will be more powerful than all the evil of heaven and earth."

Arrogantly yet playfully, Jesus spit on the floor and left.

Satan chuckled to himself. "Gotta give it to the kid. He has balls."

CHAPTER 25

The Twins

As Jesus left, the twins could see in their father a change. He seemed to age at a great rate. He spoke to them. "Boys, I need you to go and perfect your powers of influence. I used my great power in the courtyard with the Roman guards. Do you both remember?"

Mathew looked at William, pushing his giant wings out and pushing his brother, and said, "Yes, father, I remember. I doubt if my brother does."

With that being said, the twins began to grapple with each other. They were rolling on the floor, a flash of fangs from William, a bat of a wing from Mathew. Satan was now on the back of his throne, perched like a vulture. He was swinging his arms and squealing. He was in total awe of his boys; it brought him back from the ages.

He screamed, "Enough! You will kill each other, and I need both of you. There are a few laws in my realm, and one is, you are your brother's keeper."

Both William and Mathew stopped, looked at their father, and hissed at each other.

Satan spoke. "There are hardly any souls in my top two levels of hell.

My princes are getting complacent and bored. I will not have that. You, my flesh of flesh and blood of my blood, will redeem hell. You two will make it the place that is feared of all humanity. That fucking Jesus made this place a mockery, and I will not stand for it."

Mathew said under his breath, "Then sit, old man."

Satan heard his son and leaped from his throne and threw his son to the floor. "Remember, boy, my body may get old, but remember I am *pure* evil and you are not. Understand?"

Mathew struggled under his father's grasp and said, "No, old man, you cannot rule anymore, and I will take this place from you."

Satan's eyes widened, and he pulled his son's face to his and whispered, "You were not there when the archangels of heaven battled. You were not there when Jehovah was scared of the reign of hell. You were not there for the birth of the four horses. You know nothing, boy!"

Satan threw his son against the wall and scorched his face and wings.

"Now you know my true power, and you will respect it, or you will perish by it."

Satan stood and huffed at his crumpled son and turned and looked at Mathew. William, ever loyal, with his hand on the hilt of his sword, looked at his father. Satan went back in time in his mind, back to the court and back to his brother Michael and his Father. A large sigh exited the prince of darkness as he took his son's hand.

"You are my warrior-demon. I can sense it."

William, with his hand still on his sword, looked over his father's shoulder and could see his twin giving Satan the finger behind his back. Not one but two. Mathew cowered in the shadows.

Satan sat back in his throne and sighed and began to speak. "Come here, boys. I need to tell you something and need you both to perform a task."

The boys came to their father's feet and sat. Ears wide open, they listened.

"Remember me telling you of the war in heaven? I did omit quite a bit to save you, as you were too young to know the full truth. I was winning the war until my Father ruined my beautiful mess of blood-soaked clouds. You both should have seen heaven proper with its streets of mist covered in angel blood. The great battlefields were so rancid with the smell of decaying blood. Both evil and righteous. My asshole Father made sure to cleanse the clouds with a great storm. He made a giant rainstorm douse the entire planet with the blood. Fucking asshole! How I hate him and his fucking humans. I would've won that war if the disturbing sights that I left were visible. True fear would have run rampant through the streets of heaven. As the storm raged, pools of blood began to form. The blood separated into good and evil. Like water and oil, it just doesn't mix. There are pools up on that cursed planet, both righteous and evil. I need you both to go and locate them. I would send Raqael, but she is worthless and weak."

Satan sat back, his sons looking at him. "I can feel you have questions. William, you go first."

"Father, with your power and the power of the apocalyptic steeds, how were you possibly defeated?"

Satan scratched at his chin and said, "I was betrayed. I was stabbed in the back by my most trusted. It is an awful feeling knowing that all you have done was beginning to unravel. Even my beloved stud, Death, betrayed me in the end. Remember, boy, history is written by the victorious, so I'm sure my name is either feared or respected." Satan sat back down. "Even my own brother betrayed me. I murdered that fucking Michael and his arrogance. But my very own brother resurrected him. He saved his life and stole mine. When I finally get back to heaven, Raphael will be the first I kill. My beloved brother, who was my greatest general, betrayed me. He stole three-quarters of my army and defected. Saraqael will be the second I kill."

William lowered his head, and Satan said, "My son, you will learn of betrayal. It will be a tough life lesson. Mathew, you have a question?"

Mathew spoke. "How can a brother betray his own brother? Its completely confusing to me. I would never betray you, William."

Satan said, "The only sibling I had loyal to me was Raqael. My sister Uriel, the bitch, escaped my grasp, and she was always faithful to my Father. She had help escaping. All my brothers . . . remember these names, as I'm sure they will make themselves known to you on the planet. Michael, Gabriel, Uriel, Saraqael, Ramiel, and my trusted Raphael. They all betrayed me. Power is a great motivator, boy. Always remember that. My loyal Raphael and Saraqael were with me until the tides of war swung and I began to lose. I know, I can sense that, as I can sense that a brotherly appearance will come to you both. I am not the strongest psychic, but I can feel a brotherly confrontation coming. I know my brothers are going to try to stop you. Tread carefully on the planet. I will give your wings, tails, and horns invisibility so if you encounter humans, they may avoid you but will not fully know what you are. Mathew, you will go first. You have a better sense of smell."

William leaped up. "What the fuck? I'm the eldest!"

Satan smirked and said, "Yes, William, you are the eldest, but if you hadn't been in level 6 all the time with the whores, you would probably smell better. All you ever have on your mind is pussy. I am sure you will be seeking out female companionship while on the planet."

William glared at his father and bowed, but the seed of hatred had been sown.

The boys, enveloped in invisibility, left for the planet. They appeared upon the earth, and the sun was so bright it burned their demon eyes. They looked around and saw the pyramids.

Mathew said, "Ah, William, we are in Egypt."

"How the fuck do you know that?"

"While you were with your sex girls, I was reading in the libraries of hell. I know this place from ancient texts. This once was the land of the pharaohs and great rulers. Our grandfather had a massive attack on the Egyptians. It was the main reason Father lost the trial."

William shrugged and said, "Okay, nerd, whatever. Use your fucking smell that Father thinks is greater than mine and find what we are looking for. I hate it up here. I really don't want to be here long. The repulsive smell of humanity is making me sick."

Mathew began to sprint, William close behind.

"Over here, brother, I can smell it."

All William could smell was the scent of sin and cunt. "Here, brother, here." Mathew pointed.

William excitedly went to the discovery and threw himself upon the sand, laughing uncontrollably. Grabbing at his stomach, he said, "This is what you fucking smelled? A fucking puddle?"

Mathew could smell more. "Go tell Father that we have found one already, although small. We are on its trail."

Although William wanted to take credit, he could sense his brother's anxiety and chose to stay and protect him. William drew his sword as they approached an even larger pool. This time it was bigger than a puddle, yet Mathew was repulsed by the smell.

"Brother, do not touch that. It's righteous blood. It will turn you to dust with one touch."

William, being the soldier, dipped the claw of his upper wing into the blood. He could smell the horrible goodness. The claw of his wing disappeared as the desert wind took it.

"I told you! You are all brawn and no brains. I told you not to touch it."

William, wounded and irritated, pushed Mathew out of the way, sheathed his sword, and said, "I had to see for myself. That's some powerful shit."

They located several pools of both good and evil. They were on the trail as they rested for the night.

As dawn approached, Mathew said, "Go tell Father and come back to me. We have done him proud."

William disappeared and approached Satan from the darkness. He spotted the old man asleep in his throne. He quietly came to his father. With his face almost against his father's, Satan woke.

"What are you doing, boy?"

William's cock got hard as he missed his chance to be ruler of hell. "Father, I have found several pools and puddles of both good and evil. We are on its trail. We will find the large ponds in no time. Just wanted to give you an update."

As William turned and sucked at his fangs, he thought, *It will all be mine, old man, all mine.*

He appeared in front of his brother in the Carpathian Mountain Valley. Mathew was standing before a gigantic sea of glorious evil blood. He smelled and inhaled deeply.

"Brother, this is magnificent! I told Father of our great location of this small sea."

"Thank you, brother. However, I can smell a giant righteous pool across the planet. We have discovered all we will here."

They flew like rockets across the planet, soaring above the human stench. They landed in mid-America and saw a large river. Mathew went over and dipped his hand in and drank. "You are a moron! It's just water."

William raised his talons, ready to make his brother pay. "I was fucking thirsty, you sanctimonious, insulting fuck!"

Mathew just grinned and shook his head. "Brother, across the river. It's a puddle." Mathew sniffed the American air and said, "It's fucking righteous! Let's avoid it."

William said, "Let's fucking find the end."

They scanned and walked the planet, finding larger and larger pools of righteous and cursed blood. They searched, knowing, with Mathew's extraordinary sense of smell, they would find what their father was looking for. A complete and total gift to their father.

Mathew said, "With your brawn and no brains, I can read you, brother."

William knew his brother was no match for him. Mathew was avoiding the shores. "I can feel you're betrayal, motherfucker. Really? You are mimicking the war."

"You know, brother, this is the perfect time to eradicate you from this world and make me the sole heir of hell."

Mathew, with his broadsword drawn and in a defensive stance, said, "Bring it, you big stupid asshole! My cunning is Father's. Your brawn is from Michael and our bloodline."

This enraged William. He started to advance at his brother. Mathew took a defensive stance and lifted his large broadsword out against his brother. William was a bit perplexed. "Really? You have to wield your mighty fucking weapon of death with two hands? Brother, you really are no match for me."

Up in heaven, Jehovah could see the planet and went to the Rocky Mountain Valley to watch the scene unfold. Michael stopped the Almighty before he went to the planet.

"Father, where are you going? You always need me with you."

The Almighty grabbed his ever-faithful Michael's face and kissed it softly. "My wonderful, loyal son, I am just going down to observe. This intrigues me as this is Cain and Abel reincarnated."

Michael went to a knee and kissed his Father's hand. "All you have to do is think of me and I will be there. I love you, Father. Be careful."

William leaped toward Mathew, his broadsword raised over his head. Slashing as he landed, he sliced him deeply in the forearm. Mathew said, "Brother, my brother, stop. You are just mimicking the war that Father despises. Just stop! We can rule together."

But what he saw in William's eyes was pure hatred and complete takeover. Mathew struck at William, holding his large sword with two hands, deflected, and swung. Mathew's sword, shining in the moonlight, lunged at his brother again and pierced his leathery wing. William screamed in pain and slashed at his brother, cutting him open at the shoulder. In the air, Mathew would have the advantage. Being smarter and more cunning, he was able to outwit his bigger, stronger brother. Mathew sprang up and began his flight. William, in quick pursuit, caught his brother by the foot. Mathew kicked wildly at William's face and caught his brother's chin and sent him flying toward the ground. William was too strong to go down that easily. They were rolling through the air. Swords meant nothing with these close quarters. Mathew had to release himself from William's grasp. He was almost away, and William grabbed his younger brother, and they both tumbled to the planet. In a huge puff of dust, they both let out a large sigh as they hit the ground. They both stood and went after each other again. Screaming and hissing, exchanging blows. William grabbed a handful of sand and threw it at his brother's eyes. William staggered around as the sand began blinding him. Mathew screamed in agony as William head-butted him and wrapped his hands around his throat. William squeezed until consciousness left his brother. William had cheated, like his father did in the war.

William grabbed his lifeless body and slapped his face a few times. Mathew began to wake and said, "Brother, why? Why? Why?"

"You wanna know why, you weak and pathetic fucking demon? It's going to be mine and all mine. You are just the first casualty. Father is next."

The shocked looked on Mathew's face was all the gratification he needed. He grabbed his brother by the balls and throat. William wanted to watch his brother die. "I fucking hate you. You will never come back home." He mercilessly tossed him into the righteous blood, and with one large flame in the middle, an excruciating scream emerged. He stood there and watched as his brother tried to escape his inevitable demise. In no time, Mathew was consumed. All that was left was a bit of a greasy spot floating on the top.

A huge stone hand with talons burst out of the rock behind William. It grabbed him by his wings and brought him into the planet. He bounced and was smacked on the stone. His human side began to emerge as he began to become wounded. Blood spewed from his forearms, nose, and knees. William's talons were being torn off as he tried to release the stone hand's grip. He could hear his wings crunching as they were being crushed. It was relentless. Down, down, down it went, all the time hitting and cracking him off the stone walls deep within the earth. Finally, he landed in hell in a heap, his enraged father above him.

Jehovah, sitting on the mount above, was in awe of what had just transpired. "Wow! Now it begins, not with the half-demon, half-human I was expecting, but things happen for a reason." He went back to heaven and consulted with Michael immediately. Michael laughed when the Father told him of what had happened on the planet.

Michael giggled and said, "Serves Lucifer right for being such an arrogant prick his entire life. Wow, Father, fate certainly works in a mysterious way."

Satan stood over his boy and said, "What did you do?"

William, showing his weak and vulnerable human side, could only stand there as Lucifer berated him. His father hissed at him, "How fucking dare you kill the one that was to be my heir! Brains are more important than brawn. It's just like the ancient war." Satan looked at his pathetic son and added, "Mathew was the one to lead our realm in the apocalypse, not you. You are stupid, no brains. You played right into his hand. I did not want this! You big dumb fuck mimicked the exact occurrence of Cain and Abel. You make me sick! I should kill you myself. But as I've said before, even hell has its rules. I loathe the fact that I am left with you."

Satan paced back and forth in front of his son, trying desperately to control his anger but failing miserably.

"Father, I am a worthy candidate. I am still the firstborn."

Satan responded by leaping onto the unsuspecting William's chest and sinking his talons into his son. He brought his face close to his and whispered, "I won't kill you, but you will pay with your skin and wings. Oh, the agony you will endure!"

Satan wished he could bring Mathew's body back to hell. Instead, he could only bring the soul of Mathew down to hell. Releasing his son, Satan spun from him, gritted his teeth, and vanished.

William thought, *What did he mean "wings and skin"?* He thought he could make a break for it and go to his Grandfather. Maybe he would be welcomed up there. As soon as the thought escaped his mind, Baal and his two hellhounds appeared.

"You really are stupid," Baal said. "You stand a better chance facing your father than running away. Your Grandfather would burst you into flames or send your uncle Michael after you." Baal stood guard until Satan appeared again.

Satan came back up to retrieve his son's soul and own it once and for all. William spoke to Baal, who was ignoring him. "Are you kidding me? Really? He is so unworthy to be here. I am the eldest, yet I am the one being punished."

Satan brought Mathew's soul and laid it at William's feet. "Look what you did to my boy. Now it's time for you to face your punishment. I am banishing you to the planet. For all eternity, the humans will be above you in my heart. Which isn't saying much, as I released my archangel for my hatred of them. You will have to endure lifetimes of humans. This punishment is so fantastic I sure am happy It never thought of this. You are no longer welcomed here in your home. I am also banishing you from all forms of light. I cannot take the illumination of fire from you. As you were born of fire and grew strongly here, your only food source will be the humans that you and I loathe. For eternity you will be subjected to the stench of mankind."

As Satan said that, he raised his hands, and William was gone. Satan sat back upon his throne and wept, large sulfur tears running down his face.